MY GIFT TO YOU

TRACIE DELANEY

CHAPTER ONE

TODAY WAS A VERY GOOD DAY—BECAUSE Livvy realized she didn't want to die. As the startling thought took hold, a long-forgotten feeling settled in her chest. She searched her memories for the last time she felt this way, but every time the far reaches of her mind touched it, the reason vanished.

Then it came to her. Contentment. She was content. But as quickly as she recognized the miraculous feeling, it was replaced by feelings of guilt. Was this the beginning of the end? Would her memories of Mark and Daniel start to float away like driftwood on the tide, becoming smaller and smaller until they disappeared completely?

A tightening sensation clamped around her heart. Her mouth dried up, and she absentmindedly pinched the skin at the base of her throat. She couldn't allow that to happen. They were a part of her—the best part. She could not, *would not*, let them simply fade from her memories.

She shoved her sunglasses on top of her head and reached into her bag. Her fingers closed around her journal, and she lifted out the worn, brown leather book and opened it towards the back.

She read through page after page, checking out the numbers in the top-right margins—lots of twos, threes, and a couple of fours. She had to flip through several sheets of paper before she found a seven. She checked the date and saw that it was three months ago.

Despite her panic, change was coming. Today was definitely an eight, or maybe a nine. But was she really ready to move on with her life? Could she leave the nightmare of what had happened two years ago, allow herself to live, and maybe, one day, be happy again?

She pressed the pen to the paper. Carefully she drew *8/9* followed by today's date. Her therapist thought that it was a good idea to score her moods, to help her identify when to reach for guidance so things didn't get out of hand.

She raked the tip of her forefinger over the faint pinkish lines on her left wrist. For some reason, the scars on that wrist were healing faster than the ones on her right. In fact, one or two had turned silvery white, a sure sign that her skin was healing even if her heart still had some serious catching up to do.

"Hey, beautiful. Usual?"

Livvy dropped her sunglasses back in place and smiled at the barman. "You read my mind, Sam."

Two minutes later, a virgin berry cocktail was set down in front of her, condensation dripping down the sides of the glass. Livvy sipped her drink through a straw as she watched the skillful Californian surfers ride the crest of the waves. Their long, sun-bleached hair flowed behind them as they weaved their way to shore before heading back out into the Pacific Ocean once more.

She bent her head and began writing, the nib of the pen making scratching noises on the paper as she recorded her road to recovery. Well, maybe it was too early to use the word *recovery*, but at least she no longer walked around like a zombie—a beating heart without a soul.

A shadow fell across the page, and someone cleared his throat. She glanced up to stare into the greenest eyes she'd ever seen. They sparkled in the sunlight, glimmering shards of emerald buried in a face so handsome that it couldn't be real. Except it was, and so was he.

"Is this seat taken?" He spoke with a drawl, and although she didn't quite have American accents down pat yet, she would guess that he was from somewhere in the southern states— Texas, maybe.

"Um, no. Help yourself." She waved her hand at the chair but couldn't help glancing down the long bar at eight other empty chairs.

He smirked. "Yeah, you'd think I would, right? But as you're sittin' in my chair, the best I can do is park my ass next door."

Livvy inwardly groaned. *Great. A cocky egomaniac—just what I don't need.* She narrowed her eyes and clenched her jaw. "Your chair? Sorry, I must have missed your name on it when I sat down."

"Maybe you didn't look hard enough, darlin'," he murmured, staring at her with an intensity and overfamiliarity that set her teeth on edge.

She resisted the urge to stand up and look at the bloody seat in case his name actually was on it. Instead she gave a nonchalant shrug. "You can sit there"—she pointed at the seat beside her—"or in any of these other empty chairs." *Hopefully he'll choose the latter.*

His eyes twinkled with mischief. "I could just remove you."

Livvy's heart stuttered. The thought of having another man's hands on her, even in a completely nonsexual way, made her hyperventilate. "Just try it," she muttered, turning her back to him. She needed this guy to get the message. She wasn't interested in conversation—or banter.

She buried her head in her journal, and he… well, he

3

chuckled. Then the chair next to hers scraped along the floor. *Damn it.* He *was* going to sit there. Livvy sensed his eyes on her, and her body responded in a way that someone who looked like he did was most likely well accustomed to. Her pulse increased, a slight flush crept over her chest and worked its way up her neck, and her skin was heated not from the sun but from *him.* She stared at the blank page, willing her pen to move and write any old thing, but it stubbornly refused to make a single mark.

"Well, well, if it ain't Gabe Mitchell. Good to see you, man." Sam leaned over the bar, and the two men shook hands. "Usual?"

"Yeah."

Livvy furtively watched Gabe as he dropped a twenty-dollar bill on the bar. Tanned hands gave way to strong, muscled forearms. Livvy's stomach fluttered in appreciation, accompanied by a tightness across her chest that she recognized as guilt. She rubbed her forehead as a headache began to form behind her eyes.

After Sam set a beer in front of him and swiped the money, Gabe picked up the glass and took a long drink then wiped his mouth with the back of his hand.

With his thirst quenched, his attention once again turned to Livvy. "So, darlin', you know my name. What's yours?"

Livvy put away her journal and drained the last of her drink before pushing her glass across the bar. Keeping her gaze as steady as she could, she looked Gabe straight in the eye. "Number one, I am not your darling," she said in her best clipped English. "Number two, I have no intention of telling you my name, as what good would it do when we are never going to see each other again? And number three, I'm leaving now, so you can have your precious seat back."

She scrambled down from the high-backed chair with what she hoped was a modicum of grace, threw some money on the bar, and with her shoulders set back, she stalked towards her car. She had no idea why he'd irked her so much, but in a way, she reveled in the anger. It was good to *feel* again, even if her therapist would probably tell her to focus on more positive emotions.

She climbed into her car and drove out of the parking lot. As she reached the road, she couldn't resist glancing back towards Sam's. She expected to see him enjoying his beer and the ocean view. Instead, she found him staring at her, his eyes piercing, his lips curved upward into a small smile.

At his scrutiny, heat rushed into her face, and her heartbeat kicked into overdrive. She quickly turned away from his stare and hit the gas pedal. Only once she'd put some distance between herself and the bar did her breathing return to normal.

But the anxiousness churning in her gut, mingled with a long-forgotten tingle of excitement that began in her toes and slowly crept upward, was far from normal. She could sense change was in the air. Had it arrived with Gabe Mitchell?

CHAPTER TWO

GABE SIPPED HIS BEER, his gaze following the Chevy until it turned left at the end of the road and disappeared from view. That woman might have been uptight, like a lot of English women were, in his opinion, but there was something more to her, something inherently sad in her eyes. He recognized the flat, empty stare because he saw it in his own gaze every morning. She'd suffered, and by the looks of things, she still was. The scars on her wrists hadn't passed him by, either.

"Hey, Sam." He invited over the barman. Not much happened around here without Sam knowing about it.

"Another?"

"Yeah, and some information."

Sam grinned. "Intriguing, isn't she?"

"You could say that. What do you know about her?"

"Not much. She's been coming here every Tuesday for about six months, but she's always alone. She buys the same drink, orders the same meal—apart from today, thanks to you scaring her off— and writes in her journal. She's polite but standoffish. You know, the sort that screams 'stay away,' and you can't help but draw closer."

"What's her name?"

"Olivia Hayes."

Gabe stared off into the distance as Sam poured a fresh beer. *What's your story, Olivia Hayes?*

He was jolted from his daydreaming when Sam put the fresh glass in front of him. "I worry about her."

Gabe frowned. "Why?"

"Because if the poor girl has caught your attention, she doesn't stand a chance." Sam fluttered his fingers. "Like a moth to a flame, she's gonna get burned."

Gabe flipped Sam the bird, and the bartender barked with laughter as he walked away to serve a waiting customer.

Gabe's thoughts turned once more to Olivia. He usually found vulnerable, damaged women a turnoff, preferring someone he could spar with rather than having to watch every word that came out of his mouth. But she wore her sadness like a cloak, and Gabe had an urge to free her from the weight of it. And who knew? That might mean he could throw off his own demons.

He took his phone out of the back pocket of his jeans and flicked through the contacts list until he found his publicist's number. There couldn't be too many English women called Olivia Hayes living close to Huntington Beach.

"Alex," he said as soon as his call was answered. "I need a favor."

Alex groaned. "What story do I need to quash this time?"

"I see my reputation precedes me. No story, at least not yet. I need you to find someone for me."

"Shall I instruct your lawyer to prepare a defense against a restraining order at the same time?"

Gabe chuckled. "Since when has my attention ever been unrequited? Give me some credit."

"Okay, what info do you have?"

"Her name's Olivia Hayes. She's mid to late twenties.

English. I saw her in the Huntington Beach area, so that might be where she's living. I need an address."

"Shouldn't be too hard. Give me twenty-four hours."

"You've got twelve."

Alex sighed loudly. "Fine. I'll call you later."

Gabe hung up and finished his beer. He tossed some money on the bar and said goodbye to Sam. Pulling his baseball cap down low and hiding his eyes behind a pair of aviators, he set off for home, his mind swirling with images of Olivia Hayes.

AFTER A RESTLESS NIGHT'S sleep caused by intrusive images of the handsome stranger who'd ticked her off so much the previous day, Livvy decided to go for a run. She needed to do something to calm the agitated feeling making her stomach churn and her skin prickle. She dressed in athletic gear and pulled on a pair of well-worn sneakers. As she passed the fridge, she took out a cold bottle of water.

After locking the apartment door behind her, she jogged down the stairs and onto the street. The temperature was already well into the eighties. Despite that, she set off at a fast pace, desperate to quiet the unwelcome voices in her head.

Ninety minutes later, she returned to her apartment block, sweaty and out of breath. But at least the pit of anxiety gnawing at her had receded, and her body and mind were exhausted too. Maybe now she would be able to relax.

She stepped out of the elevator and trudged along the corridor towards her apartment. As she turned the corner, her eyes widened in astonishment. She paused, wondering if she should turn around and run away before he spotted her. *Too late.* His eyes lifted and met hers, and he flashed her a brilliant smile.

Goddammit. Gabe Mitchell.

Livvy stood absolutely still, holding her breath, unable to

move. What the hell was he doing there? And more importantly, how the hell did he know where she lived?

Gabe's tall, muscular frame was casually leaning against her door, his feet crossed at the ankles. He seemed unable to contain his amusement, his lips twitching upward as he gave her the once-over.

Livvy resisted the urge to tidy her hair or swipe at the rivers of sweat running down her face. She cleared her throat and tried to find her voice. "How…"

He pushed himself away from the door. "It's not as hard as you think, Olivia," he said, edging closer.

Shit. He knew her name and where she lived? What else did he know? Was he some kind of stalker? As he reached her, he held out his right hand, palm up. Livvy frowned, still frozen to the spot, and looked at him questioningly.

"Give me your key," he said. "You look like you're going to drop at any minute. You should be careful running in this heat."

"I'm not giving you the key to my apartment. You could be a murderer, a rapist, anything."

He threw back his head and laughed, the action causing her eyes to slip to the long column of his tanned throat. She swallowed, and her tongue briefly swept over her lips.

"You're perfectly safe, I promise you."

Livvy averted her gaze from the way his Adam's apple bobbed as he spoke—because she didn't like the thoughts that popped into her head—and planted her hands on her hips. "That's exactly what a murderer would say."

He laughed again. "I'm one of the good guys. Promise. And considering I was asking Sam about you yesterday, I'd guess that if any harm were to come to you, I'd be suspect number one."

She narrowed her eyes. "Why were you asking Sam about me?"

He reached out his hand once more. "Come on. Give me your key. We need to get you a drink before you pass out."

With a heavy sigh, and without understanding the reason for

her capitulation, Livvy took the key out of her pocket and dropped it into his outstretched palm.

He turned around, walked back to her apartment, and opened the door. Glancing over his shoulder, he cocked his head to the right. "Coming?" he asked, walking inside.

Livvy's hands formed into fists, and her chest burned. She'd thought him arrogant the previous day. This morning, his arrogance was on bloody steroids.

When she stepped into her apartment, he'd already opened the fridge, removed a carton of orange juice, and was pouring some into a glass that had been draining on the side of the sink. He extended the glass of juice towards her.

Unbelievably, she found herself taking it from him. "Thanks." She took a swig. "I need to shower."

He arched an eyebrow. "Don't let me stop you."

"Oh, I don't think so." She stalked to the door and opened it, inclining her head. "Out."

He smirked, and for an awful moment, she thought he wasn't going to leave. She began running scenarios in her head for how to deal with the situation, when he shrugged.

"Okay. I'll wait outside." He clipped her under the chin as he passed then pulled the door closed behind him.

For a few moments, Livvy stared at the door. Who was this guy? His overfamiliarity towards her was more than a little unnerving. Maybe that was why she felt so wrong-footed. Or perhaps it was his composure and poise that was throwing her off.

She jumped into the shower and let the cool water wash over her. She stood there for a minute or so, trying to put her scattered thoughts into some semblance of order. Less than twenty-four hours ago, they'd met at Sam's, and she was certain she hadn't told him her name. Or had she? God, it was so hard to remember. Regardless, her name was one thing; her address was quite another. Had he followed her home after she left the bar? No, he couldn't have. Yet there he was. What could he possibly want?

She dried herself off and quickly dressed. Maybe he hadn't stuck around. As quietly as she could, she opened the door and peered through the crack. Damn, he was still there, lounging against the wall, tapping on his cell phone. As if sensing her scrutiny, he lifted his head and met her eyes, an amused expression curving his lips. He gestured towards the door with his chin, his instruction clear.

Livvy ground her teeth and opened it fully. "Signing in to stalkersRus.com?" she asked.

His answering smile could have turned the hardest of hearts to mush. "No. They canceled my account for using it too much. Feeling better?"

She held her breath as a warm feeling swarmed through her veins, and her fingertips tingled with an urge to touch, to explore. Grimacing as guilt slammed into her, she bit down hard on her bottom lip. Her reaction to Gabe was purely physical, nothing more. *No need to get all of a dither.* He was simply a good-looking guy. And that smile…

"Yes, thanks."

"Good." He sidled past her before she could stop him. "Would you like another glass of juice or water?"

Was this her apartment or his?

"No, I'm fine. What are you doing here, Mr…"

He cocked an eyebrow. He knew that she was faking her lack of memory. "I'm here to see you, Olivia."

She refrained from telling him she preferred Livvy to the much stuffier Olivia. He didn't need any more encouragement. "How do you know who I am and where I live?"

He shrugged. "As I said before, it wasn't very hard to find out." He gestured for her to sit, which totally pissed her off. Even so, she obeyed, glowering at him as he plunked himself down beside her.

"You rushed off so quickly yesterday, just as we were starting to get to know each other. You left me no choice." His jade-green eyes twinkled. "Despite your absolute certainty we would never see each other again, here we are."

His light repartee gave her goose bumps. He was teasing her, but she wasn't in the mood to banter. Still struggling to come to terms with her reaction to him, the last thing she needed was to share a joke. She needed him gone.

She snatched the glass of orange juice from his hand and slammed it on the table. A little spilled over the top. "You've got a bloody cheek. You turn up here, unannounced and uninvited. You take over my home, put your feet up on my sodding table, and help yourself to my juice. I don't even know you, and you certainly don't know me."

He took his feet off the table and fixed her with a long, intense stare. "But I want to know you," he said finally.

"Do you always get what you want?" she asked, unable to keep the irritation out of her tone.

He shrugged. "Mostly." Then he grinned. His teeth were straight and white, probably designed by an expensive orthodontist. "And what do you want, Olivia?" he asked quietly.

"I'd like you to leave," she hit back.

Those green eyes settled on hers again, firm yet kind, determined yet soothing. He rubbed his chin. "Can I be honest with you?"

"If you must." She hated the sarcastic tone to her voice but needed the protection it offered.

His lips twitched up again. Clearly her snotty attitude wasn't bothering him in the slightest. He tilted his body forward, and Livvy fought the urge to lean back.

"When I met you yesterday and you looked at me, your eyes were so sad even though you were clearly pissed off. I found myself wanting to see them smile. And I will… if you give me a chance. I don't know why you're unhappy, but I'd love the chance to put the sparkle back into those baby blues of yours."

Livvy's nostrils flared as she breathed out heavily. She

clenched her hands into fists, holding them close to her sides so one wouldn't shoot out and hit him on his perfectly square chin. Who the hell did this guy think he was? And the worst thing was he'd seen straight through her armor. How he'd managed to achieve that wasn't a question she wanted to examine too closely.

"I'm fine," she said between gritted teeth.

Gabe shook his head. He captured a lock of her hair and slowly fed it through his fingers. Livvy held her breath, unsure what her next move should be. Should she knock his hand away? Tell him—no, order him—to leave? Instead, she sat there like a deer in the headlights, allowing him to touch her.

"No, you're not. You're a beautiful, sexy woman on the outside, but inside, you're an empty shell. You can't be happy living like that, just existing. Don't you want to feel vibrant, alive?"

Livvy jerked her head back, freeing her hair from his long, lean fingers. "Who do you think you are? I am perfectly happy with my life, thank you."

"Don't lie," he said. "You're not very good at it."

Livvy launched to her feet, strode across the room, and flung open the door. "I want you to go."

Gabe slowly eased himself to a standing position. He looked down at her, and their considerable height difference gave her the shivers. "If you give me a chance, I will change your life for the better. A lot better."

"Pretty sure of yourself, aren't you?" she asked with a sneer.

"Well, I don't lack confidence if that's what you mean." He was teasing her again, a mischievous grin sending his full lips curving upward. He really was stunning—so stunning that Livvy wondered why he was there, wasting his time with her. He *had* to have an ulterior motive. What would a guy like him want with a girl like her? She was only half a person, and despite the great strides she'd made since that drunk driver wrecked her life almost two years earlier, she still had a hell of a long way to go.

"Why me? You don't even know me."

He blinked several times and rubbed his chin. "I don't know. I feel a connection to you, and I have no clue where it's coming from. It hit me like a truck yesterday in the bar. I really wasn't expecting it. I'm not in the habit of tracking down beautiful English girls I don't know and offering to be some sort of emotional crutch. But there's something about you—I can't put my finger on it—and I know that if you let me in there, let me past the armor you're using to protect yourself, I think we could have a lot of fun together."

His honesty disarmed her, and when his hand came up to brush a lock of hair out of her eyes, she stilled. "You feel it too, don't you, Olivia?" he murmured.

"I don't know what you're talking about," she whispered.

A faint smile touched his lips. "How about dinner tonight? No strings. Sound good?"

"No. It sounds completely crazy."

Gabe laughed, the sound rumbling deep and low in his chest. "Don't you eat?" There he went again with the teasing.

Despite a burgeoning smile that threatened to emerge, Livvy kept her face straight. "Yes, I eat."

"So let me buy you dinner. What harm could it do?" When she remained silent, Gabe continued. "I'm very persistent, so it might be better—and definitely less exhausting—to give in now. I'm offering steak and salad, not whips and chains."

His comment finally made her break a smile, and before she knew it, she accepted his invitation. "Fine."

"Great," he said with a quick glance at his watch. "I have to go. I'll pick you up here at eight."

He strode across her apartment as if she had just been acquired in a business deal. Now that she'd signed on the dotted line, it felt as though he'd lost interest. She wrapped her arms around her body. What on earth had she agreed to?

"Dress for a nice restaurant," he said, glancing over his shoulder as he walked through the door. Then he was gone.

Agog, Livvy sank into the space Gabe had recently vacated. The fabric still felt warm from his body heat. She'd been railroaded, and yet she wasn't sure how he'd managed it. Still, she could always cancel... damn, she didn't have his number. Then again, he'd found her, so surely she could find him.

She grabbed her computer, opened Google, typed "Gabe Mitchell" into the toolbar, and hit return.

Hundreds of pages were returned in a nanosecond.

Gabe Mitchell: Five things you may not know about the business tycoon.

Gabe Mitchell breaks into the Forbes top-ten list of the richest people in the world.

Gabe Mitchell and Tabitha Hale finally call it quits.

60 Minutes *with tech tycoon Gabe Mitchell.*

Another sultry brunette on the arm of business leader Gabe Mitchell.

That was why he'd looked familiar. He was one of America's top businessmen. But unlike a lot of CEOs that preferred to conduct their business behind closed doors, Gabe Mitchell sought out media attention, and in the States, at least, he was seen as more of a celebrity than a businessman.

Livvy clicked on the last story and was faced with hundreds of images of Gabe at various events, with different beautiful women dripping off his arm. She looked closely and noticed that he was very rarely seen with the same woman twice. About two years ago, he'd had a serious relationship with someone called Tabitha Hale. Since their breakup, Gabe looked as though he'd had nothing more than a long series of temporary distractions.

A chill crept up her spine. Gabe Mitchell was a womanizer, a man who chewed through women like candy. And he'd set his sights on her.

Oh shit. What the hell had she gotten herself into?

CHAPTER THREE

GABE SMOOTHED a hand down the front of his shirt before running the same hand down the back of his head. Women didn't make him nervous, so why the hell was his stomach fluttering as if a swarm of butterflies had set up home?

He knocked on Olivia's apartment door and waited. The chain rattled, and as she opened it, those damn butterflies went crazy, their wings quivering against the walls of his stomach.

"Hi." She met his gaze. "You're right on time."

"Olivia." His eyes skimmed over her from head to foot. "You look lovely."

"Thanks. You look… nice," she mumbled.

He grinned. "Wow, nice. One of my favorite adjectives."

Her cheeks flushed. "Let me grab my purse, and then we can go, if that's all right?"

"Take your time."

As she turned around, his eyes fell to her ass swaying beneath the mint-green flared dress she'd chosen, and his stomach jolted. The style of the dress was casual, but paired with sparkling silver four-inch heels that enhanced her shapely legs, she'd more than met his instructions.

Gabe held out his hand, indicating that she should go on ahead, and together, they strolled to the elevator in companionable silence.

"I hope you like Italian food," he said, pushing the button for the third time.

"Yes, I do. Very much."

"Good. I'm taking you to my favorite Italian restaurant. It's off the beaten path, but the food is outstanding." He pushed the elevator button once more.

"It doesn't do any good, you know."

He looked down at her and frowned. "What doesn't do any good?"

"Pushing the call button over and over. It'll get here when it gets here."

The elevator dinged to signal its arrival, and the door slowly shuddered open. Gabe stared at her in mock horror. "Is it safe?"

"Safe but slow," she replied with a giggle. "Although I have gotten stuck in here once or twice."

"Is that so?" He raised one eyebrow. "Well, I'm sure we'll think of some way to pass the time if we get stuck tonight."

A beautiful flush crept up her neck, inching over her cheeks. Jesus, she was adorable. She wasn't a virgin—his experience had taught him that—yet she gave off a pure and honest air that was enchanting.

After an interminable wait, the elevator reached the ground floor, and the door jerked open. Gabe caught Olivia's hand in his and strode across the parking lot. As he unlocked the car, he caught her surprised expression. "What?"

Olivia's brow creased. "This is your car?"

"Yes. Why?"

She shook her head. "I imagined something more… pretentious."

He laughed. "You pictured a Ferrari?"

She chuckled. "Maybe. I definitely didn't picture an SUV."

He helped her climb in, and after he slid behind the wheel,

he gave her a quick glance as he fired up the engine. "I thought this type of car might make you feel more comfortable."

Her eyes widened, and then she smiled. "Read minds, do you?"

He tried to ignore what her smile did to his insides as he pulled out of the parking lot and merged onto the highway. Once they were underway, he put his hand on her knee. When she almost jumped through the roof of the car, he quickly removed his hand.

"You're safe with me, Olivia, I promise you."

A frown drifted across her face before she smoothed her expression. "I know."

"Good."

Twenty minutes later, he turned onto a gravel driveway and parked the car in front of a rectangular sign—Giovanni's Ristorante.

"Stay there," Gabe ordered as he got out of the car and walked around to her side. He opened her door and helped her out then once again took her hand in his.

"Is this okay?" he asked as they strolled to the entrance, nodding to where their fingers were knitted together as he tried to ignore how good it felt to touch her. It was one dinner. Nothing more.

She nodded, and relief rushed through him as he led her into the restaurant. He loved coming to Giovanni's. The inside was dimly lit, giving it an air of intimacy, and there were only twelve tables, which meant that it wasn't full of people. Olivia was skittish, so he needed to take things slow and easy with her. A busy restaurant filled with people he knew, who would probably ask pointed questions about his date, wasn't the way to go.

"Gabe? Is it really my old friend Gabe Mitchell?" Giovanni clapped him on the back several times. "I saw your name in the bookings, and I thought, 'No, it can't be! He hasn't been to see his buddy Giovanni for such a long time.'"

"As usual, Giovanni, you bend the truth. I've been working

overseas, so it's difficult to fly back just for a bowl of your delicious pasta."

Giovanni grinned broadly. "Non importa." He turned his gaze to Olivia. "Well, well, and who is this beautiful lady?"

"Giovanni, this is Olivia Hayes. Olivia, this is Giovanni Tortorici. He owns this place."

"Bella, Olivia." Giovanni enthusiastically grabbed her hand and kissed it. "Welcome to my restaurant. Come, come this way. I have the best table for you."

He began to walk away, still holding Olivia's hand, until Gabe stopped him and gently gripped his forearm. Giovanni grinned, understanding, and with a bow, released her. He led them to the very back—a private table hidden from the rest of the diners by a wall of fake foliage. Giovanni pulled out one of the chairs with a flourish and gestured for her to sit down.

"Sit, sit, bella Olivia. I have a very special evening prepared for you." He unfolded a napkin and, with a flick of his wrist, laid it in her lap.

"What would you like to drink, Olivia?" Gabe said.

"Whatever you're having is fine."

"A bottle of Barolo and two orders of the fettuccini Alfredo." Then as an afterthought, he turned to her. "That's okay, isn't it?"

"Yes. Sounds lovely."

He nodded. "Good. Giovanni makes the best pasta in the West."

Giovanni grinned widely, pleased with the compliment. "Coming right up."

Before they had time to say more than a couple of words, Giovanni returned and poured their wine. Then with a cheerful, "Enjoy, amici," he left them alone.

Olivia sipped her wine, and Gabe couldn't help but notice a slight tremor to her hand as her lips pressed against the glass. He found it difficult to drag his eyes away from her mouth, but when she noticed him checking her out, she gave him a tight smile.

"Don't be nervous. I don't bite. Well, not on a first date, anyway," he added with a wicked grin.

A flash of anguish crossed her face. "It's not a date. It's dinner."

Gabe inwardly cursed his poor choice of words. This one was different from the usual women in his life, and therefore, *he* would have to be different. If he came on too strong, he would just see her back as she walked away.

"Of course. I'm sorry."

She jutted her chin in a show of bravado that was betrayed by her tense body language. "Why am I here?"

He frowned. "What do you mean?"

"I didn't recognize you before. I mean at Sam's or at my place. But now I know you're some hotshot businessman. I have no idea why you would want to bother with someone like me."

Her choice of words was incredibly revealing. Whatever had happened to this girl had impacted her life dramatically.

"How did you figure out who I am?"

She flashed a quick grin, but it disappeared before he could savor it. "I was going to cancel so I Googled you to try to find your address or phone number."

He tilted his head to the side as he considered her previous statement. "Why were you going to cancel?"

She shrugged. "I changed my mind."

Gabe leaned back in his seat. "And yet here you are. Why?"

"Because I couldn't find a way to contact you."

"You could have told me no when I came to collect you."

She nodded. "But that would have been rude."

Gabe laughed. "So your English sensibilities mean you'd rather go to dinner than tell me that you'd changed your mind?"

She glanced down at her fingers fiddling with the tablecloth. "I have a feeling that if I'd said I'd changed my mind, you wouldn't have taken no for an answer."

A dart of surprise hit him in the chest. "I can accept a no when someone means it."

She fixed her gaze on him, her gorgeous blue eyes like a deep pool of water he could drown in. "Can you?"

"Yes." Silence stretched between them until Gabe sighed. "Okay, if you'd told me you'd changed your mind, I would have done my best to change it back."

Olivia laughed. "And we're back to 'why me'?"

Gabe rubbed the tips of his fingers over his mouth. "Tell me about yourself."

She shrugged. "There isn't a lot to tell, to be honest."

"I'm sure that isn't true at all. And in my experience, people who end a sentence with 'to be honest,' usually aren't being honest."

She winced at his directness, and he kicked himself for his lack of tact.

"That was unfair. Forgive me."

Olivia paused and looked at him, a small smile curving her lips upward. He would love to put his mouth on those lips, but it was unlikely he would get the chance if he didn't filter his comments.

"You don't strike me as a man who makes many apologies. Was that painful?"

Gabe chuckled. "Extremely. Okay, let's start again. What are you doing in California?"

She glanced down and began feeding her napkin through her fingers. "It's as good a place as any."

"It's a great place, but why did *you* choose it?"

Her tongue swept over her lips, and his stomach clenched. "It's peaceful here."

"Why are you looking for peace?"

She stared at her hands. "I'm recovering."

"Recovering? Like from an illness?"

She paused, her brows pinched together in a frown. "Not exactly. Something awful happened to me, and before you ask,

I'm not getting into it with you, so don't bother asking. I needed to get away from England, that's all."

Gabe gazed at her, saying nothing. Then he reached across the table and clasped her hand in his. He squeezed, and a thrill ran through him when she didn't shake him off. "I'm sorry," he said. "Of course I'm not going to ask you. It's your business."

A wave of sadness crossed her face before she hid it behind her perfected mask. "Tell me about how you started your business."

Gabe picked up on her cue to move on. Here was a subject he could talk about for hours, and he got the distinct feeling that she preferred not to talk about herself. If he got the chance for a second, third, and fourth date, he would gradually work up to further probing, but for tonight, he'd let it lie.

"I wasn't very studious at school, but once I left and escaped the constraints of people who constantly told me what I could and couldn't do, it gave me the freedom to take risks. I don't come from a wealthy background—far from it—but I caught a lucky break when I saw an advertisement in a paper looking for entrepreneurs with ideas but no money. I went along to the job fair, and the rest, as they say, is history. That's not to belittle how tough it's been, but without that first opportunity, it would have been very difficult to get started."

"I guess everyone needs a helping hand."

Gabe nodded as Giovanni appeared with their food. He watched as Olivia picked up her fork, wrapped the fettuccini around it, and lifted it to her mouth. Her eyes fell closed, and she made an appreciative sound at the back of her throat as she chewed, a sound that made his eyes widen and his cock stiffen.

As she opened her eyes, she caught him staring at her and frowned. "What?"

"I don't think I've ever, in thirty-five years on this earth, seen anyone look so damned sexy while eating pasta."

She took a sharp intake of breath then began to choke. Coughing and spluttering, she grabbed her napkin and put it over her mouth, desperately trying to catch her breath. Gabe got up from the table and struck her firmly on the back. As he swept her hair away from her face and held it in a makeshift ponytail, his gaze fell on a tattoo on the back of her neck. Five stars cascaded downward in an S shape, all in decreasing sizes.

"Sorry," she spluttered. "Pasta went down the wrong way."

"Better now?"

She took a sip of water. "Yes, thank you."

Gabe retook his seat as Olivia began to eat once more. He looked directly at her. "You don't seem like the type of girl to get tattoos. Is there a meaning behind it?"

Her hand froze on the way to her mouth, and an expression of despair crossed her face. She dropped her fork, pushed back her chair, and with a muttered apology, ran for the door.

CHAPTER FOUR

LIVVY FLUNG OPEN the door to the restaurant, her breathing labored. She hadn't been prepared to answer questions about her tattoo. She should have brushed it off with a quip instead of freaking out, which would no doubt raise his curiosity, leading to more questions. She barely knew the guy, and after her performance tonight, she was unlikely to see him again.

A jolt of disappointment surprised her. Despite her initial reservations, she'd enjoyed spending time with Gabe Mitchell. She hadn't made any friends since arriving in California six months earlier, preferring to keep to herself, and apart from the odd chat with Sam on Tuesdays, she barely spoke to a soul. Gabe was good company, very easy to be around, and until he'd inadvertently stumbled upon a difficult subject, she'd felt at ease.

Without a clue where she was, she decided to head for the highway in the hope of flagging down a cab.

"Olivia, wait. Please?" Gabe shouted over the sounds of the passing traffic.

Embarrassment swamped her. He'd think she was crazy, and right then, she concurred. With no intention of sticking around and facing his inevitable questions, Livvy upped her pace. She scanned the highway for any signs of a taxi, but there were none. Dammit, what should she do now? She set off walking down the sidewalk, but before she got very far, Gabe caught up to her.

He put a hand on her shoulder. "Stop, please."

She drew to a halt but kept her eyes on the ground. "I'm sorry," she muttered. "I need to go home."

He gently cupped her chin and lifted her head until she was forced to meet his gaze. "Then I'll take you."

She shook her head. "I've put you out enough already. A cab is fine." She glanced up and down the highway once more.

"A cab is *not* fine." With his hand firmly on her elbow, he propelled her back towards the restaurant car lot. His touch made her shudder, and he must have felt the tremor running through her because he let her go.

Exhausted and mortified at her not-so-minor freak out, Livvy got in the car.

Gabe started the engine, paused, then turned to her. "Okay?"

"Yes. I'm okay."

He hesitated, obviously wanting to say something but unsure of her reaction. She watched him as he wrestled with his thoughts, her breath in her throat at the thought of him pushing her for an answer she wasn't ready to give. Not an honest one at least.

"I shouldn't have pried," he finally said.

"No, it's my fault. You asked an innocent question, and I freaked out." She couldn't help a small smile from creeping across her lips. "You must think I'm a madwoman."

Gabe smiled back at her, and an uncomfortable feeling stirred in her chest at the way that smile made her feel. He tucked a lock of hair behind her ear. "Compared to the circle I usually mix in, you're the most normal woman I've spent time with in quite a while."

His easy manner made her shoulders relax, and the tension

in her spine lessened. "I forget it's there most of the time. I'm sorry. I wasn't prepared to answer questions about it. My reasoning is rather personal, you see."

Gabe held his hands in the air in a pacifying manner. "Like I said, none of my business." He reversed the car out of its parking spot and merged onto the busy highway.

They traveled in complete silence, both deep in their own personal thoughts. As nice and friendly as Gabe seemed, Livvy was nowhere near ready to share her story with him. He was clearly concerned about her extreme reaction, but with any luck, he wouldn't press her. She was tired, overwrought, and craving isolation.

She risked a peek sideways. Gabe's gaze was focused on the road ahead, although a nerve twitched in his right cheek, most likely from his firmly clenched jaw. Livvy faced forward once more. Silence as a companion was better than the alternative.

About twenty minutes later, they pulled up outside her apartment building, and Gabe parked in the same space they'd left not two hours before.

He killed the engine and turned to face her. "Home, safe and sound."

Livvy stared at her hands. "Thanks for tonight. I had a nice time."

Gabe sighed. "Did you?" She opened her mouth to answer, but before one word spilled, he continued. "Look, I don't know what happened in your past, and I don't want to know until you're ready to tell me." He chuckled. "Be honest, though. I bet you've had better nights."

She tried to force a smile as a heavy sadness settled in her chest. "And much worse ones," she said, staring out of the window.

He briefly touched her arm, withdrawing his hand the moment she faced him. "You intrigue me. I'd like to see you again. Do you think you can trust me enough to say yes?"

Livvy paused. She was so lonely, and the chance to spend

time with a good-looking guy who was also great company was one she found she couldn't say no to, even if she was at the end of a long line of women. If anyone could resist the charms of a man like Gabe Mitchell, she could. After all, she had guilt, heartbreak, and sorrow as her protectors.

"I'd like that." Livvy reached for the door handle but then turned back in his direction. "Goodnight."

"'Night, Olivia. I'll be in touch. Soon."

She nodded and stepped out of the car. As she headed towards the elevator, she risked a quick glance over her shoulder to see if he was watching her, but she was greeted with a view of car taillights as he drove away. She quelled an unreasonable stab of disappointment that he hadn't stuck around to make sure she got safely inside, then she jogged upstairs.

She made herself a hot drink and went to bed, but, desire to know more about Gabe kept her from falling asleep. She grabbed her laptop from the living room and snuggled back under the covers, resting the computer against her bent legs. The web page from earlier in the day was still open. Images of all those women—so many women—hit her. Each and every one had been fleeting alliances, except Tabitha Hale.

She should leave it there and close the laptop. *Don't feed the desire to know the details.* Yep, she *should* leave it alone. But she didn't. Instead, she searched for information about Gabe and Tabitha.

The woman was beautiful. Actually, that adjective didn't do her justice. Stunningly perfect was a better description. She and Gabe had made such a striking couple, and they seemed happy in the pictures, always laughing, touching, and sharing secretive glances. What could possibly have happened to split up such an ideal pair? The Internet was full of speculation, although neither Gabe nor Tabitha had shared any details. A publicist had issued a banal statement from Tabitha's point of view. "With love and respect, Gabe and I have decided to take a break from our relationship." Absolutely nothing had been released from him, not even a confirmation of their split. And clearly that "break" had turned into something a lot more permanent.

With a sigh, she closed the laptop. It was utterly pointless to compare herself to someone like Tabitha. Livvy couldn't hope to compete with the beauty or confidence Tabitha projected. Still, her earlier unanswered question seemed even more poignant now. Why her? She was nothing like Tabitha or the multitude of women Gabe had been with since. What could she possibly offer a man like him other than a whole set of baggage he had absolutely no idea about?

She scooched down under the covers and closed her eyes. As she drifted off, her cell dinged with an incoming text, dragging her away from much-needed sleep. She picked it up off the nightstand. It wasn't a number she recognized. She swiped the screen.

Olivia, thank you for this evening. I'm looking forward to next time.

Gabe

A lightness sped across her chest. He'd texted her. *How did he even get my number?* Stupid question. The man had found out her name and address in no time. Her cell phone number wouldn't exactly be a challenge. She saved his number to her contacts list then penned a quick reply.

Thanks for dinner. Oh, and my friends call me Livvy.

Within seconds he replied.

Good to know you consider me a friend, Livvy.

A warm feeling started in her core and spread outward but was immediately followed by the clawing of remorse. Was she so shallow that the first beautiful face to pay her any attention had her grasping for it as if she were drowning? Gabe Mitchell had gotten under her skin, and she wanted him.

Except he was the last thing she needed.

CHAPTER FIVE

LIVVY WOKE the next morning to bright Californian sunshine streaming through the blinds. She groaned and turned over, glancing at the clock. *Shit! Midday.* She never slept so late. She must've been so exhausted from the previous day. Plus she'd probably needed the extra rest since she hadn't been able to fall asleep.

She grabbed a coffee and headed out onto the balcony. Thanks to Mark and the provisions he'd put in place to ensure she would be okay if anything happened to him, she could afford a decent place. She winced at the thought. The old saying was true: money did not buy joy. She'd happily live like a pauper if it meant that Mark and Daniel were still alive.

She had no idea what she was going to do when her visa ran out in three months and she had to go back to cold, bleak England. She wouldn't get an extension—she'd already been told as much by the consulate office—and because worrying wasn't going to change the situation, she mostly ignored it.

She switched on her cell and saw that she had three missed calls. Before she could check who they were from, Gabe texted her.

I can't get a hold of you. Do I have to come there?
I'm worried.
G

Her skin tingled with delight. His intensity was overwhelming and absorbing in equal measure. She dialed his number, and within a few seconds, the ringtone sounded in her ear.

He immediately answered. "Livvy, are you okay?"

"Yes, I'm fine. I overslept is all."

"I was worried when you didn't answer. I was about to get in the car and come over."

Overprotective much? And if that was the case, why was she grinning like an idiot?

"There's no need. In fact, I won't be here. I'm heading to the gym."

"Oh, okay." Was that disappointment she heard in his tone?

"Why were you calling, anyway?" she asked.

"Do you have any plans for Saturday?" His voice was soft and tender, and an involuntary shiver ran through her.

"I don't have any plans."

"Good. Now you do. I'll pick you up at eight a.m. Don't be late. Dress comfortably, no skirts or dresses."

Before she had the chance to respond or ask any further questions, he hung up on her.

With a shrug, she finished getting ready for the gym. She'd worry about what he meant later.

THE NEXT TWO days passed so slowly, and Livvy found herself wearing out the carpet, pacing up and down as she tried to figure out what Gabe had in store for her.

Dress comfortably, no skirts or dresses.

She ran through various activities in her head but couldn't decide if any of them came close to what he had planned.

She hoped he had something fun in mind. She tried to settle down with a book, but not even her favorite novel could distract her. She grabbed a juice from the fridge, wandered outside to the balcony, and flopped into one of the comfy chairs.

Her thoughts turned to her regular Skype call with Ches. God, by the time Sunday came, she would have so much to tell her. She wondered what Ches would make of the couple of dates she'd had with Gabe. She hoped her best friend would be happy for her.

As she got ready on Saturday morning, Livvy considered whether Gabe would bother turning up at all. On reflection, she doubted he would be a no-show—not because she thought she was an amazing catch and worth turning up for, but because Gabe struck her as the type of man who kept his word. If he said he would be somewhere, then he would.

At one minute before eight, a knock sounded on the door. Christ, he was punctual. She opened it to find Gabe leaning against the doorjamb, looking one hundred percent like the successful man he was. He was dressed head to toe in designer gear. A thin black sweater made his shoulders look even broader, and blue jeans clung to his hips and thighs before flaring out below the knee into a standard boot cut.

A warm smile played across his lips. "Have I passed?" he asked, gesturing at himself.

"You'll do." A warm flush spread over Livvy's cheeks at how he'd caught her checking him out—and not for the first time. "Am I dressed okay?" She indicated her woolen pants and short-sleeved T-shirt.

His eyes slid over her. "Oh yeah."

She hid another blush by bending over to pull on her sneakers. Fortunately, when she straightened, her skin felt less hot. Gabe was grinning as he held the door open. She grabbed her jacket and purse and shot through it as fast as she could.

As they walked towards the elevator, Gabe coiled his arm

around her waist. Livvy twitched, but all Gabe did was pull her closer, and after a couple of seconds, she relaxed.

"So where are we going, anyway?" Livvy asked as Gabe opened the car door for her.

He tapped the side of his nose with his finger. "It's a surprise."

She grinned. "I like surprises."

As Gabe pulled into traffic, Livvy rested her head against the back of the seat and closed her eyes. A song by Snow Patrol—one of her favorite bands—came on the radio.

"Can I turn it up?" she asked, already reaching for the volume.

Gabe nodded. "Go for it."

Livvy cranked the sound up high. The car gently rocked her as she turned her face towards the sun, relishing the warmth as it shone through the windows.

About forty minutes later, Gabe turned off the main highway. "Almost there," he said as he glanced sideways, his eyes sparkling with excitement.

Livvy fed off his enthusiasm but couldn't help the bite of nervous tension clawing at her insides. What if she didn't like what he'd planned? Would she tell him or just go along with it?

The concrete road eventually turned into a dirt track, which they traveled along for a minute or so before Gabe pulled into a gravel parking lot. Small aircraft were dotted around, and as Livvy peered through a metal gate to her right, she spotted a runway.

She turned to Gabe and frowned. "Are we flying somewhere?"

"Yes and no." He climbed out of the car.

Livvy unclipped her seat belt and got out too.

Gabe met her gaze over the roof of the car, his expression unreadable. "We're going skydiving."

Livvy's heart began thudding in her chest, and she couldn't stop her mouth from gaping. This had to be a joke—a very bad joke. Her stomach cramped with nerves, and she blinked rapidly while Gabe stood there, watching her growing panic with a mixture of uncertainty and determination.

"I-I," she stammered, unable to get the bloody words out. She closed her eyes and took a deep breath. When she finally found her voice, she didn't hold back. "Are you insane? There's no way I'm going to voluntarily jump out of a perfectly functioning aircraft."

"It's safe."

"I don't care. Jesus!" She dragged her hands through her hair, tugging when she reached a knot. She brushed the torn hair to the ground. "What happened to a normal day out like bowling or the cinema or shopping, for goodness' sake?"

Gabe analyzed her, his keen gaze reading her panicked expression. "I won't let anything happen to you. I'm fully trained, and you're going to be absolutely fine." He chuckled. "It'll definitely bring some color to your cheeks."

Livvy planted her hands on her hips. "So would makeup," she said, drawing another laugh from him. "Look, how can I put this in one-syllable words so you understand? I. Am. Not. Doing. This."

Gabe strolled to her side of the car. He placed his hands around the top of her arms, his grip firm and mildly comforting. "I'll take you through the process from start to finish. It will be an amazing experience, one you will never forget, I promise you. Let's go inside, and after we've been through everything, if you really don't want to do it, then we will walk away."

Although she was terrified, his rationality was her undoing. Her knees trembled as adrenaline coursed through her body, but as she looked into his eyes, she couldn't help but notice the raw desire for her to do this with him.

"If I'm unhappy with anything, it's not happening."

"Done. Now come," he said, taking her hand in his.

Like a prisoner being led to the gallows, Livvy shuffled behind Gabe as he towed her towards a hangar. As they entered, a tall, rather reedy-looking guy greeted them. He thrust his hand out to Gabe, who dropped hers to shake his.

"Hey, Gabe. Good to see you. It's been a while."

"Hi, Ryan. Yeah, I've been overseas. This is Livvy Hayes. We're gonna do a tandem jump today. It's her first time," he added, probably to explain to Ryan why Livvy was standing there with her knees knocking and sweat beading on her top lip.

"Hi, Livvy." Ryan gave her a firm handshake. "Nervous?"

She swiped a finger over her lips. "Incredibly."

"You don't have any reason to be," Ryan said. "You'll be jumping with one of the best in the business. Let's take you through the safety briefing, and then we'll get you harnessed up."

Gabe and Livvy followed Ryan to a table with a mountain of gear piled on top of it, none of which meant anything to her. Ryan chattered away, explaining in minute detail what was going to happen and what her part in it was. Livvy forced herself to concentrate as Gabe examined the equipment. The biggest thing she took from the safety briefing was that she should try not to puke. Yeah, she could have figured that out for herself.

"Ready?" Gabe asked when Ryan finished the briefing.

"Nope," she replied.

He grinned, picked up a harness, and held it out. "Come on. Step in."

It didn't take long before Gabe and Livvy were in their harnesses. Gabe explained they would be strapped together, and the only thing she had to do was enjoy the view.

"Time to head over to the plane, Livvy," Gabe said.

"Okay." Her voice was so small that Gabe leaned closer so he could hear her. As he did, she caught a whiff of his cologne. "I like your aftershave," she blurted, immediately overcome with embarrassment. "God, sorry. That makes me sound like an idiot, but I'm freaking out here. I don't know what I'm saying."

Gabe laughed. "You're far from an idiot, and the nerves

you're experiencing are normal. Try to relax. You're safe with me, darlin'."

Livvy nodded briefly, too anxious to say anything else. Gabe took her hand and set off towards a small plane. As they got closer, Livvy's breathing escalated. Her heart began to pound, and she briefly wondered how many beats a minute a twenty-nine-year-old could take before her heart gave out.

"Am I too young to have a heart attack?" she asked, causing a gruff laugh to come from Gabe.

"Stand in front of me," he said.

Livvy frowned. "Why?"

"Well, unless you want your first jump to be solo, I need to strap us together."

An involuntary shudder coursed through her. This would be the closest she'd been to a man since Mark, and she feared her own reaction. She might be grieving, but she still had a pulse, and Gabe was very attractive. She instinctively knew her body would react and her head would revolt.

She did as he asked and squeezed her eyes closed. His fingers skimmed over her body as he fed several straps through buckles and tightened them. Warmth spread through her core at his touch, even as a simultaneous slug of guilt made her chest tighten and tears prick her eyes. After the trauma she'd suffered, she had honestly never expected to find herself attracted to another man again, yet she couldn't lie to herself any longer. She was definitely attracted to Gabe Mitchell.

"Okay?" he murmured, his breath feathering the back of her neck. Livvy broke out in goose bumps as she nodded, not trusting herself to speak.

Gabe eased her forward. "Let's go."

As they climbed up the metal steps and onto the plane, her limbs began to tremble, and her heart almost punched out of her chest. Even Gabe's supreme confidence didn't reassure her that she would be fine.

The plane engines roared to life, and Gabe shouted something to the pilot, but Livvy paid no attention. She chose instead to concentrate on managing her escalating pulse and on taking deep breaths through her nose.

The plane launched down the runway, and as it reached optimum takeoff speed, the wheels lifted. Livvy's stomach sank as the ground disappeared beneath her. As the plane ascended, she peered through the tiny window at the patchwork of green fields below them.

"Great view, huh?" Gabe asked. "It'll be even better when we jump."

Livvy grimaced. "I prefer it from in here."

Gabe laughed, and Livvy realized she was beginning to crave the sound, looking for ways to amuse him so she could hear it again.

"Trust me. When the parachute deploys and nothing except beauty and silence surround you, I bet you change your mind."

"Don't bank on it," Livvy muttered as her heart started banging against her rib cage once more.

Gabe must have sensed her growing unease because he moved his mouth right next to her ear. "It's okay, Liv. Relax. I promise you on my life nothing is going to happen to you."

Her head bobbed in agreement even as her mind screamed, *Are you crazy?*

At about three thousand feet, Gabe pointed. "Look. You can see the LA skyline."

Livvy glanced out the window and saw downtown LA in all its glory. The often-present smog didn't give her a clear view, but she could just about make out the US Bank Tower, the seventy-three-floor skyscraper situated in the heart of the city.

Too soon, they reached their jumping altitude of ten thousand feet. As the door was opened, wind whistled through the plane. *Fuck. This is it.* Livvy began to pant. *I am so not ready for this.* Regardless, it was going to happen. Like being on a rollercoaster that had already left the platform and was climbing to the first drop, the only way she was getting off now was when the ride finished.

The noise inside the plane was so loud, Gabe had to shout to make himself heard. "Ready?"

Livvy shook her head. She felt Gabe's smile against her neck.

"Too bad. Only one way down."

"That's not true," she shouted.

Gabe laughed as he shuffled towards the huge gaping hole in the side of the aircraft, taking Livvy with him. Every fiber of her being was telling her that this was madness. *Stupid. Dumb. Fucking crazy.* Her blood migrated south, leaving her light-headed. Christ, she was sick with fear. She'd never been so scared in her whole life, not even when she was trapped in the car after…

Gabe had moved until they were right in the doorway. He was holding on to the sides. "This is it, Livvy," he hollered.

Before she could reply, he jumped.

CHAPTER SIX

THEY PLUMMETED TOWARDS THE EARTH, freefalling from ten thousand feet after having jumped out of a perfectly functioning aircraft. Buffeted by the wind, Livvy squeezed her eyes shut. They streamed despite being covered by protective glasses. Sound roared in her ears. Gabe was shouting something, but his voice was carried away on the wind. He tapped her on the shoulder, which she remembered meant he was about to deploy the parachute.

Livvy gripped tightly onto the harness as she was swept upward. In an instant, the wind dropped and their speed slowed. She glanced up to see the bright-red parachute above her that would see them safely to the ground. Exhilaration swept through her, and she began to yell and scream with pure excitement now that she'd survived the terror of freefalling.

"Oh my God," she cried out. "This is awesome!"

"Look around you, Livvy," Gabe said in her ear. "Take in the view."

The silence and peace as they floated towards the ground made her eyes water for a different reason. This time, she was overcome with emotion. Gabe had been right. The jump out of the plane was a leap into the unknown but also a decision to choose life. She was finally coming to the realization that Mark wouldn't want her to mourn forever. He would want her to live, to be happy and fulfilled... and to find someone else.

Before she was ready for the experience to be over, the ground rushed towards them, and she pulled her legs up as Ryan had instructed her to during the safety briefing. Gabe expertly brought ss to his sides, which slowed them even more. And then... touchdown. They hit the soft grass of the landing site, and a rush of emotion so strong sped through Livvy that she had no words to describe it. Gabe unhooked them, and as soon as she was free, she couldn't hold back.

She dragged off the safety helmet and pitched it to one side. "Oh my God! Oh my God! That was *amazing*. The adrenaline rush was *unbelievable*. When can we do it again?"

Gabe started laughing as he unfastened his helmet. "Whenever you want to." He playfully nudged her shoulder. "I knew you'd love it. You were scared shitless, and yet with no hesitation, you jumped. And look at you. Your eyes are sparkling. Your skin is glowing. You look *alive*, Livvy."

The incredible buzz racing through her body and the sincerity with which he spoke to her were her undoing. She threw her arms around him and hugged him close. For a moment, he froze, then his arms came around her waist.

Desire swarmed outward from her core as his firm body pressed against hers. God, she'd missed this—the warmth and solidity of being in a man's arms. She nuzzled into his neck and let out a sigh of contentment.

Then she almost drowned in a swathe of guilt that weighed her down so heavily, she buckled beneath the pressure. She tore out of his arms. Her legs shook, and she bent over, bracing her hands on her knees.

"Livvy?" Gabe's concerned voice reached her. "What's wrong?"

She straightened. "I shouldn't have done that." The wind

had tugged some of her hair free of the hair tie, and she pushed it away from her face.

Gabe sucked in a shuddering breath before gently tilting her chin upward. Under the intense gaze of his vibrant-green eyes, Livvy squirmed. She tried to drop her chin, but he wouldn't allow it. No, she'd started this, and Gabe wasn't going to let her hide.

"I'm sorry," she said. When he remained silent, Livvy decided to pick imaginary fluff from her skydiving suit.

"What happened to you?" he asked softly.

Livvy paused for a moment. The thought of offloading was extremely tempting, but then she shook her head and kept her gaze averted. "Thank you for making me do it. You were right. It was wonderful, but I'd like to go home now, please."

Gabe reached for her hand. When he folded her small one inside his much bigger one, she didn't pull away. She should have, but something about the gentleness with which he held her hand made tears rush to her eyes. She was so lonely, stuck in no-man's-land, wanting to move forward yet allowing the past to hold her back.

"Come on," Gabe said. "Let's get changed, and then I'll take you home."

As they reached the hangar, Ryan came out to meet them, wearing a beaming smile. "Wow! You landed like a pro. How was it?"

"It was great." Livvy tried for a smile, but she figured it had fallen short when a frown drifted across Ryan's face. He looked over at Gabe, who gave the smallest shake of his head.

"Okay, well." Ryan shifted from foot to foot. "I hope we'll see you again."

"Maybe," Livvy said.

"Do you want to stay for a drink?" Ryan asked Gabe.

Gabe shook his head. "We're going to get changed, and then we have to go."

"Another time, then?"

Gabe gave a curt nod as Livvy trudged towards the changing area. Her clothes were hanging where she'd left them, but after she struggled out of the dive suit, her energy waned and she sank onto the wooden bench.

She was so confused, so tired, and so fed up with living this life. But every time she thought about moving on, an invisible force hauled her back. She closed her eyes and allowed her head to rest against the wall. "Mark, help me," she whispered. "Please don't hate me. I'll never forget you or Daniel, but I'm so lonely. I deserve to be happy, don't I?"

Although only silence greeted her, she knew the answer. Whether she would act on it was another matter entirely.

Livvy quickly dressed and stepped outside to find Gabe waiting by the door to the hangar. He waved her over and held out his hand, which she didn't hesitate to take. Her acquiescence brought a small curve to his lips.

"Buckle up," he said as she climbed into the car.

Gabe reversed the car out of its parking space and set off up the dirt track. They fell into silence, and the rocking of the car sent Livvy into a doze. As the car drew to a halt, she pushed herself upright and rubbed her eyes. She looked out of the window to find Gabe had parked outside her apartment building.

"Why am I so exhausted? It's not even midday."

"It's the adrenaline. Come on. I'll walk you up, get you something to drink, and then let you rest."

She leaned on Gabe as the ancient elevator stuttered on its way up to the thirteenth floor. He settled her on the sofa and brought her a glass of chilled water. She drank until it was all gone even though her eyes drooped towards the end.

Gabe pulled a blanket off the back of the couch and covered her with it. "I'll let you get some sleep."

"Don't go," she blurted as an overwhelming urge for company hit her out of nowhere.

Gabe shook his head. "You need rest. Your first skydive is a very emotional, exhausting experience, and you'll need a few hours to recover. I'll call you later."

He started to leave, but Livvy clutched his forearm. "No, please. Stay with me. I don't want to be by myself." Christ, who was she turning into? She craved the feelings this man was stirring in her, yet she feared them at the same time. The push and pull was exhausting.

He smiled softly and sat down beside her. His hand swept over her hair, his touch tender and comforting. "Okay. I'll stay until you fall asleep."

LIVVY GRABBED a glass off the drainboard and filled it with water from the faucet. How long had Gabe stayed after she'd begged him not to leave her alone? *Well done, Livvy. Great way to look needy and desperate.*

She took her water out to the balcony and settled down to watch the sun disappear over the horizon. Five days had passed since she'd met Gabe Mitchell. Five short days in which she'd changed beyond recognition. The reconciliation she now needed to make was between her attraction to a man who was clearly attracted to her, and the overwhelming sense of guilt that felt like barbed wire tearing at her insides.

Her mind turned to the following day. She was due to Skype her best friend—and boy, was Livvy going to have a lot to talk about. Normally, their calls revolved around Ches regaling Livvy with what she'd been up to, who she was seeing, who she'd slept with, and what they were like in bed. It wasn't because Ches had no interest in what was happening in Livvy's life. It was because nothing ever *did* happen in Livvy's life. Their calls always began with Ches asking, "So, Liv, what's been going on with you this week?" And her reply was always, "Nothing much. What about you?" Then Ches would sigh, give Livvy *that* look, and launch into the details of her week. But this time, Ches wouldn't get a word in edgewise.

Livvy took a quick shower and dressed for bed, a little disappointed that Gabe hadn't called her. But when she picked up her cell, she realized the battery was dead. It took about ten minutes before she remembered where she'd left her charger. She plugged it in, and as soon as the battery sparked to life, a text came through.

You looked so peaceful sleeping. I hope this morning was as wonderful for you as it was for me. Truly a time I will never forget. Call me when you wake.

G

Livvy shivered as a thrill ran through her. She reread the text once more. With a steadying breath, she pulled up Gabe's number and hit dial. His phone rang twice before he answered.

"Hey, how are you feeling?" His voice was deep, smooth, and downright sexy.

"I've only just woken. I can't believe I slept all day."

"You needed it after all the excitement from earlier."

"I wish you'd been here when I woke up." She surprised herself with her honesty, especially when she realized she meant every word.

After a pause, he asked, "What are you doing tonight?"

"Nothing. Why?"

"Good, because I'm coming over. I'll cook. See you at seven."

CHAPTER SEVEN

LIVVY PEERED through the peephole then opened the door. Gabe had a large tote bag slung over his shoulder, two other bags in either hand, and he was alone. No cook or butler followed him. Shit, he'd meant it when he said he would cook. Livvy surreptitiously gave him the once-over. He was dressed casually, in faded jeans and a black T-shirt that clung to his firm, hard chest, leaving little to the imagination. Here was a man who took care of himself and found the time to work out despite his busy life.

"Can I come in?" Gabe asked with a smirk and an arched eyebrow.

Livvy's face heated as she realized she'd been gawking without actually saying a word.

"Yes, of course you can." She stepped backward as Gabe entered. Even though she was sure she'd given him enough room, his body brushed against hers, causing a delicious shiver to run down her spine. He dropped the bags on the kitchen countertop and turned to face her. His gaze skimmed her from head to foot, almost invasive in its intensity. She averted her eyes and willed her flushed skin to settle down.

"You look lovely, Livvy."

Livvy laughed. "What, this old thing?" She smoothed down the material of her lemon sundress. She'd never been very good at receiving compliments, and she was finding it even more difficult when they were from him. He moved closer and traced his knuckles down her cheek. A swarm of butterflies set up camp in her belly at his gentle touch.

"The color really suits you. It brings light to your eyes."

Livvy stepped back, causing Gabe's hand to fall to his side. She mourned the loss of contact, even though she'd been the one to cause it.

"Thanks," she muttered, feeling off kilter. Why did he make her feel so gauche, like a teenager? She was twenty-nine years old for goodness' sake, and she should be able to hold her own, yet she couldn't. He paralyzed and dazzled her.

"Why don't you organize the drinks, and I'll get started in the kitchen? A gin and tonic for me, please. I wasn't sure whether you'd have any alcohol so I brought some along. They're in that bag." He pointed with his chin as he grabbed two other bags and moved them to the opposite side of the kitchen, where she had her food-preparation area.

"You're really going to cook?" Livvy asked. "You weren't joking?"

Gabe chuckled. "No, Livvy. I wasn't joking. I am *really* going to cook. I think you'll find I'm very handy in the kitchen. In fact, I love to cook. It's soothing and a good de-stresser at the end of a long, hard day."

Livvy poured herself a vodka and prepared a gin and tonic for Gabe. She set down the drink next to where he'd already started chopping vegetables.

He placed the knife on the chopping board and lifted his drink. "Cheers." He held his glass in the air, and she clinked hers against his.

This felt so normal yet surreal at the same time. What the hell was she doing there? More importantly, what the hell was he doing there? Even though she'd thought about this several times, she still couldn't work out why he seemed interested in her. Surely, he could have whomever he wanted—and already had if the images on Google were to be believed. Yet there he was, in her kitchen, cooking a meal for them both. Livvy was having real trouble getting her head around it.

"Why are you here?" The words were out before she could stop them, and when he glanced over at her with a furrowed brow, she wished she could take them back.

"Haven't we had this conversation?" He raised his eyebrows in inquiry. "Why do you think, Livvy?"

"Well, if I knew the answer to that, I wouldn't have asked, now, would I?" Her words came out harsher than she'd intended, and his eyes narrowed, although a smirk lurked around his mouth.

"It's good to know that you have claws," he said with a laugh. He placed his drink on the counter and moved towards her, but his approach was tentative, almost as though he wasn't sure whether she would run or knee him in the balls.

Livvy held her ground and met his gaze. He cupped her face in both of his hands and dropped a kiss on her forehead. "I'm here, Livvy Hayes, because you are quite simply the most beautiful, interesting, kind, sensitive, funny, and frustrating woman that I've ever had the good fortune to meet. And quite frankly, I can't stay away from you. Does that answer your question?"

Well, she hadn't expected those words to fall from his perfectly formed lips. Her knees trembled, and she sucked in a steadying breath as, once more, her stomach flooded with desire. She searched for an appropriate response.

"Yes" was the best she could manage. She stared at her feet, mortified. *Way to go, Livvy.* She seemed to be struck dumb every time he spoke to her. If she carried on like this, he would begin to think she was an imbecile, incapable of having an adult conversation.

Gabe tucked a finger underneath her chin and applied a

little pressure until she had no choice but to meet his gaze. His eyes bored into hers, the green inflected with specs of aqua, like the sea on a stormy day.

"Someone as lovely as you should never spend any time looking at her feet. Look up with confidence, Livvy. I mean every word. You've bewitched me. You're so different from the sycophants that follow me around like puppies without a mind of their own. There's an innocence and yet a wisdom about you. The conflict is intoxicating."

Her breath caught in her throat. The blazing look in Gabe's eyes scorched her, and she couldn't tear her gaze away from his. She didn't have to, because he made the first move by dropping his hand and turning his attention back to chopping vegetables.

Livvy swallowed her disappointment. She'd been sure he was about to kiss her, but something had changed his mind. Maybe he'd seen a hint of panic cross her face.

She moved to stand beside him, watching as he prepped the food. "How did you learn to cook?" she asked as he wielded the knife like a professional chef.

He shrugged. "I'm self-taught. I'd love to take a course, but I can't commit to such a length of time. My work takes me all over the world. I'm not in the same place long enough to attend a series of classes."

Livvy internally winced. She hadn't thought about the fact that he might be there one day and gone the next, but he didn't exactly have a nine-to-five job. She was falling for his charms, yet any day, he could be gone. By the time he got back, her visa would probably have expired and she would be back in England.

A wave of depression washed over her. "When are you away next?"

Gabe glanced sideways at her. "Not sure yet. Why? Will you miss me?"

"No. I'd enjoy the peace," she lied.

Gabe chuckled, the sound rumbling through his chest. He returned his attention to the chopping board.

"What are you making, anyway?"

"A one-pot chicken recipe I created myself. It's got a bit of everything—peppers, onions, cheese, lots of herbs and spices."

"Oh, I'm so sorry. I should have mentioned that I'm a vegetarian."

Gabe turned to her with an expression of horror on his face. "Shit." He sifted through the bags on the floor. "If you have any pasta, I can throw something together. Or we can go out."

He was so earnest that Livvy couldn't keep up the pretense. She started to laugh. "For a worldly wise guy, you're pretty gullible."

Realization crossed his face. "Oh, you play dirty."

He stalked towards her. Livvy backed away, still giggling. Gabe's arm shot out, and he snagged her around the waist. She found herself pressed up against him, so close that she could feel every single muscle. Her pulse jolted as Gabe lowered his head until his mouth was only an inch from hers. She parted her lips in anticipation of his kiss, her heart thudding in her chest. Excitement caused dampness at the apex of her thighs. She could have sworn a spark of electricity passed between them.

Gabe stared into her eyes. "Breathe, Livvy," he whispered, then his mouth closed over hers.

Her arms curved around his neck of their own accord. Her fingers found their way into his hair, and she clung to it as her knees trembled. A quiet moan eased from her throat as Gabe deepened the kiss. His tongue briefly swept inside her mouth, but then at the most inopportune moment, her stomach rumbled.

He drew back. "Sounds like I need to get back to cooking. You're very distracting."

Livvy made an attempt to pull herself together as Gabe started to add ingredients to the pan. Within seconds, the food was sizzling and the most delicious smell made its way over to her. Livvy sipped her drink as she watched him move about her kitchen, looking as far removed from a top-notch businessman as she could imagine.

After several tasting sessions, Gabe served up the food, and they sat down to eat at Livvy's small glass dining table.

She dipped her head and sniffed the food appreciatively. "This smells incredible."

Gabe nodded at her plate. "Let's hope it tastes good too."

Livvy forked a piece of chicken. The minute she put the food in her mouth, her taste buds were flooded with intense flavor. She chewed slowly, savoring the best-tasting food that she'd eaten in a very long time, including the pasta she'd eaten at Giovanni's.

"Wow! You weren't kidding about being able to cook. This is fabulous."

"Glad you like it."

"You can cook for me every day, if you like."

"Deal." The look in his eyes smoldered with an intensity that made her toes curl.

After they finished eating, Livvy cleared away the dishes. "I've got ice cream if you want dessert," she said as she piled the plates in the sink.

"I can't eat anything else." He rose from the table and settled on the couch, patting the space next to him. "Come sit with me."

Her pulse jolted as she settled down beside him. Every time she was within touching distance of him, her heart rate increased and her palms became clammy. Gabe crossed one leg over the other. He looked as though he were about to say something but then changed his mind.

"What?" Livvy asked.

Gabe shook his head. "Nothing."

She laughed. "Isn't that usually a woman's line? Saying nothing when there's clearly something?"

Gabe took a sip of his drink before fixing his gaze on her. "Look, I don't mean to pry…" he said before he broke off.

Livvy's spine stiffened as she guessed what subject he wanted to discuss. Was she ready to tell him? Maybe it would do her good to share with someone who hadn't known her back then. She was feeling much stronger, much more able to think about Mark and Daniel without a searing pain ripping apart her insides. She didn't owe Gabe an explanation, of course, but he also didn't deserve a brush-off.

"You can ask me," she said.

His gaze softened, his green eyes deepening in color. She could drown in those eyes when she finally removed the sackcloth and ashes she'd worn for the last two years. Maybe that time had finally arrived.

"What happened to you?" he asked.

Livvy took a deep breath and steeled herself to share the most heartbreaking, painful time of her life.

"I had a husband, a really wonderful man named Mark. We met during my first year of university, and as soon as we graduated, we got married. Mark was training to be a lawyer, and I went to work for a marketing firm. We didn't have a lot in the beginning, but we were really happy. I desperately wanted kids. We started trying, but after two difficult miscarriages, I couldn't quite dredge up the emotional strength to try again, so we decided to take a break."

She reached for her drink and took a sip. Gabe's eyes never left her face, but he made no move to interrupt or ask any questions.

"About a year later, I fell pregnant for the third time. The first few months were awful because I couldn't relax, couldn't enjoy any part of my pregnancy. I felt no joy, only fear and panic of it all going wrong again. But it didn't. We found out we were having a little boy, and we named him Daniel."

Livvy briefly closed her eyes as the memories crowded in, as clear today as they'd ever been. She felt Gabe's hand on her arm, and he gave her an encouraging squeeze.

"You don't have to go on."

She shook her head. "It's fine." She inhaled a deep breath and continued. "When I was eight and a half months pregnant, I accompanied Mark to a work function. He wanted me to stay at home, especially as I was huge by that time, but I was going stir-crazy sitting around the house all day. So after I nagged him —a lot—he gave in." She smiled at the memory. "I always could twist him around my little finger."

Gabe raised an eyebrow. "I'll bet."

Livvy chuckled at his teasing, but then her smile fell. "We were on our way home at about eleven in the evening, and we almost got there. Almost." Her vision blurred, and she blinked back tears, but despite her best efforts, they spilled down her cheeks. She dashed them away with the back of her hand. "We were hit by a drunk driver. Mark died instantly, so they told me later, and I had to be cut from the car. They rushed me into hospital and performed an emergency C-section, but it was too late for Daniel." Her voice broke as more tears fell. "He didn't make it. My baby didn't make it."

She found herself in Gabe's arms. His embrace was warm as he whispered in her ear. "I'm so sorry, Livvy. I'm so very sorry."

She let herself absorb his strength for a few seconds before she pulled back and rose to grab a box of tissues. She blew her nose and wiped the tears away from her face before sitting back down.

"That was quite cathartic, actually," she said, meeting Gabe's concerned gaze. "It felt good to talk to someone who wasn't there at the time, someone who's not a family member waiting for me to throw myself off the nearest building, or a shrink watching for signs of a complete mental breakdown."

"How long ago did this happen to you?"

"Two years."

Gabe reached for her hand. He turned it over so the palm was face up and gently traced the scars on her wrist with his thumb. "And these?"

Embarrassed about what she saw as weakness, Livvy tried to tug her hand from his grasp, but he tightened his hold and continued to trace the red and silver lines.

"I did that about a year ago. I couldn't go on. After the hospital released me, my best friend sat me down and gave me a few hard truths as only best friends can. She made me face up to the fact that I had to find a way through. That's when I sold everything back home and came here."

"And where are you now on the road to recovery?"

Her mouth creased in thought. "I'm doing okay. In fact, in the last five days, I'm doing better than okay."

A smile edged across Gabe's face as he realized what she meant. "Glad I could help."

"You should know I'm messed up. I still have very dark days where I find it difficult to imagine a life without them, and I can sink into a pretty deep depression when those times come." She inadvertently touched the back of her neck.

Gabe's gaze followed her movement, and he grimaced. "The tattoo. It's for them?"

Livvy dropped her chin to her chest. "Five stars for all the people I've lost. Mark, Daniel, my two other babies... and me."

"Oh hell," Gabe muttered. He shuffled closer to her, and once more, she found herself encased in his arms, her head resting against his broad chest as he stroked her hair. "I'm glad you told me."

Livvy nodded. "Me too."

CHAPTER EIGHT

THE FOLLOWING MORNING, Livvy almost bounded out of bed even though the sunlight had woken her long before her alarm.

A slow smile built across her face as her mind turned back to the previous evening. Sharing her past with Gabe had been the right thing to do because she felt lighter—as though a weight had been lifted from her shoulders. Finally, she could stand tall and almost pain free. She could barely believe they'd met less than a week ago. He was incredibly easy to talk to. He didn't interrupt, and he gave her his full attention. Those intense green eyes read every nuance in her body language and every inflection in her voice. He understood the things she'd said, as well as the things she hadn't.

And to think she'd assumed he was an egotistical dick after their initial meeting at Sam's bar. Oh, she had no doubt he had a big ego—What successful businessman didn't?—But he was also thoughtful, kind, caring… and hot.

Livvy climbed out of the shower and dried herself off. After slipping into a T-shirt and shorts, she padded into the kitchen and stuck two slices of rye bread into the toaster. While she waited for the toast to pop, she picked up her phone. No missed calls or texts from Gabe, although when he'd left the previous night after her "on-the-cheap" shrink session, they'd made no further plans.

Livvy rubbed the back of her neck as a heaviness settled in her stomach. Why hadn't she asked him to call? What if she'd scared him off with her neurosis and he decided he didn't need a complication like her in his oh-so-wonderful life?

She chewed on the inside of her cheek. When they were together, he pushed away all negative thoughts, but when he wasn't around, she was fraught with self-doubt. All of the uncertainty about why he wanted to spend time with her came flooding back, and the heavy burden of guilt that returned when he wasn't close made her stomach twist with anxiety. And that brought its own concerns. She was enjoying being with Gabe a little too much, already relying on him to make her feel better. Maybe some distance would do her good.

After eating her breakfast outside, she wandered into the kitchen, leaving the door open so that she could hear the birds tweeting. Her phone dinged with an incoming text. She glanced at the banner across the screen—Gabe. With sweaty palms and trembling hands, she swiped at her cell.

Hope you're feeling okay today. Are you free later? Say around twelve?
Livvy twisted her hair into a knot before she typed a reply.
What did you have in mind?

She stared at her phone, willing it to make the text sound she realized she was starting to crave. Such a simple sound had a hell of a thrill attached to it. She didn't have to wait long.

Do you own a pair of hiking boots?
She tapped a response. *No.*

She hung on, waiting for another text from him, but when one wasn't forthcoming, her shoulders dropped. She picked up the latest novel that had captured her attention and headed back outside. She still had an hour before her Skype call with Ches, and she wasn't in the mood for a run.

She'd only read a couple of chapters when she heard a

knock at her door. She put the book down beside her and climbed to her feet, a frown drifting across her face. She wasn't expecting anyone. Then her pulse jolted. God, maybe it was Gabe. She took a quick glance at her reflection, tucked a few strands of stray hairs behind her ears, and cursed the lack of makeup on her pasty face.

With a deep breath, she peeked through the peephole. It wasn't Gabe. Leaving the chain on, she opened the door and peered through the gap.

"Miss Hayes?" the guy asked.

"Yes," she replied in a suspicious tone.

"I have a package for you."

Livvy raised her eyebrows. "I'm not expecting anything."

The delivery guy shrugged. "Can you sign here?" Through the small gap in the door, he passed her a clipboard with a pen attached by a grubby piece of string. Livvy scrawled her signature and handed it back.

He held up the large box. "Want me to leave this here?" He seemed legit, but she had no intention of taking any chances.

"Please." She waited until he'd disappeared around the corner before closing the door to remove the chain. After picking up the box, she took it inside and went to the kitchen drawer that contained all manner of paraphernalia. She grabbed a box cutter and sliced through the tape.

She folded back the cardboard and pulled out reams of packaging. Nestled at the bottom were a pair of stout-looking hiking boots and a set of thick socks. Livvy's mouth fell open. This couldn't be a coincidence. Not thirty minutes before, Gabe had asked her if she owned a pair, and now, miraculously, a pair had been delivered.

She turned them over and looked at the sole and saw they were a size seven. Goddamn, the man had even picked the correct size.

"What the hell?" she muttered to herself. She reached for

her phone and stabbed out a quick text. *Ask me again about the boots.*

Within seconds, he replied.

Do you own a pair of hiking boots?

Livvy began typing but then changed her mind about what she was going to say. Finally she typed out a text.

No, I don't. However, rather worryingly, I've just had a pair gifted that happen to be my exact size. Oh, and socks too. Care to comment?

Yeah, he replied. *Be ready by noon.*

Livvy clenched her jaw. She almost called him but decided to wait until they were face-to-face. Then she would have a serious conversation with him about boundaries.

The reminder on her phone popped up, telling her it was time to call Ches. Livvy settled down in front of the TV and went into her apps. She dialed Ches's number and waited for her connection.

Ches's face appeared on the screen, and Livvy's irritation with Gabe's high-handed approach faded into the background.

"Hey, my lovely. Good to see you."

Livvy grinned. "You too, Ches. Looking good, hon."

Ches rolled her eyes. "You obviously can't see the spot right in the middle of my forehead that decided to spring up from nowhere on the very day I have a date."

Livvy leaned forward. "A date? Tell all."

Ches looked at her directly. "I will… after you tell me what's made your eyes sparkle in a way I haven't seen in far too long."

Livvy laughed out loud. She'd never been able to keep anything from Ches, who'd always seen through her as easily as looking through clear glass.

Livvy nibbled on her thumbnail and gave a coy smile. "I might have sort of met someone, although not really. Honestly, I'm not sure what it is. Could be nothing. Could be something."

Ches's face grew larger as she crept closer to the screen. "I want to know everything. Spill."

Livvy gave a quick recap of the last few days.

Ches's shocked expression when Livvy told her she'd jumped out of a plane was priceless. "So who is this miracle worker who has brought out an adventurous side of you that I've never seen?"

Livvy inhaled a deep breath through her nose. "His name's Gabe Mitchell."

Ches wrinkled her nose. "What does he do?"

"He owns a company," Livvy said.

"What sort of company?"

When Livvy mentioned the name, Ches's eyes widened. "Livvy, that's one of the biggest companies in the world. Hell, that company makes the bloody phone I'm talking to you on."

Livvy giggled. "I know."

"Holy fuck." Ches's mouth parted, and she shook her head as though she had water in her ears. "Hang on. I'm Googling him."

Her face disappeared for a few minutes. When she returned, the previous delight had faded, and in its place was a very serious-looking Ches. "Oh, Liv, are you sure? I mean, he seems a bit of a playboy. According to Google, he's only had one serious relationship, and that seems to have been with a woman whose face looks so stiff from being injected with Botox, I'm surprised she can move it at all."

Livvy tensed her spine. "I've only had one serious relationship."

"It's hardly the same," Ches said with concern. "This guy seems to go through women as fast as I go through wine. They're all one-date wonders."

"Well, as I'm on date three today, I'd say I'm not doing too badly."

Ches gave Livvy a pained stare. "Be careful. That's all I'm going to say. Don't get me wrong, Liv. I'm beyond thrilled you're finally coming out the other side of a hell that would have finished off most people, but please take care on this one. I say that from a position of love, not because I'm such a bitch that I want to strip the first genuine smile from your face I've seen since Mark died."

Livvy rubbed at her eyebrow. "I know you are, and I will be careful. I promise. I only want to have a little fun."

"As long as you tell yourself that's all it is, then go for it. God knows you deserve all the happiness you can find. But do me a favor, please. Keep reminding yourself that this guy doesn't do relationships. As long as you have that at the forefront of your mind, then when he moves on, you'll have at least protected yourself."

A hollow feeling spread through Livvy's stomach—a sensation that scared the hell out of her—because she knew that Ches was right. Yet the level to which her words stung was worrying.

"I promise." She kept her face neutral and her tone light. "Now, let's hear all about this date of yours."

Fifteen minutes later, Livvy ended the Skype call. She looked forward to her weekly chats with Ches but wished she hadn't bothered today. Ches's frankness was something she hadn't wanted to hear, even though she knew her friend only had Livvy's best interests at heart. She'd spent the last two years in such terrible pain and turmoil, most days not wanting to live, yet the last few days had taught her that she had so much to look forward to. She didn't expect this thing—whatever it was—with Gabe to last, but that didn't mean she shouldn't go with it and live a little. Her heart was so damaged anyway that she was sure another few cuts wouldn't make too much of a difference.

Half an hour before noon, she got ready, pulled on the hiking boots, which fit perfectly, and waited for Gabe to arrive.

CHAPTER NINE

THE KNOCK at Livvy's door shot her heart rate into overdrive. She took a calming breath before opening it. Gabe stood on the other side, wearing a smirk, board shorts, a navy T-shirt, which stretched across the tight muscles of his chest, and a pair of stout walking boots.

His gaze skimmed over her, settling on her boots for a second, before he lifted his eyes to her face. "Oh, good. They fit. Ready?"

His laissez-faire attitude triggered her annoyance scale, which was quickly climbing upward. Livvy crossed her arms over her chest. "A little presumptuous of you, don't you think?" She fixed him with a hard stare.

A brief frown drew down his brows, then he hit her with a smile so dazzling, she considered putting on sunglasses. "You're wearing them now, so I can't take them back."

Livvy expelled an irritated sigh. "It's not about that."

"Then what is it about?" he asked. But before she could answer, he said, "Let's have this argument on the way. We need to get going."

Livvy gritted her teeth as she grabbed her keys. "Fine. Do I need anything else?"

Gabe shook his head. "It's all in the car."

He turned around and set off towards the elevator. Livvy slammed the door to her apartment and marched after him. Something about Gabe had changed. Since she'd told him about the accident, he'd stopped treating her with kid gloves. This Gabe was much more authoritative, and if she were being honest with herself, she kind of liked it. He was very different from Mark, not only in looks, but also in personality, which was a good thing. She didn't want to be reminded of Mark when she was with Gabe. It made the swathes of guilt easier to keep at bay, almost as if she'd split herself in two. The Livvy who'd been married to Mark wasn't the same Livvy who was trotting after Gabe.

By the time she reached the elevator, he'd already pressed the call button. His lips twitched as he caught sight of her face, which continued to reflect her irritation.

"A good hard hike up a mountain should get rid of all the negative energy you're dragging along, Livvy. It's a pair of boots. Get over it."

Yep, she'd been right about his change in attitude. A shiver crept up her spine, which, on examination, she recognized as excitement. Most people she knew had walked on eggshells around her for more than two years, and their careful treatment of her had gotten much worse after she'd tried to kill herself. As she peeked into the light and realized she had a chance for a future, she knew she didn't want to be treated like that anymore. She wanted to be called out on her shit. The only one who came close to doing that was Ches, and even she considered every word spoken for fear Livvy would regress and try to take her own life once more.

But ever since Livvy had met Gabe, she could feel herself changing—and that thrilled her.

As they stepped out into the dazzling sunshine, Gabe

dropped his aviator sunglasses into place. They hid his sharp green eyes, making him harder to read, though his twitching lips told her he still found her annoyance amusing.

He held open the car door and gallantly waved his arm. "I take it this is okay? Or would you prefer to open your own door?"

Livvy's first response was to narrow her eyes, but as his lips curved even further upward until he was full-on laughing, she cracked a smile. "You're an ass."

He gave her a playful nudge with his shoulder. "I thought you British types preferred 'arse'."

"Ass suits you better, especially as it doubles up as another name for a mule."

Gabe's laughing grew louder as he closed the door behind her and walked around the hood before climbing in the driver's side.

"Where are we going, anyway?" Livvy asked as he clipped his seat belt in place and fired up the engine.

Gabe glanced over his shoulder and began reversing. "Echo Mountain."

Livvy wrinkled her nose. "Never heard of it."

He glanced over at her. "It's in the San Gabriel Mountains —my namesake," he said with a wink. "It's a hard hike, but I think you're up to it. I've brought a picnic, which we can eat at the top. The views are amazing." He pulled out onto the highway before joining the interstate and heading north.

Livvy stared out the window as they left the city behind. The closer they got to the mountains, the more her restless legs began to twitch. She'd wanted to hike the mountains behind Los Angeles ever since arriving in California, but hiking on her own didn't appeal. Some activities were better when shared, and she was really looking forward to sharing this one with Gabe.

He eventually pulled into a small parking area and cut the engine. As Livvy stepped outside, the sun beat down on her. She reached back into the car for her baseball cap and pulled it on, feeding her ponytail through the gap at the back. Gabe opened the trunk and lifted out a sizeable backpack. He dug into one of the side pockets and passed her a tube of sunscreen.

"Thanks." She layered a decent amount on all exposed skin before passing back the tube to Gabe, who followed her lead. They both had a quick drink before Gabe shrugged into the backpack. He took hold of her hand, and they set off up the trail.

As they walked, he pointed out the odd landmark, but mostly they climbed in silence, for which Livvy was grateful because her lungs were burning with a combination of effort and the intense heat from the sun. Every once in a while, they stopped to take in fluids before setting off once more.

When they reached the summit, Livvy planted her hands on her hips and took a moment to catch her breath. It hadn't been a long climb, but it had been steep, and her lungs were protesting the effort. Gabe, on the other hand, appeared completely unaffected.

"You're very fit," Livvy said between panting breaths.

Gabe waggled his eyebrows at her. "Thanks, darlin', although you're not the first woman to tell me that."

Livvy rolled her eyes. "I meant exercise-wise."

Gabe chuckled. He set the backpack on the ground and pulled her close. The peaks of their baseball caps clashed, and Livvy giggled.

Gabe twisted his cap back to front then dropped his hands to her waist once more. "Got your breath back?"

Livvy nodded, her giggles receding as Gabe looked into her eyes. His earlier mirth had disappeared. He stepped closer to her and bent his head. His lips hovered inches away before he brushed them softly over hers. Livvy's stomach clenched deliciously, and she pressed herself closer to him, but Gabe disappointed her by stepping back.

He righted his cap and bent down to pick up the backpack.

"Follow me." He pointed straight ahead. "It's quieter over there."

He stopped at a relatively flat area and unzipped the backpack. He reached inside and pulled out a blanket, then lay it on the ground and and indicated for her to sit.

In minutes, he'd set up a whole picnic with tasty sandwiches, pastries, and fruit, along with a half bottle of champagne, two glasses, and a large bottle of water.

"I can't believe you hoisted all that up the mountain," Livvy said.

Gabe winked. "I'm fit. Remember?"

Livvy groaned. "Not going to live that down in a hurry, am I?"

Gabe shook his head. "Nope."

Livvy grabbed a sandwich and bit into it. "Did you pack this yourself, Mr. Chef Extraordinaire?"

Gabe tilted his head to one side. "Are you mocking me, Hayes?"

Livvy grinned. "You make it too easy."

"Hmm, we'll see about that. Actually, no, my housekeeper did."

She nodded. "Well, tell her…" She paused. "Her, right?" When Gabe nodded, she continued. "Tell her she's a bloody marvel. These sandwiches are amazing."

Gabe chuckled. "You're very easily pleased." He uncorked the champagne bottle without spilling a drop then poured her a glass and passed it across to her before filling his own. Livvy took a sip. The champagne was delicious. She finished her sandwich then reached for a huge strawberry.

After they'd eaten and finished the champagne between them, Gabe insisted she take on plenty of water as he cleared away and stuffed the trash into the backpack. He zipped up the bag, picked up a bottle of water for himself, and took a long pull. Livvy's eyes fell to his throat as he drank. She wanted to put her mouth on it and taste him, but her natural hesitancy prevented her from acting on the urge. Instead, she dragged her gaze away and finished her own water. She handed him the empty bottle, which he slotted into a side pocket.

"Full?" he asked.

"Couldn't eat another thing."

Gabe lay back on the blanket and raised his face to the sun. Livvy stretched out beside him, a contented sigh escaping from between her lips.

"This is heaven," she murmured. "I wish we could teleport back down."

Gabe turned onto his side and propped himself up on an elbow. "Tired?"

She shook her head. "A bit lethargic. The food, the sun. I'm feeling lazy."

"You're different," Gabe said. "Much less uptight."

Livvy pushed her sunglasses on top of her head and squinted at him. "I know."

"Why?"

She shrugged. "Not sure. Maybe it was sharing what happened to me. It's easier talking to a stranger than those who know me well."

A frown drifted across his face. "Do you consider me a stranger?"

"No. Not now. Although I don't know very much about you, so you're not exactly a close friend, either."

His frown deepened. "I don't like the sound of that."

His body shifted, and before Livvy could figure out what he was going to do, he kissed her. Butterflies swarmed through her stomach as he traced his tongue across her bottom lip. She started to wrap her arms around his neck, but he gripped her wrists and held them against either side of her head, pinning them to the ground. His body covered hers, his erection pressing against her hip. He slung his thigh over her leg, easing her knees apart.

Livvy expected to panic, but instead, hot, powerful desire

made her crave more of what this man was giving her. Wetness pooled between her legs, dampening her underwear, and a soft moan eased from her throat. Gabe's response was to almost growl, the sound rumbling through his chest.

He tore his mouth away from hers and cursed. "I have horrible timing." He brushed a thumb over her swollen mouth, inflamed by his kiss. "And you are far too intoxicating."

He sat upright, rocked back on his heels, and rose to a standing position. Livvy tried to pull herself together. Her eyes fell to his groin, and when she looked up again, he was grinning.

"Looks like I'll have the advantage climbing down too." When she frowned, he tipped his head forward, indicating the unmistakable bulge in his shorts. "Third leg."

As Livvy creased over in laughter, Gabe held out his hand. Still chuckling, she gripped it as he helped her to her feet. "Are you ready to go?"

She nodded as Gabe folded the blanket and tucked it away in his backpack. The journey down was easier than the hike up, and they reached the bottom in no time. Livvy's eyes began to droop on the way home, and she allowed herself to fall into a doze.

Gabe's hand on her arm woke her, and she forced her lids open and gave him a shy smile. "Thanks for taking me out today. I really enjoyed myself."

Gabe took a deep breath. "Want to stretch out the day?"

Livvy pushed herself upright and glanced out the windshield. Instead of her beige thirteen-story apartment building greeting her, she was faced with what could only be described as a mansion—a large structure set in its own grounds. And what grounds they were. From her limited vantage point, she couldn't see another dwelling.

She turned towards Gabe. "Where are we?"

"My place."

Livvy's eyes widened. "This is your house?"

He nodded and unhooked his seat belt. "Want a tour?"

Hell yeah.

"Sure," she said nonchalantly.

"Great. Let's go." Gabe took her hand and led her into a huge foyer.

As they moved from room to room, he told her he'd designed the house and even had a hand in building parts of it. Once again, overwhelming feelings prodded at Livvy, making her feel out of her depth. Irritated with herself, she pushed them to one side.

They finished the tour in the backyard, where an enormous swimming pool dominated the space. A line of palm trees had been planted along one side of the pool, giving a sense of the tropics, and outdoor furniture made for plenty of seating. A large Jacuzzi was built into the side of the pool.

"What's that?" Livvy pointed to an outbuilding with a triangular-shaped roof.

Gabe looked over at where she was indicating. "Steam room, sauna, and changing facilities. Saves walking through the house with damp feet."

He led her to a shaded area, where a large jug of what looked like homemade lemonade had been placed along with two glasses. He pulled out a chair for her and took the seat opposite.

He lifted the jug and poured them both a glass. "So what do you think?"

She took a sip and placed her drink on the table. "Of your place? Fabulous. Although it's a lot of space for one person," she said, giving him a suspicious glance.

Gabe laughed. "I like space. Remember I told you I didn't have much growing up?" When she nodded, he continued. "Well, that was an understatement. I was very poor. I was one of three siblings, and we lived in a two-bedroom shack a couple of miles outside Austin. With the profits from my very first business deal, I rented a four-bedroom apartment, even though a one-bedroom would have worked just fine. I was ecstatic with the amount of space I had. When you've lived on top of your family members without an ounce of privacy, believe me, you crave it."

Livvy stared at him. She didn't have a clue about his background or what made him the man he was today. Yet with one little sneak peek, he'd given her more than a glimpse into the man behind the success.

"And where is your family now?"

He grimaced. "My father died a few years ago, no doubt because of the poor living conditions he'd had to put up with for most of his life. Sadly, my success came too late to help him. He was only forty-eight."

"How terrible. Gosh, you wouldn't think such things could happen in modern society."

He blew out a slow breath, almost as though he were trying to regain control. After a few seconds, he managed to collect himself, and when he met her worried gaze, he smiled. "My mom is amazing, though. I hope you'll get to meet her sometime. I'd love for her to move to LA, but she's a Texan through and through."

Livvy repressed a moment of panic. Meeting family members put any relationship firmly into the "serious" bracket, and she and Gabe were far from being at that stage.

"What about your siblings? Do they live locally?"

He stared at his hands for a few seconds, and when he looked up, his features had hardened. "My younger sister, Sophia, died when I was eighteen. She was only fifteen."

Livvy briefly closed her eyes. Having had no sisters or brothers, she couldn't understand his pain, but she could empathize.

"I'm sorry." She curled her fingers around his. "What a tragedy."

"My mother never got over it, although she hides her pain extremely well."

"She must be a remarkable woman."

He gave her a tight smile. "She is."

"And what about your brother?"

Gabe's eyes darkened, and his jaw clenched. A nerve pulsed in his cheek. "He's a piece of shit. If he ever shows his face around here, he'll be sorry."

His vehement response sent a quiver of fear through her, and even though it was none of her business, she couldn't help asking, "Do you want to talk about it?"

He blew out a slow breath. "Not really, but as you've been honest with me, I guess I owe you the same."

Livvy shook her head. "You don't owe me anything."

He grimaced. "Sorry. I didn't mean it like that." He rubbed the tips of his fingers over his mouth as a shadow crossed his face. "Sophia had cystic fibrosis, so I'm sure you can imagine, with two older brothers, she was sheltered. Sometimes her health wasn't too bad, and she could carry on like any normal teenager, but at other times, she'd spend weeks in the hospital, which put a terrible strain on a family who was already dirt poor.

"After yet another stay in the hospital, she hadn't been home very long, when a group of girls from school invited her to the movies. It was difficult for Sophia to make friends because she spent so much time away from school, and you know what kids are like. Anyway, she was thrilled, and even though she hadn't fully recovered, my mom relented. I dropped her off, and Aaron, that's my brother, said he'd pick her up."

Livvy began to get a really bad feeling about where this was going, but she didn't want to interrupt him, so she sipped her lemonade and waited for him to continue.

"Cutting a long story short, Aaron was on a date, and he lost track of time. Sophia waited for him, but when it began to rain, she set off for home. Our house was five miles from the movie theater, and she walked the whole way. By the time she got home, she was soaked through, shivering, and couldn't catch her breath. My dad took her straight to the hospital. She caught pneumonia, and with her lungs already so damaged from the cystic fibrosis…" He broke off, staring at his hands. After a few seconds, he lifted his head, his eyes going to hers. "They did everything they could, but she didn't make it."

"Oh God," Livvy murmured.

Deep pain scored Gabe's face as he relived the memories. "My brother chose his dick over his sister. I couldn't bring myself to forgive him then, and I still can't."

"What about your mum? Does she still see him?"

"Yes. You'll understand when you meet my mom. She's an incredible woman with a huge heart and a capacity for forgiveness that I simply don't possess. In the early years, she tried to make us reconcile, but now…" He shrugged. "She accepts and respects my point of view. Anyway, what about you?" he asked, making it clear he wanted to move on. "Any sisters, brothers?"

Livvy shook her head. "I was an only child. My dad died when I was very young. He was a soldier and got killed during a training exercise. My mum was heartbroken. She never really got over losing him. She died when I was at university."

An expression of sorrow crossed Gabe's face before he smoothed his expression, correctly guessing she wouldn't want his pity. "You've had it rough" was the only acknowledgement of her difficult past.

"Sounds like we both have." She shrugged. "But they make 'em tough in England."

His lips lifted at the corners. "And in Texas."

Livvy nibbled at the inside of her cheek. There was one person she was desperate to ask about but didn't know what Gabe's reaction would be. The closer she and Gabe became, the more curious—and envious—she was of Tabitha. Which was silly because Tabitha wasn't there and Livvy was. But she couldn't help the growing curiosity about what had happened to the perfect couple.

"What about Tabitha?" she asked, plunging in. "Do you regret things not working out between you?"

Gabe's expression darkened, and pure venom blasted out of

his eyes, sending a blaze of fire careering towards her. "No," he snapped.

Determined not to be put off, Livvy pressed on. "But you looked so happy in the pictures I saw of you on the Internet. I mean, I'm not prying—"

"Yes, you are," he said, cutting her off. His voice sounded pained, making Livvy regret her questioning.

She tucked her chin to her chest. "Forget it."

Gabe reached out to her, his hand curving around her cheek. "I'm sorry, darlin'. I shouldn't have snapped. It's just that wasn't a great time in my life. I'd prefer not to talk about it or her." He almost spat the final word.

Livvy forced a tight smile and refrained from reminding him that she'd shared her entire past—every sad, depressing, devastating moment. "It doesn't matter."

"Come on." He got to his feet as if the altercation hadn't happened. "I haven't shown you the best part of the tour yet." Gabe curled his fingers around hers and led her down a gravel pathway. He unlocked a wood-paneled door and pushed it open.

Livvy followed him inside, and as she took in what he wanted to show her, she couldn't stop her mouth from falling open. "Wow," she said, glancing around at the garage full of cars. "How many does one man need?"

Gabe laughed. "I know it's indulgent, and it probably makes me a bit of a dick, but I adore cars, and choosing only one when I didn't have to seemed silly."

Livvy trailed her hand across the candy-apple-red paintwork of the nearest car. "You have far too much money if you can afford a Bugatti Veyron."

Gabe's head spun around so quickly, he must have cricked his neck. His eyes widened. "You know about cars?"

Livvy nodded. "Mark was a real petrol head—that's what we call car enthusiasts in the UK. He'd buy every car magazine going, and because it was a hobby of his, as his wife, I felt it only right to pay attention. After a while, I found I loved them as much as he did."

Gabe's broad smile made his eyes sparkle. "Wow. You're full of surprises. It's not often I get blindsided."

Livvy moved farther into the garage, her eyes darting everywhere. If a supercar existed, Gabe owned it. The contents of his garage must have been worth millions, but it was the car—although *car* wasn't the right word—tucked away on the far wall that caught her attention.

On tentative feet, she moved closer. "Oh my God," she whispered. With an excited glance over her shoulder, she shook her head. "How did you get a hold of a 2006 Ferrari F1?"

Gabe's stunned expression indicated she'd surprised him twice in a matter of minutes. He moved closer and caught her hips with his hands. "I think you may be my perfect woman."

Livvy laughed, but as his face fell serious, so did hers. He moved slowly until their lips were almost touching, then a groan eased from his throat. His mouth covered hers, softly at first, but then harder, more insistent. Livvy went along with it as desire powered through her, making her knees tremble and her head spin.

When Gabe pulled back, his neck was flushed, his gaze intense. He lifted her hands to his mouth and kissed the back of each one. "I want you," he said. "But I understand if it's too soon. I'm more than prepared to wait."

"I don't want to wait," Livvy said, surprising herself more than Gabe.

He hesitated for the briefest moment before Livvy found herself being towed out of the garage. She had to jog to keep up with him, but as they reached the bottom of the winding staircase in the center of Gabe's home, he bent his knees and swept her up into his arms.

Livvy repressed a surprised squeal as Gabe took off up the stairs. On the top floor, at the end of the corridor, he kicked open a door, and Livvy found herself in what had to be Gabe's bedroom.

"Are you sure?" he whispered as he placed her feet on the floor. He flicked her hair over her shoulder, his fingers lightly brushing her neck, sending delicious shivers over every vertebra in her spine.

Unable to find her voice, she simply nodded.

He pulled her into his arms, his mouth seeking hers. His tongue surged inside, tangling with her own. Sure and steady fingers snaked beneath her T-shirt. He gripped the hem and, breaking their kiss, tugged it over her head. His eyes fell on her breasts, the soft swells peeking over the top of cream lace. He groaned as he buried his face between them, his thumbs brushing the stiff peaks of her nipples through the satin. A sharp spike of desire curled within Livvy's abdomen, and she clamped her thighs together to relieve the sweet agony.

He sank to his knees and unlaced her boots, removing them one at a time before tossing them to one side. Her socks followed. He reached up and unfastened the button on her shorts, yanked down the zipper, then slowly peeled them down her legs.

In partial disbelief at what was happening, Livvy stepped out of them as Gabe slowly got to his feet. He must have recognized her semi-paralyzed state because he undressed himself until, like her, he was naked except for his underwear. Her gaze swept over him. She'd been right. He was a man who took care of himself. She wanted to sink to her knees and lick every single ridged muscle in his abdomen, but unfortunately, she was too damned scared, too frozen, and too bloody English.

His hands were warm and comforting as he led her to the enormous bed, which overlooked the backyard and the Hollywood hills visible behind the house. He encouraged her to lie down.

Livvy let her head sink into pillows so soft, they felt like clouds beneath her. In a dreamlike state, she closed her eyes as Gabe kissed her mouth, her shoulder, and the dip of her cleavage. Her bra loosened around her chest, then her breasts were bare. But as he went to remove her panties, panic bubbled up inside Livvy. Her mouth filled with saliva, and her heart rate spiked.

"No," she mumbled, but he mustn't have heard her, or he was lost in his own desires because his lips continued to blaze a trail over her body.

"God, you're beautiful," he muttered, but when the tip of his tongue traced her C-section scar, Livvy lost it.

"No," she yelled. Her legs scrambled beneath her as she shot backward, curling her knees to her chest. She wrapped her arms around them. Her back was ramrod straight against the headboard, and her chest rose and fell with the effort of breathing through her panic.

Gabe held his hands out in front of him as though calming a startled mare. "It's okay, Livvy. You're in control. Nothing needs to happen."

Embarrassment swept over her in waves. He'd asked her if she was sure, and she'd said yes. At the time, she thought she was, but the intimacy of feeling his tongue against the scar that had allowed her dead child to be removed from her womb... it was all too much.

"I'm so sorry," she whispered as her face began to burn.

Gabe said nothing as he climbed off the bed and disappeared into an adjacent room, but he was back seconds later, holding a bathrobe.

He passed it over to her. "Here. This will make you more comfortable."

Livvy clutched the gown against her, which at least allowed her to cover her modesty, and when Gabe turned his back, she could have wept at his thoughtfulness. She quickly shrugged into it and fastened the belt around her middle.

She swung her legs over the bed and began gathering her

clothes, averting her gaze from him. "I'll get dressed and then be out of your way."

"Stay, please," Gabe said gently. "I don't want you to go, not like this."

Livvy's chin dropped to her chest. "I'm so sorry for leading you on. It's just… I can't…" She covered her face with her hands. "Oh God."

Gabe's fingers curled around her wrists, and he tugged her arms apart. As they fell by her sides, he clipped her under the chin. She tilted her head upward as her eyes went to his.

"No, I'm sorry. I shouldn't have pushed. You're right. It's far too soon, but please don't go. I want you to stay."

Feeling an overwhelming need to explain herself, Livvy gave him a wry smile. "It's my scar, you see. I—"

Gabe placed his forefinger over her lips, silencing her. "You don't need to justify anything to me."

She frowned. "Why aren't you more angry? I led you on and then didn't follow through."

Gabe's eyes flashed. "Now *that* makes me angry. Jesus, Livvy, you have the right to say no at any time. You didn't lead me on —you simply changed your mind." His gaze softened then, and he chuckled. "I might need to engage in a little… self-service later, and I can't promise that I won't be thinking of you when I do."

Livvy laughed, and as she did, the tension in the room evaporated. "You're quite something, you know."

Gabe leaned forward until their lips were close, but he didn't let them touch. "I'll wait, Livvy. As long as it takes." He moved back and rubbed at his chin, his gaze thoughtful. "You're so different from what I'm used to, so refreshing. You let me know when you're ready, and I'll be waiting."

And with that, he turned his back and left the room, leaving her alone to dress.

CHAPTER TEN

GABE WAS as good as his word, and he gave Livvy space to come to terms with her minor—okay, major—freak-out. Over the next few weeks, whenever he had the time, he arranged lots of fun and interesting things for them to do together, and while Livvy kept waiting for him to get bored of her company, not to mention the serious lack of physical contact, he showed no signs of that happening.

One Saturday evening after another fun outing that culminated with Gabe persuading her to ride on the Ferris wheel at the Santa Monica Pier, Livvy sat with her head on his shoulder as he read through a contract for a company he was considering buying. He'd told her he had to do a site visit in the next week or so, but fortunately, the company was based in LA, which made Livvy feel both relieved and scared. She was relieved that he wouldn't be going away, especially because her visa would run out in six weeks, and she needed to grab every precious moment. However, she was scared because she didn't know how she would cope without him when she returned to England.

"Good day?" Gabe asked as he leaned forward and refilled her wine glass.

"Mm-hmm," she replied.

Gabe nudged her with his shoulder. "What's the matter, Livvy?"

"What makes you think anything's the matter?"

"Because you've been pretty quiet all day, apart from when you screamed like a banshee when I rocked the Ferris wheel."

She gave him a look of disdain, which made him laugh. "That was a mean trick."

He held his arm out, and she took his invitation, folding herself against his chest. "Come on. You can tell me."

"I'm going home soon."

Gabe's arm tightened around her. "What?"

She nodded against his chest. "My visa is up in six weeks."

"So extend it."

"I tried, but I got turned down."

"When was this?"

"A few weeks ago, not long after we met."

Gabe rose from the couch and picked up his phone from the coffee table. Without saying a word, he left the room. Livvy crossed her legs and chewed on her fingernails, wondering whether she should follow him or let him be. The fact that he didn't seem happy about her impending departure made her heart squeeze with sorrow. Their time together had been a wonderful interlude, but she was up against the clock, and it was ticking down.

Gabe returned about ten minutes later, a broad grin on his face. "Problem solved," he announced, looking very smug.

Livvy frowned. "What do you mean?"

"Your visa has been extended for a year, and if that isn't enough, then it'll be extended again, for however long you want."

Livvy's eyes widened. "How did you manage that?"

Gabe chuckled. "I know a couple of people at the State Department. Your passport will need to be updated, but I can get it worked out for you. It's a shame you didn't tell me earlier. I could have saved you the worry."

Livvy shook her head as relief at not having to go home yet rushed through her. "That's some power you have."

He grinned and ran his finger tenderly down her cheek. "Well, darlin', it's a selfish act, really. I like having you around, and I don't want our time together to end yet."

Livvy repressed a wince, but Gabe seemed unaware of the effect his last word had on her. Still, he'd never made her any promises, and even if it all finished tomorrow, at least she got to stay in California for another year.

She hugged herself and grinned back at him. "I don't know how to thank you."

Gabe held out his arms, and she scrambled to her feet and pressed against him, her hands tucking into the back pockets of his jeans. A rush of desire caught her by surprise. She didn't know whether it stemmed from gratefulness, happiness, or good old-fashioned need, but she wanted to feel close to him. He'd waited long enough, and so had she. Their abortive attempt from a few weeks ago seemed as if it had happened to a different person.

She tilted her head back and cupped her hands around the back of his neck, easing his mouth to hers. For a moment, Gabe hesitated, but the pause didn't last long. He knitted his fingers into her hair and took control, his mouth moving over hers, his tongue lapping inside. He grew hard, and his erection nudged at her belly. Desperate to give him a sign without having to say the words, Livvy hooked her legs over his hips. His hands automatically cupped her backside, supporting her as she rubbed herself against him.

Gabe tore his mouth from hers. "Jesus," he groaned. He tried to put her down, but Livvy squeezed with her thighs and held on.

"I want you." She poured as much sincerity into her voice and her eyes as she could.

Uncertainty swept across his face, and he gave a small shake of his head. "You don't have to do this."

Livvy chuckled. "Oh, I know. But I *want* to do this, and I want to do it with you. I'm not changing my mind, not this time."

A soft noise eased from his throat. He set her on the ground and led her upstairs. Livvy hadn't been in Gabe's bedroom since that fateful evening, but this time, the panic was notably absent, and the desire was very much present.

Gabe pressed his lips to her neck, but then he pulled back. His gaze swept over her from head to foot, and he crossed his arms over his chest.

"Okay, Livvy, this time you're taking the lead. We're going at your pace." When she frowned, he continued. "You undress yourself, and you undress me *when you're ready*. We have all night. There's no rush."

Oh, he had to be kidding.

Livvy shook her head violently. "No. I want you to lead."

Gabe caressed his top teeth with the tip of his tongue. "Not happening."

Livvy's stomach rolled. This wasn't her bag. She'd never been good at taking the lead, even with Mark. She was too *English*, too *uptight, and* too *goddamn scared*.

She took a step forward, then another. With fingers that felt as if they'd been fused together, she tried to unbutton Gabe's crisp white shirt. After she had several fumbles, he took pity on her and deftly unbuttoned it but left it hanging open.

Livvy slipped her hands inside and over his broad shoulders, and when he shuddered and closed his eyes, his head falling back, she trembled in response. She slid the shirt down his arms and let it fall to the floor.

Her eyes flickered to his, but Gabe's were still firmly shut. Forcing a deep breath into lungs that wouldn't expand, she tackled his belt first, which unfastened without any trouble, then she groaned.

"Button fly," she muttered under her breath. "You have *got* to be kidding me."

Gabe's warm chuckle reduced her nerves a touch, but when she struggled to unfasten even the first one, she let out an irritated sigh and yanked the material apart.

"Someone's in a hurry," Gabe murmured, and when she looked up, his eyes were twinkling, although desire had darkened them to a deep jade rather than their usual soft emerald.

Livvy peeled Gabe's jeans down his legs. He stepped out of them and stood back, waiting for her to undress. An urge to slow this down and draw it out slipped into her mind, but her nerve wouldn't hold. She dragged her T-shirt over her head, unfastened her jeans, and threw them on the floor near Gabe's clothing. She slipped off her bra, but there was something about the final step of being totally naked that made her leave her panties in place.

She crossed her arms over her chest, and a hot flush spread from her neck to her cheeks as Gabe slowly appraised her.

"Panties on. I can work with that," he said, a glimmer of a smile tugging his lips upward. "What next, Livvy?"

She gave him a panicked look. "I did what you asked. Now it's your turn."

Gabe wagged his finger in the air. "Uh-uh. You're in charge from beginning to end. What do you want me to do to you?"

With a look of dismay, Livvy chewed on her cheek until an idea came to her. She held back a grin, which might have tipped him off as to her intention. "So you have to do everything I say?" She glanced up at him through her lashes in the best innocent stare she could muster.

He nodded. "Yep. Everything. Anything. It's your call."

"Good," she said. "Then I order you to take over."

Gabe paused for a beat then threw his head back and laughed. "Goddamn smart woman." His arm shot out, and he snagged her around the waist, pulling her into his body. Gabe had muscles on top of muscles when fully dressed. When he was naked, she could feel every hard edge of him. A tremor ran through her as he gathered her hair into a ponytail before gently tugging back her head until she had no choice but to look at him.

"I may have to make you suffer for that little stunt," he said with a wink in case she took his words literally. Before Livvy could respond, his mouth covered hers in a kiss that demanded she comply. There would be no backing out. She wouldn't run this time.

He leaned into her, forcing her to walk backward. When her knees hit the bed, she fell onto the soft mattress.

"Now, how shall I make you pay?" Gabe straddled her and tilted his head to one side as he pretended to consider her punishment. Then he leaned forward and pulled her nipple into his mouth.

The abruptness of the action made Livvy's back arch and her toes curl as a low moan fell from her lips. She'd forgotten the sheer bliss of a man's touch. Her core clenched as Gabe rolled his tongue over her pert nipple before grazing it with his teeth.

"God help me," Livvy muttered as butterflies swarmed her stomach.

Gabe lifted his head. "We can stop at any time."

Livvy responded by pressing his head back to her breast. She felt his smile against her flesh before he lavished her nipple once more.

He traveled south, his mouth and his tongue sending her nerve endings into overdrive. She didn't know whether her body had forgotten these sensations or whether they were completely new experiences, but as fire licked through her veins, she almost lost her mind.

Gabe's fingers snaked inside her panties. He pressed his thumb to her clit as his middle finger slipped into her wet heat. Livvy's hips rose from the bed of their own accord, although even through her hunger, she sensed him giving her scar a wide berth.

She let her hands wander over his muscled back, his broad shoulders, and his thick, soft hair. She was almost fevered in her exploration of him, as though she couldn't get enough... as though she'd been starving and was suddenly being presented with a buffet fit for a queen. When he replaced his finger with his tongue, she tried to clamp her legs together. The intimacy of the act with a man she'd known for only six weeks overwhelmed her.

"Gabe... no."

He lifted his head as he heard the uncertainty in her voice. "No because you want me to stop completely, no because you don't like it, or no because it's too intimate?"

Jesus, could he read minds?

"The last one," she mumbled as heat flooded her face.

He grinned against her inner thigh. "Relax," he murmured. "Intimacy is good, Livvy."

She squeezed her eyes shut as he returned to his previous... activity. As his tongue penetrated her once more, she forced herself to focus on the sensations rushing through her rather than the more-than-a-little-embarrassing situation. *Must be an English thing.* Mark hadn't been massively interested in oral sex, so she didn't have a whole lot of experience with it. But once she put aside the apprehension of having Gabe's mouth on her most intimate parts, dear God... it... felt... good.

Her body began to crest, climbing higher and higher, until she peaked and exploded. Lights flashed behind her eyelids as if she were watching her own personal fireworks show. Her toes curled, her legs twitched, and her core clenched repeatedly around his tongue.

She'd barely recovered when Gabe moved over her. But as she prepared herself to welcome him into her body, he dropped a quick kiss on her forehead and rolled to the side.

"What are you doing?" she asked, more than a hint of frustration leaking into her tone.

He pulled her into his arms and rested her head against his

chest. "No fucking condoms," he said with a chuckle. "You kind of took me by surprise."

Livvy smiled against his heated skin. "I'm on the pill. You're good."

Gabe shook his head and kissed her temple. "I'll grab some tomorrow. That is if I haven't scared you off completely."

Livvy raised herself up on her elbow. "There's no risk of pregnancy, Gabe."

"I'm not concerned about that."

Livvy frowned, then realization swept through her. He was talking about STIs—or whatever the Americans called sexually transmitted infections—which meant he'd had sex with someone else recently. Unprotected sex. Or worse, he thought she had.

Livvy sat bolt upright and pulled a sheet around her. Gabe was lying on it so she yanked hard then wrapped it around her chest. She almost ran to the adjoining bathroom. As she slammed the door, she fumbled for the lock and turned it.

Her legs wobbled, and she allowed them to give way beneath her as she plunked down on the toilet seat. How long ago had he had sex? Today or yesterday? Last week? Her stomach rolled, and she swallowed down bile. God, she'd let him put his tongue inside her. Where else had that damn tongue of his been?

Gabe knocked on the door. "Livvy, what's going on?"

She ignored him, instead turning the faucet on full blast and making a big production of flushing the toilet. She needed to play this cool, to show him his philandering didn't bother her one little bit.

After taking a deep breath, she opened the door and stepped back into the bedroom. Gabe was standing off to the side, still wearing his boxer shorts, his arms folded across his chest. "You okay?" he asked in a low voice as though testing the water.

Livvy gave him a bright smile. "Absolutely." She began to

pick up her clothes from the floor but hadn't gotten far in dressing when his arms came around her.

He tore her bra and T-shirt from her grasp and tossed them behind him. "Don't lie to me." His lips caressed the shell of her ear, causing a tremor to travel through her body. "Is this about the whole condom thing?"

Livvy managed to wriggle from his grasp. "Don't be silly," she said, hiding her anguish behind a too-bright smile. "We're not exclusive, particularly as I haven't been exactly... forthcoming. You're free to sleep with whomever you choose. I really appreciate you putting my health first."

She bent down and picked up her bra then put it and her T-shirt on before glancing around to see what had happened to her jeans.

"Livvy." Gabe had a sharpness to his voice that hadn't been there before. "For fuck's sake, stop getting dressed and talk to me."

Livvy ignored his request. She spotted her jeans and dragged them over her legs, giving him another dazzling smile. "About what?"

Gabe planted his hands low on his hips, irritation written all over his face. "I haven't slept with anyone since I met you at Sam's."

"Okay," she said, looking around for her purse.

"Livvy!" Gabe clamped his hands around her upper arms and gave her a quick shake. "I never have unprotected sex. Ever. Just because I wanted to use a condom doesn't mean I have anything. Nor does it mean I think you do, either."

"Good to know." She spotted her purse on the floor, picked it up, and slung it over her shoulder. "Thanks for a lovely day. I'll ring for a cab."

She headed for the door, but before she reached it, Gabe's arms came around her. His warm breath on her neck sent shivers up every single vertebra of her spine. "Don't go. Not like this."

Livvy repressed an urge to lean into his embrace.

"Please," he said. "Stay the night. I don't want to wake up without you tomorrow. I want to spend the night with you in my arms."

She wanted to. The idea of being held by Gabe as she fell asleep, of feeling safe and warm and protected was one hell of a draw. She hated sleeping alone, had never gotten used to it after Mark died. Without making the conscious decision, she found herself nodding, and Gabe's unmistakable sigh of relief bolstered her slightly battered ego.

His fingers closed around hers, and he lifted them to his lips, grazing the back of her hand with a kiss. He gently removed her purse from her shoulder and tossed it on the bed. "Come on. I'll get dressed and then make us some dinner."

GABE LAY AWAKE, listening to Livvy's steady breathing. He'd tried to stay calm during her brief meltdown, but his underlying panic when he thought she might walk out merited further examination. He had not found himself attracted to a woman on an emotional level since Tabitha, but he'd known Tab for years. Livvy was another prospect altogether. She'd gotten under his skin—that much was obvious—and the temptation to ignore his rules and have sex with her anyway had almost finished him off.

He'd also lied to her. He didn't bareback… not now. He'd learned his lesson the hard way. But to say he didn't *ever* had been a lie.

Her reaction to him refusing to have sex had surprised him, but on reflection, it shouldn't have. She was so fragile in lots of ways, and yet in others, she was as tough as they came.

He turned onto his side and rested his head on his elbow. Moonlight shone on her face, replete in sleep, and his stomach tightened. She was so different from the hardened, vacuous women with whom he'd sought temporary solace after his relationship with Tab had gone horribly wrong. Livvy wasn't just relationship material. She was *marriage* material. This was a girl who didn't do casual. She felt deeply, and when she committed, she would be all in.

Gabe sighed. Livvy might be marriage material, but was he? For sure, something about her called to the very core of him. He wanted to protect her, to heal her, to make her eyes shine and keep them shining. He'd felt it from the second they met, and every day since then, the urge had grown. But he just wasn't sure if that amounted to a future together.

She rolled over in bed, a contented sigh escaping from her lips. As she snuggled close to his side, her arm came across his waist. Gabe placed his hand over hers as a wave of pure joy washed over him. The feeling was so alien that it took a second or two for him to recognize it for what it was.

He closed his eyes and allowed sleep to claim him.

A LOUD RINGING made Livvy stir, but she struggled to open her eyes. She groaned, half in, half out of sleep, willing the damned noise to stop. She was lying across Gabe's chest, the warmth from his body seeping through the cotton T-shirt he'd loaned her to sleep in.

Reluctantly, she rolled over and fumbled around on the floor for her purse.

"Hello?" she mumbled into her phone as she sat up and rubbed the sleep from her eyes.

"Livvy, is that you, darling? It's John."

Livvy's eyes sprang open. She was immediately awake and alert. Her father-in-law never called her. He hated speaking on the phone. He always had Beth call if they needed anything.

"John, yes, it's me." She fumbled for the lamp in the dark. "What's wrong?"

Gabe sat up beside her, his brow wrinkled in concern at her worried tone.

"Oh, Livvy," John said. "It's Beth. She's in the hospital. They think she's had a heart attack. Livvy, her heart stopped." John's voice broke on his last word.

"Oh God," she whispered as her body broke out in a cold sweat. She blindly felt for Gabe's hand and held on tight. "John, tell me she's all right."

"They don't know, sweetheart. She's in intensive care. She needs you, Livvy. Will you come?"

"Of course I'll come. I'll be on the next plane over. Hang in there, okay? I'll call you when I land."

She leaped out of bed and began scrabbling around for her clothes.

Gabe had tuned in to her panic. "Livvy, what is it? What can I do? What do you need?"

She shook her head, feeling as if she had water in her ears as fear swamped her. *Breathe, Livvy.* She Googled the airport number and hit dial. "My mother-in-law is in the hospital. She —hello, yes," she said as flight reservations answered her call. "I need a flight to London, the first one you have. Any class, I don't care. What? That's the first one going out? Nothing sooner? What about Manchester or Birmingham?"

She began to pace as she barked questions at the poor reservations clerk who was trying to apologize for the lack of flights. No seats were available that day or the next one.

Without warning, Gabe eased the phone from her grasp. He hung up and wrapped his arms around her. "Livvy, I'm here. I have a plane. It will take you anywhere you need to go. Please tell me what's going on."

Her head began to swim as a wave of nausea rolled through her stomach. She couldn't lose Beth, not after finally finding her feet and moving on after Mark and Daniel. She wasn't strong enough to deal with that. Beth and John were her rocks, her safe place to land, her lifeboat that had saved her from stormy seas.

She bent over and clasped her knees as the room pitched back and forth. "My mother-in-law had a heart attack, and they don't know whether or not she's going to make it. Please, help me."

Gabe, still clutching her phone in his hand, stabbed at the screen. A few seconds later, he was talking rapidly into it, snapping out instructions. Satisfied with the outcome, he threw her phone on the bed and pulled her into his arms once more.

"My plane will be ready at the airport in one hour, waiting to take us to London."

Livvy lifted her head. "Us?"

"Yes. I'm not letting you go through this alone."

Livvy began to protest, but then her shoulders sagged. It would be good to have someone to lean on, someone who could take control, because her head was all over the place. She had no idea what she would say to John about who Gabe was, but at this point in time, there were much more important things to do, like being there for Beth.

She can't die. Livvy could not lose yet another important person in her life. Hadn't she suffered enough?

CHAPTER ELEVEN

THE FLIGHT to London seemed to take forever, but Gabe's comforting presence soothed her on a level she didn't quite understand. He talked when she wanted to talk and stayed silent when her fears made it difficult to form words. At those times, he simply held her, his thumb caressing the back of her neck in a show of affection that made her heart ache.

Beth. Poor, beautiful Beth. She'd been through so much, as they all had. The loss of Mark had almost been too much for Beth to cope with, and when Livvy had selfishly tried to end it all, Beth had sunk further into a deep depression. Livvy would always blame herself for that. She'd piled more worry and sorrow onto a woman who'd had more than her fair share of it already. It had been John, along with Ches, who had insisted that Livvy needed a change of scenery—and not just a couple of weeks lying on a beach in Spain—but really getting away. John had been the first to suggest that Livvy sell the home she'd shared with Mark, something that had hurt Beth deeply. But John had insisted it was the right thing to do. He'd always put Livvy first, even though his idea meant he lost his daughter-in-law, for all intents and purposes.

Livvy began to mutter prayers for Beth. She had to come through this. Livvy feared for John if she didn't. Losing their only child had aged them both far beyond their years, but John had also had to be strong enough for Beth to lean on. If he lost her too, Livvy didn't know whether he would be able to cope.

The plane touched down at a private airfield north of London a little after midnight. As the doors opened, an immigration official—at least that was who she assumed it was—boarded and checked their documentation before leaving. Gabe folded Livvy's hand into his own and led her down the aluminum steps. Instead of joy at being home, she felt only despair. It was chilly, despite being the middle of July, and the rain was falling in heavy droplets as Gabe ushered her into the back of a waiting car.

In a little under an hour, the car pulled up outside the hospital. Livvy leaped out and burst through the front doors with Gabe at her heels. She headed for the only reception desk she could see, with no idea whether she was in the right department.

"Hi. I'm looking for Beth Hayes. She was brought in yesterday with a suspected heart attack. I'm her daughter-in-law."

The receptionist nodded at Livvy and began tapping on her keyboard. "She's on the third floor. The lifts are right around the corner."

Livvy turned on her heel, wanting to run but settling for a fast walk instead. As soon as the elevator reached the third floor, Livvy hurried down the corridor, spotting another reception area straight ahead. She repeated her question and waited again for more keyboard tapping before being guided to the right room.

She paused outside, her palm flat against the door, and took a deep breath. Gabe's warm hand curved around her neck, and he brushed a kiss to her temple. "I'm here," he murmured. "Lean on me."

Tears pricked her eyes, and not trusting herself to speak, she nodded. With a firm shove, she pushed open the door to Beth's hospital room and stepped inside with Gabe next to her. A gasp fell from her lips at the sheer number of tubes keeping her mother-in-law alive.

"Livvy!" John scrambled to his feet. Livvy dashed across the room and flung her arms around his neck, holding him tightly to her.

"Oh, Livvy. Thank you so much for coming," he murmured in her ear.

She extricated herself from his embrace and gave him the once-over. Dark circles beneath his eyes gave him a tired, almost defeated look, and the skin was baggy around his mouth. His gaze fluttered over to Gabe, and a question flashed across his face.

"This is Gabe Mitchell, a friend of mine."

"Sir." Gabe held out his hand, which John shook.

"How is she, John?" Livvy asked as she pulled a chair close to the bed and wrapped her hand around Beth's. It was cold, and Livvy absentmindedly rubbed it, trying to get some warmth into her.

John sighed as he sank back into his chair, his brief interest in Gabe waning. "She had a massive cardiac arrest, so they're not sure yet what the long-term damage will be to her heart, but the fact that she's survived this long is encouraging, apparently."

"Oh God. I'm so sorry I wasn't here for you. I should have been here." Livvy began to cry, silent tears slipping down her cheeks. Her shoulders shook until Gabe gave her a comforting squeeze. Livvy allowed herself a moment to absorb his strength before she wriggled away. She didn't want John to start asking questions yet.

"It isn't your fault, Livvy. You have to live your own life. Mark would have wanted that for you, and Beth and I want that for you. You're here now. That's all that matters, okay?"

Livvy nodded silently as a nurse brought in a third chair for Gabe. He sat down beside her, close enough for her to feel the warmth from his body but not so close as to raise suspicions about the depth of their relationship. As exhaustion swamped her, she laid her head on her arms and, keeping hold of Beth's hand, slipped into a restless sleep.

When Livvy woke, morning had arrived. The rain that had battered down during the night had evaporated, and bright sunshine shone through the window, warming the room. Her head snapped up, and she glanced around. John was sitting opposite her, his skin pallid and gray, worry lines drawing his mouth downward. She shot a glance to her left. Gabe was nowhere to be seen.

"He's gone to get coffee," John said, nodding at the empty chair.

Livvy rubbed her eyes. "Oh, good. I need the caffeine." Her gaze turned to Beth. "No change, then?"

John shook his head. "He seems nice."

It took Livvy a second to figure out who John was talking about. A warm flush spread across her cheeks, and she ducked her head and fiddled with Beth's sheets.

She shrugged. "I guess."

"It's about bloody time," John said, his gaze full of love as he looked across Beth's hospital bed at her. "You've suffered enough, Liv."

She grimaced. "Haven't we all?"

"Is it serious?"

Another shrug. "I don't know. It's early days." She stood and stretched out her back.

"Why don't you go for a walk? Go find your man."

Livvy gave him a glimmer of a smile. "I don't want to leave her."

John cocked his head at the door. "Go on. Give yourself five minutes."

"Have you had five minutes?"

He nodded. "Your man insisted I take a break during the

night. It did me good. If it makes you feel better, I could murder a bacon sandwich."

"With brown sauce?" Livvy asked, holding back surprise that Gabe had managed to persuade John to take a short break from Beth's bedside. Then again, he did have excellent powers of persuasion. She should know.

"Of course," John scoffed. "It's not a bacon sandwich without brown sauce."

Livvy giggled and stepped out into the hallway. Gabe was coming towards her, three paper cups held expertly between his fingers in a triangular shape.

He smiled as his eyes fell on her. "Hey, how are you holding up?"

She took one of the coffees from him. "I'm okay. It's him I'm worried about." She jerked her head towards the hospital room behind her. "The good thing is he's hungry, so I'm going to grab him a sandwich."

"Hang on. I'll come with you. Let me drop off his coffee first."

Gabe was back seconds later, and he threaded his fingers through hers, an action Livvy found she was beginning to crave.

"Here, you sit," he said when they reached the cafeteria, pointing at a spare table by the window. "What do you want to eat?"

Livvy shook her head. "Let's just grab something and go."

"Livvy." Gabe jabbed his finger at the chair. "Sit down. You'll be no use to either of them if you don't look after yourself."

Reluctantly, Livvy did as he asked, causing Gabe's lips to twitch.

"I expected more of an argument," he said. "Now, what do you want to eat?"

She shrugged. "A croissant or a Danish pastry." Gabe gave her a look of admonishment. "I'm not hungry," Livvy added in explanation.

When he returned with the food, the two of them sat in silence, each mulling through their own thoughts. Livvy picked at her croissant before pushing it away. Her stomach kept churning with unease, and the greasy pastry didn't help. A couple of times, Livvy began to stand until Gabe's firm grip tugged her down again. After her third attempt, he gave in. She grabbed a bacon sandwich for John on the way out, loading on the brown sauce exactly as he liked it, before they both headed back upstairs.

As they stepped out of the elevator on the third floor, Livvy was almost knocked over by at least three nurses and a couple of doctors who were sprinting down the corridor.

"What the hell?" Then she spotted them going into Beth's room. "Oh, no, no, no, no," she shouted, sprinting after them.

The paper bag holding John's sandwich slipped between her fingers. She didn't stop to pick it up. She followed the medical staff inside, but Beth had so many people around her bed, Livvy couldn't see her. John stood off to the side, a look of sheer horror and despair on his face as he repeatedly ran his hands through his thinning hair. Machines were going off, and doctors barked out orders as they applied compressions to Beth's chest. John's body sagged, and Livvy managed to reach him just in time to stop him from falling to the ground.

She put her arms out to steady him. "John, what's happening?"

"She's gone, Livvy. She's gone."

Livvy gave Gabe a helpless stare as the medical staff kept working on Beth until the doctor in charge stood back and held up his hand.

"Everyone, stop please." The room went quiet. "I'm calling it. Time of death"—he glanced at his watch—"9:56 a.m."

"No!" Livvy yelled. "Keep going. You can't stop yet."

Gabe touched Livvy's shoulder. She shrugged him off and pushed past the various medical staff. She pressed her palm against Beth's still warm cheek. She couldn't be gone. It wasn't possible. Pain seared across her chest, burning, agonizing. How much more suffering would be loaded on her and John? Wasn't it someone else's turn to experience heartache?

Like an early-morning mist that burned away when the sun came up, the staff dissipated, leaving the three of them alone with Beth.

Livvy spun around and stared helplessly at John. He'd crumpled in on himself. He looked like a broken man, and her heart squeezed painfully. She'd left him to go through this alone while she'd been enjoying a leisurely breakfast with Gabe.

Her eyes went to Gabe's. He reached out a hand, but she recoiled. If he hadn't insisted she take a break, she would have been here with Beth at the end. Hurt crossed his face at her rejection. He opened his mouth to say something but then seemed to have second thoughts.

"I need some air," Livvy choked out before blindly walking to the door and reaching for the door handle. She careened through the door, into the hallway, her sneakers squeaking on the highly polished floor as she broke into a run.

"Livvy!" Gabe's voice held a tinge of panic, but she didn't turn around. She heard him, though, gaining on her.

She wrenched open the door that led to the stairwell and sped down the three flights of stairs. As she spilled outside and began to gulp down the warm, humid air, Gabe reached her, and his arms came around her waist.

She shoved hard at his chest until he stepped back. "Don't touch me," she hissed.

"Liv." His tone was calm, meant to soothe, but all it did was ratchet up Livvy's anger.

"This is your fault." She pointed her finger at him. "If you hadn't insisted I stay and eat something, I'd have been with her at the end. She died without me. Because of you!"

Visitors and staff milling about the entrance looked over, a mixture of interest and embarrassment crossing their faces. When Livvy caught the eye of a particularly intrusive stare, she glared until the young man had the good grace to blush and turn away.

She focused her anger back on Gabe. Deep down, she knew it had nothing to do with him and everything to do with rage at the unfairness of it all. But he was there—solid, dependable, composed—whereas she was fracturing inside.

"Liv." He reached for her again. "Use me, darlin'. I'm not going anywhere, so give me all you've got."

Livvy let out a wail of despair, and her hands curled into fists. She pounded them against his strong chest. For his part, Gabe simply held her as she took out her anger and hurt on him. When she was spent, she collapsed against him. As she cried, he stroked her hair and murmured soothing words in her ear.

He eventually eased her back and dried her tears with his thumbs. Her eyes were stinging, and exhaustion washed over her. But as she looked at Gabe's grave and sincere face, a wave of affection rushed through her. Lesser men wouldn't have let her blame them for something they had absolutely no control over, let alone take the physical onslaught she'd given him. This one was special—a keeper.

"What do you need, Livvy?" he asked. "Whatever it is, I'll do it."

"You," she said. "I only need you."

GABE'S PLANE came in to land, and as it hit the ground, Livvy's heart mirrored the resounding thud. Leaving John behind after Beth's funeral had been terrible. Mark's death had stripped him of so much, but without Beth, he seemed shrunken somehow, a shadow of the man he used to be. She'd begged him to come to California with her, but he'd steadfastly refused. She would have to make sure she headed home more often. At least he had Ches to keep an eye on him.

As Livvy and Gabe descended the steps of the plane, the sky overhead was unusually dark and gloomy, reflecting her mood perfectly. How much more death would she and those she loved the most have to suffer? Yet another special person in her life was gone—one who could never be replaced.

Gabe's fingers reached for hers, and he squeezed them hard. Since Beth's passing, every day had gone by in a devastating, painful blur, but the one constant had been this amazing man. He'd stood by her side the whole time, even though his business interests had demanded his attention back in LA. Her life had become a dichotomy of extremes—terrible, devastating sadness, and ecstatic, thrilling joy.

"Don't go back to your apartment," Gabe said as they settled into the back of the waiting limousine.

She twisted in her seat. "I don't have any clean stuff."

His lips twitched, a much welcome moment of amusement. "I have this amazing invention in my house. It's a machine that cleans clothes."

Livvy dug him in the ribs as a bright smile spread across her face. It felt good to laugh. Joy had been sadly lacking in recent days, and her mood instantly lifted.

She gave him a stern look. "Very funny."

"So you'll come back with me?"

Too tired to put up much of a fight, she nodded. Gabe made a satisfied noise and slipped his arm around her shoulder. She leaned into him, taking the strength he was so willing to give.

After the limo pulled up in front of Gabe's house, he eased Livvy out of the car and led her inside.

He wandered into the kitchen, with her trailing behind. "Hungry?"

"A little."

"How about a snack? What would you like to eat?"

She slid onto one of the stools at the breakfast bar and rested her chin on her hands. "You," she said quietly.

With his head in the fridge, Gabe froze before slowly turning around. In his hands were plates of meat and cheese. He put them on the counter before walking around to her side of the kitchen. He threaded his hands into her hair and kissed her, his mouth firm then demanding against hers.

Livvy eased off the stool and pressed herself up against him. They'd waited long enough. Tonight, this man was hers. She wanted him, *all of him*. Waiting was no longer an option. Life was far too short. She'd already known that with the loss of her babies and Mark, but Beth's passing had been a poignant reminder. *No more procrastinating.*

Gabe's tongue surged inside her mouth, taking, possessing, and owning. God, the man knew how to kiss a woman so that her toes curled and her spine tingled. His hands moved lower over her back as he circled his hips against her, pressing his erection against her in a way that had a moan easing from her throat.

Livvy was so lost in Gabe's expert touch that she failed to hear they had company until a broad Texan accent drawled, "Well, well, darlin'. When you decide to take your tongue out of that poor girl's mouth, you can introduce us."

Livvy leaped away from Gabe, an undoubted look of horror on her face as she came face-to-face with a petite woman, who looked to be in her early sixties. She was no more than five feet tall, and her hair was styled in a bob, dark in color but streaked with caramel. She popped her hands on her hips and gazed at them with a perfectly arched eyebrow.

Gabe, on the other hand, looked highly amused. His lips twitched as he reached for Livvy, pulling her to his side again. "Heard of knocking, Mother?"

Mother? Oh shit!

Livvy glanced up at him then back at the woman standing in front of her. Fortunately, his mother had an amused look that rivaled Gabe's.

"Good to see you too, darlin'. So…" Her gaze flitted between Gabe and Livvy then back again.

"Mom, this is Livvy Hayes. Livvy, this is my mother, Heather Mitchell."

Heather stepped forward and held out her hand. The two women shook briefly.

"Hi, Livvy. How lovely to meet you. My son is notoriously tight lipped when it comes to his private life, so I'm afraid it falls to you to fill in the gaps. Now come, sweet pea. Tell me everything."

She tucked Livvy's hand into the crook of her arm, patted the back of it, and started to head out of the kitchen. "Darlin'," she said with a casual glance over her shoulder. "Get me some tea, will you?" And without uttering another word, she walked into the hallway, towing Livvy along with her.

CHAPTER TWELVE

GABE REPRESSED a groan as he found Livvy and his mother in the living room. The two women had their heads together, both chatting away as if they'd known each other for years rather than mere minutes.

As she heard him enter, his mom glanced over her shoulder and held her hand out for her tea.

"Over here, darlin'," she said as he placed the cup in her outstretched hand.

He set a coffee in front of Livvy and sat down to sip his own drink. "To what do I owe the pleasure?" he drawled at his mother.

She tsked. "If I left it up to him"—she cocked her head in Gabe's direction—"I'd be lucky if our paths crossed once a year."

Gabe refrained from rolling his eyes. "I have a business to run, Mother."

"I know you do, darlin'. But really, how much time does it take to pick up the phone once in a while and make sure your old ma is still breathing?"

Livvy snickered. Gabe shot her a look that made her smile spread further instead of having the intended reaction.

"Point taken," he said begrudgingly.

"And do tell," she continued. "How long were you going to keep this gorgeous girl from me, huh?"

"We just got back from England. Give me a break."

His mom looked at Livvy then back at Gabe. "Taking vacations together already?" She clapped her hands. "Oh, this is *marvelous.*"

Gabe let out a frustrated sigh. Time to rein in his mother from getting ahead of herself and launching into wedding arrangements. "Actually, Livvy recently lost someone very important to her. We were over in England for the funeral." Not exactly the full story, but he didn't want to explain the details of the last few weeks.

"Oh, no." She picked up Livvy's hand and rubbed it between both of hers. "I'm so sorry, sweet pea. How awful for you."

Livvy nodded. "It's been a tough few weeks." She looked over at Gabe, her face full of… appreciation? "But your son was wonderful throughout."

A thrill of excitement crossed his mother's face, and this time, Gabe didn't withhold a groan. "Stop, Mother." He knew exactly where her thought process was heading. Livvy gave him a confused look, but he just shook his head.

Heather clasped a hand to her chest. "Stop what?" She took a sip of her tea and gave him an innocent stare over the rim of her cup.

"Livvy and I have only known each other a matter of weeks." *And haven't even had sex yet.* "Give us a break."

She tsked again and waved her hand in the air in the dismissive way she'd mastered over the years. "Time waits for no man." She turned her attention back to Livvy. "It could be over in a flash for any of us."

Gabe couldn't hold back a sharp inhale as Livvy paled. She

scrambled to her feet, coffee spilling over the sides of her mug as she almost dropped it onto the coffee table. "Excuse me a moment," Livvy mumbled as she darted from the room.

Gabe gave his mother an exasperated look. "Terrific," he said before clambering to his feet. He wasn't sure whether Livvy had been thinking of Beth or Mark and her unborn child, but regardless, Heather's comment was far from welcome.

"I'm so sorry, darlin'," she said, attempting to stop him as he started after Livvy. "I didn't think."

"Don't worry." He put a hand out, stopping her in her tracks, and patted her shoulder. "Stay here. I'll be back in a minute."

He found Livvy in the kitchen, and relief poured through him. She could be so skittish at times, especially where her grief was concerned. Gabe wasn't yet sure how she would react in certain situations.

"Mom feels terrible." He held his arms out, his worry ebbing away when she folded herself inside them. "Her heart's in the right place, though."

Her shoulders shook. At first he thought she was crying, but when she looked up at him, her eyes were sparkling with laughter. "It's fine. She didn't say anything wrong. It's me. I'm too sensitive. I needed a moment to gather myself. Your mum is right—life is too short. I, more than most, understand that."

Her hands curved around his cheeks, and she urged him towards her. His stomach clenched as their lips met in an all-too-brief kiss.

"I'm ready," she said, making him frown until she finished her thought. "And this time, you'd better have condoms."

———

HEATHER STRETCHED her arms overhead and yawned. "Well, darlin', I guess I should be off."

"You can stay if you want," Gabe said, although if she accepted his offer, he would disown her.

With a twinkle in her eye, she shook her head. "You don't want an old girl like me cramping your style." She rose to her feet. "I'm meeting a friend for lunch, and I want to get some shopping done before then."

Livvy stood, and Heather gave her a warm hug. "I hope we'll be seeing a lot more of each other, Livvy."

Gabe rolled his eyes and took her by the arm. "Give her a break, Mother." He walked his mom to her car, readying himself for a grilling. He knew her too well.

Precisely on cue, as he opened her door, she rested a hand on the roof of the car. "How long have you two been together?"

"Only a few weeks."

Heather's eyes bored into his. "She's the special one, though, isn't she?"

Gabe blew a breath through his nose. His mother had always been able to read him. He nodded. "She's had it tough, Mom, and yet she's a survivor." He looked down at the ground, trying to find a way to verbalize his inner feelings. He lifted his head. "From the first day I met her, I knew. Something about her calls to me. I can't explain it. She reminds me of Sophia. Not in looks or personality, but in the way she copes with being dealt the shittiest hand. She refuses to let her demons drag her under."

His mother winced a little at the mention of his sister. She reached up and touched his cheek. "Livvy is your soul mate, darlin'."

Gabe chuckled. "You old romantic."

"Just like I was for your father, and he for me."

This time, it was Gabe's turn to wince. "I know you miss him."

She nodded. "I do. So please, make every moment count." She climbed into the car, closed the door, gave him a quick wave, and drove away.

Gabe watched pensively as the car disappeared down the driveway, his mother's comments spinning around his head. It was just like her to put into a couple of words feelings he'd been struggling to understand for weeks.

With a soft smile, he went back in the house. Livvy was putting the coffee cups in the dishwasher. He slipped his arms around her and spun her around. His lips brushed hers in a featherlight kiss.

"Are you sure?" he asked. "Really sure?"

She nodded. "With everything that's happened, it's made me realize I need to take more risks and live life more fully than I have been doing. I'm sorry I've pushed you away all these weeks and given you so many mixed signals. I'm lucky you've stuck around. Lesser men would have gotten bored by now."

"You could never bore me." He took her hand and led her upstairs. Once inside his bedroom, he wrapped his arms around her again. This time when he kissed her, he didn't hold back.

As her tongue tentatively reached out to meet his, Gabe groaned, desire rushing through him. Every touch, every sensation, every feeling with Livvy was heightened to an almost painful level. He broke away from her mouth and covered her face in kisses. As his lips met her neck, she threw back her head. The low, husky moan that escaped her throat made him want to record it so he could play it back on repeat.

"Do that again." She tilted her head to one side, giving him better access. "I *love* having my neck kissed."

Gabe smiled against her skin as he obliged her request. He kissed and sucked at the delicate skin, and the resultant noises Livvy emitted made his cock thicken and lengthen.

Livvy's hands feathered up and down his sides before she gripped the hem of his shirt and lifted it over his head. She tentatively reached out and touched him, her fingertips fluttering over his tanned, smooth chest before venturing farther south. She ran the tip of her nail inside the waistband of his jeans. His stomach clenched, making his abs ripple.

She pressed the flat of her palm against the ridged muscles of his stomach. "I want to lick these."

"Darlin', I ain't gonna stop you."

Livvy smiled as she sank to her knees. Gabe threaded his fingers into her hair, as much to anchor him as to support her, while Livvy flicked her tongue over his abdominal muscles, paying attention to each and every one.

"Jesus, you're killing me," Gabe gritted out. He released his hold on her head to unfasten his belt and tug his jeans down his legs. He kicked them to one side, and as he glanced down at Livvy, still on her knees, he had to refrain from yanking down his boxers and asking her to wrap her mouth around his dick. It would be a mistake. She was still too jumpy and nervous, and he was worried that he would scare her off if he pushed her too soon. Even though she'd been married for years, instinct told him that she didn't have a lot of experience—maybe two or three lovers at most.

He was about to help her to her feet, when her hands fisted the material of his boxers. In one swift movement, she pulled them down to his knees, wrapped her hand around the base of his cock, and took him into her mouth.

"Holy fuck."

What the hell did he know? Either he'd been wrong, or she was acting on intuition and hitting the mark.

Gabe moved his hands back to her head as she took him deep into her mouth. But as his balls tightened, he eased back. He slipped his hands under her armpits and helped her to her feet.

Her teeth grazed her bottom lip, and she gazed at him from under her lashes. "What did I do wrong?"

Gabe's eyes widened. "Not a goddamn thing, but I don't want our first time to be like that. I want to be inside you."

"I want that too." She shrugged out of her clothes and knitted their fingers together as she led him to the bed.

"You're so beautiful, Livvy," Gabe murmured, his gaze raking her from head to foot as she stretched out in front of him.

She beckoned him to her, and he went willingly. "Make me forget, Gabe," she whispered in his ear as her fingers traced the outline of his face. "Make me forget everything except you and me and this moment."

Gabe covered her body with his, and their eager tongues tangled with each other. He slid his hands down the sides of her slender waist. The feel of her skin beneath his palms sent shivers up his arms and made his head spin.

He trailed kisses down her neck, and Livvy arched her back, pushing her breasts against his chest as a soft moan tumbled from her lips. Gabe let out a low groan as he took her nipple between his lips and used the tip of his tongue to bring the peak to a hard point.

"Don't wait," Livvy whispered as she tilted her pelvis. "Don't make me wait any longer."

Gabe lifted his head and met her eager gaze. She nodded in encouragement as his eyes searched her face, looking for any signs that she had the slightest doubt. When he found none, he reached for a condom and tore the silver packet with his teeth. He leaned back on his heels and slid the condom down his shaft. Livvy reached out, curling her hands around his length as she eased him inside her warm, wet heat.

Gabe clenched his jaw as his balls tightened once more. He rested his weight on his elbows and thrust his hips. As Livvy's teeth grazed her lower lip and her eyes fixed on his, he almost came. To apply a level of control, he tore his gaze from hers and buried his head against her neck. He began to move faster as her body welcomed him every time he drove in hard. He nipped and sucked at the tender skin of Livvy's neck, driving her as crazy as she was driving him.

Livvy groaned as he continued to push in deep. Then she stiffened, and her whole body began to convulse around him.

When her inner muscles clamped around his shaft, he couldn't hold on anymore.

His orgasm was so intense, it felt as if an electric jolt erupted from the head of his cock. "Oh God, Livvy, you're killing me," he groaned. He collapsed on top of her, his arms holding her close, their damp bodies connecting as one. His tongue touched her neck, tasting her. Fuck, she was perfect—utterly, spellbindingly perfect.

After a few moments, he rolled to the side, his chest still heaving. As his breathing returned to normal, he lifted himself up and caressed her face. "Are you okay?"

A broad smile lit up her face. "I hope you bought a decent supply of condoms."

CHAPTER THIRTEEN

LIVVY GLANCED at Gabe and found his eyes still firmly closed. She flung her legs over the side of the bed and stretched. Her body ached, but as her mind turned to the previous evening, her abdomen flooded with butterflies. She waited for the familiar slug of guilt to take away this moment of joy, but when her mind remained free of doubt, she couldn't keep from smiling. Nothing was going to rob her of this feeling. Even as her mind turned to Beth, John's last words to her about grabbing happiness and holding on tight were the ones she decided to listen to. She could choose to be sad for the rest of her life because of what she'd lost, or she could move forward, knowing it was those experiences that had brought her into Gabe's life.

"Mornin', beautiful." Gabe wrapped his arms around her waist and tugged her back into bed.

She yelped in surprise. "I bet I don't look remotely beautiful. I think I've still got sleep in my eyes."

"You're beautiful to me." He leaned over and planted a soft kiss on her lips. Before he could deepen it, Livvy turned her head to the side.

"I need to brush my teeth."

Gabe laughed. "Darlin', you really think that bothers me?"

"No, but it bothers me."

He shrugged and released her. Livvy climbed out of bed. A moment of embarrassment hit her as she realized she would have to walk across the bedroom completely naked, but then she thought *what the hell* and sauntered towards the bathroom, hips swaying. Gabe's answering hiss made a smile edge across her face.

She slipped through the door and dug her toothbrush out of her wash bag. As she brushed her teeth, she stared at herself in the mirror, half expecting to see a different person looking back at her. But no, her reflection showed the same old Livvy. Her hair was ratty because she'd forgotten to tie it up overnight, and a smudge of mascara remained in the corner of one eye where she hadn't removed her makeup properly. She was far from beautiful, but if Gabe's adoring gaze meant anything, it was that he didn't care.

She filled the sink with hot water and scrubbed her face vigorously until all traces of sleep and mascara were gone and her cheeks held a healthy pink glow. As she walked back into the bedroom, Gabe was lying on his back, one arm flung above his head and the bed sheet strewn halfway across his body. His gaze raked over her as she sauntered back to bed. Warmth rushed to her cheeks—and other parts—as desire sparked in his eyes. She had to steel herself not to run and dive under the covers, but she instinctively knew Gabe wouldn't want that.

He opened his arms, and Livvy curled into his side and rested her head on his chest.

"Better?"

"Much. I hate the unbrushed feeling."

Gabe grinned. "You are so *English* sometimes."

Livvy dug him in the ribs, and he grunted.

"Hey… no violence."

"Hey… no picking on my deeply rooted English reserve."

His smile widened, and he kissed her briefly. "I'm starving, but before eating breakfast, I'm going to eat you."

He dove beneath the covers as Livvy's giggles erupted into the room.

GABE STOOD AT THE STOVE, cooking pancakes, eggs, and bacon. Livvy's stomach grumbled as the smells reached her, making him chuckle.

"It's coming," he said, dishing up their breakfast. He slipped onto the stool next to hers and poured her a coffee. "I wanted to talk to you about something."

Livvy cut into her eggs. "What?" she asked with her mouth half full. Jeez, he even managed to make the humble egg taste amazing.

"I have to go away on business in a week or so. I've been putting it off, but I can't any longer."

Livvy swallowed her food as her mood took a downward spiral. "I see."

"I thought I'd take a little time off before I go so we could do some fun stuff."

"Skydiving?" She brightened at the thought.

Gabe laughed. "If you want. I had a few other things in mind too."

She raised her eyebrow in question. "Like what?"

He gave her a crooked smile. "I thought you liked surprises."

A thrill ran up her spine. "I do."

"Then let me surprise you."

"When you go away on business, how long will you be gone?"

"Three to four weeks."

That long? She'd gotten used to him being around, and if he was going to be away for so long, she wondered how she would manage to keep herself occupied or whether the distance would ruin their fledgling relationship.

Livvy chewed on her thumbnail and stared at her half-eaten plate of food, her appetite waning. "Where are you going?"

Gabe's hand came underneath her chin, and he tilted her head up. "New York. I'm buying a company out east, and the current head offices are based in Manhattan."

"Okay," Livvy said quietly.

"I want you to come with me."

Her eyes widened. "You do?"

He laughed. "Of course. I can't imagine spending a day without you, let alone weeks at a time."

Relief surged through her, surprising her with its intensity. "Won't I get in your way?"

"No. Why would you? I won't have much time in the day, but I can make it up to you at night." He waggled his eyebrows, making her laugh. "That is, if you want to come. If you'd rather stay here, I'll understand. I won't like it, but I'll accept it."

"I'd love to come with you."

His palm skimmed her jaw, and he leaned in for a brief kiss. "Right answer."

"COME ON, Livvy. Get up. We have to be at the airport soon."

"It's too early," Livvy groaned, turning over in bed. She pulled the comforter over her head, but Gabe had other ideas. He shoved the covers to one side and moved on top of her. As he peppered her face with kisses, Livvy began to laugh.

She pushed at his immoveable chest. "Get off me, you big Texan oaf."

"Say it like you mean it, darlin'." His hands cupped her cheeks, and his mouth covered hers.

Livvy drowned in his kiss. Gabe was chipping away at her English modesty, piece by piece.

"I thought we didn't have time," she said as his hands moved down her body, sending shivers of delight through her.

"We don't." He rocked back on his heels. "But at least you're awake now."

Livvy threw a pillow at him, which he expertly ducked. "You don't play fair," she said with a scowl.

"True." He climbed off the bed and sauntered across the room. When he reached the door, he glanced over his shoulder. "Move your ass, Livvy."

She threw another pillow at him. Her aim was true, but he'd already slipped outside. She ground her teeth as she heard him laughing on his way downstairs.

A half hour later, Gabe caught Livvy's hand as they walked around to the garage. Dawn was still some way off, and the sky above was a carpet of twinkling stars.

"Where are we going, anyway?" Livvy asked as she got into the car.

"You'll see. I promised we'd have fun this week, and today's just the beginning."

Livvy stuck out her tongue, and he laughed.

"You're a grouchy little thing without sleep, aren't you?"

"It's eight hours, or everyone pays," she said. "How come you're all bright and breezy?"

Gabe started the engine and reversed until the car was facing the right way around. He set off down the driveway. "When I was building the business, I learned to survive on very little sleep. Now, I guess it's a habit."

"Not one I want to emulate," Livvy muttered, drawing another chuckle from him.

"Duly noted," he said as the gates slowly drew back and the car glided through.

The highway was virtually empty, and they reached the airport within thirty minutes. As Livvy began to wake up properly, her excitement grew. Every time she risked a glance at Gabe, he was wearing a small, satisfied smile, as though he knew a secret no one else did. Which, of course, was accurate, given that she didn't know where he was taking her.

As she settled into her seat, she hit him with her best interrogation stare. "How long is the flight?"

His lips twitched. "Two and a half hours."

"Hmm." She tried to picture a map of the US. The problem was, without knowing which direction they were traveling, it was impossible to hazard a guess at their eventual destination.

"There's no point," Gabe said with a grin. "I'm not telling. Anyway, you like surprises, or so you said. All I'm doing is going along with your wishes."

She pouted. "Yeah, well, maybe I've changed my mind."

He ignored her, and once the plane was in the air, he took a large file out of the bag he'd brought on board. "You don't mind if I do a little work on the flight, do you?"

"Of course not." She reached into her purse, pulled out a book, and smiled at him. "I have plenty to keep me occupied."

Livvy opened the book, but it didn't hold her attention. She peered over the top of it to watch Gabe. He had one ankle casually crossed over the opposing leg, completely immersed in the spiral-bound set of papers resting against his knee. When he wasn't scribbling notes in the margin, he was tapping the pen against his chin as his eyes scanned the document. Livvy found herself absorbed in watching him work.

He must have sensed her staring because he lifted his head and met her gaze. "I'm not being very good company, am I? Do you want me to stop?"

"Not at all. It's riveting to watch you."

A trace of a smile left his lips. "I can't imagine why, but from you, I'll take it."

As he went back to work, Livvy put her book down. She propped her elbow on the table and rested her palm against her cheek, focusing her gaze on him once more. In some ways, he reminded her of Mark: his intelligence, his work ethic, and his calm demeanor. In others, the two men were polar opposites.

Gabe could be intense both in and out of the bedroom. He was less tolerant of her than Mark, who had treated Livvy like a precious doll that could break at any moment. Their physical appearances were also nothing alike. Mark had had a lean body and an understated personality. Gabe was at least four inches taller than Mark, broader in the shoulders, and definitely more commanding in stature.

Livvy only realized they'd begun their descent when her ears popped. She held her nose and blew hard. Unsuccessful, she attempted a forced yawn.

"Here," Gabe said with an amused smile gracing his lips as he watched her attempts to combat the pressure change. "This might help." He passed her a piece of hard candy, which she unwrapped and slipped into her mouth.

Her left ear cleared, but her right remained stubbornly blocked. "I hate that feeling."

"We'll be landing soon."

"Landing where?"

Gabe laughed. "A little tip in the art of negotiation, darlin'. Work on your subtlety."

Livvy kicked off her shoe and trailed a toe up and down Gabe's leg. "We have a phrase in England. There's more than one way to skin a cat."

He fidgeted in his chair and cleared his throat. "And what does that mean, exactly?"

She repressed a smile. Rising slowly to her feet, she walked around to his side of the table and straddled his thighs before lowering herself onto his lap. Gabe let out a low hiss as her breasts brushed against his chest. She touched her lips to his, but as he tried to take control and deepen the kiss, she drew back, pressing her hand against his chest to keep him at bay.

"If you tell me where we're going, then I'll make sure you're suitably rewarded on the trip home. You don't have to tell me what we're doing, just our destination."

Gabe stubbornly shook his head. A low groan eased from his

throat as she slowly rocked her pelvis against his growing erection.

"How am I doing in the art of negotiation?" she asked, parroting his words as she ground down harder. She cradled his face and kissed him, her tongue sliding between his lips as she circled her hips against his fully erect penis.

He tore his mouth from hers, his chest rising and falling rapidly. "Cabo," he said.

She frowned. "Where's that?"

"Baja California."

"Oh. Cool." She climbed off his lap and gave him a satisfied smile. "See, that wasn't so hard, was it?"

"It's very fucking hard, actually," Gabe said.

Livvy laughed. "Oh, poor baby."

A sense of excitement washed over her as their banter continued. She hadn't felt so light or so free in a very long time, yet as she teased Gabe and he promised payback, she couldn't imagine that it was possible to achieve greater happiness.

The plane landed and came to a halt. As the door opened, blazing sunshine poured into the cabin.

Gabe unclipped his seat belt and cocked his head. "Ready?"

Excitement pricked her skin. "Absolutely. I can't wait."

At the bottom of the stairs, a waiting car drove them to immigration.

"I've heard of a drive-through McDonald's but never a drive-through passport control," she said with a laugh as Gabe handed over their documentation. Livvy paused for a beat, deliberating what was wrong with the picture. Then she gasped. "How did you get hold of my passport?"

Gabe tapped the side of his nose. "All part of the service, ma'am."

"Breaking and entering is not a service that you should be proud of," Livvy said, although the brevity of her tone belied the sharpness of her words.

Gabe chuckled. "I'm not sorry."

Within minutes, they were driving along a coast road. Livvy stared out the window at the breathtaking view of the coastline. White-topped waves crested an emerald-green sea—the color reminded Livvy of Gabe's eyes—and the contrast of the ocean with the clear blue sky beyond the horizon was absolute paradise. Gabe took her hand, his thumb gently brushing across her knuckles. Livvy could feel his eyes on her, gauging her reaction.

"What a view." She turned to face him. "California is beautiful, but this is something else."

He nodded. "I take it you haven't made it down here since you came to California?"

"No. Although I definitely should have."

Livvy looked out the window once more. The scenery passed in a blur as their vehicle sped down the highway.

"Are you going to tell me yet?" she asked as the car slowed and banked to the left before drawing to a stop.

Gabe tilted his head to the side. "Well, I could drag it out for a bit longer, but seeing as we're here, I may as well tell you."

When he didn't continue, Livvy huffed. "Well, come on, then."

Gabe laughed. "We're going swimming with dolphins."

A wave of emotion washed over her. She and Mark had always talked about doing that someday, but vacations had been difficult to come by for Mark as he'd tried to build a sustainable career. So they'd put it off—and subsequently, Livvy had learned a terrible lesson. She went quiet, her teeth gnawing on her bottom lip as regret made her head ache.

"What's the matter, Liv?" Gabe frowned. "Have I done the wrong thing?"

"No. No, you've done the right thing. The perfect thing," she said, her voice hitching.

"Then why do you look so sad?"

Livvy shook her head. She didn't want to get all maudlin by telling him the real reason, so she smiled through blurred vision.

"I didn't expect it, that's all. I've always wanted to swim with dolphins."

Gabe let out a huge sigh of relief and opened his car door. "Then let's go."

As they walked towards the entrance of the facility, a young woman wearing a wet suit greeted them warmly. "Mr. Mitchell, Ms. Hayes, welcome. My name is Adrianna Fabrice. I'll be your guide for the day. Please follow me. We have everything ready for you."

They followed Adrianna inside. Rows of wet suits were lined up on racks. She quickly measured both Livvy and Gabe for size then directed them to the changing rooms. After struggling into the rubber outfit—not an easy task—Livvy met Gabe outside. Her mouth went dry at the sight of him in what amounted to nothing more than a second skin.

His gaze slid over her, and when he looked up, his eyes were sparkling. "Nice outfit," he murmured.

"I was thinking the same thing myself," she said, making him laugh.

He slipped her hand inside his, and they walked to where Adrianna was waiting for them.

"Ready?" she asked. They both nodded. "Okay. Follow me."

Adrianna led them to the edge of a boardwalk, where a salt-water pool had been created with rock. A wire fence peeked out above the waterline. On the far side were two beautiful bottlenose dolphins, their sleek bodies moving effortlessly through the water. Livvy's excitement ramped up, and her heart thudded against her ribcage. She couldn't wait to get into the water with them.

Adrianna went through a short safety briefing, as much for the dolphins as for them. Livvy listened attentively, taking it all in.

"Okay, any questions?" Adrianna asked. When Livvy and Gabe shook their heads, Adrianna slipped into the water and waved for them to follow her.

Gabe held Livvy's hands as she dropped into the water.

She gasped. "It's freezing."

Gabe laughed. "Why do you think we have wetsuits? This is the Pacific, darlin'. Ice cold."

As they began to interact with the intelligent, social creatures, Livvy soon forgot the cold. Adrianna coached them through the various hand signals, which the dolphins reacted to accordingly. The highlight for Livvy, however, was when she got to hang on to the fin of a dolphin and was pulled through the water at such a speed that she lost her breath.

"Oh my God." She smiled so broadly, her cheeks hurt. "That was *amazing*."

As she swam back to the edge of the pool, Gabe drew her into his arms. He swept aside a damp lock of hair that had clung to her eyelashes and bent his head to kiss her. When a brief peck turned into something deeper, Livvy pulled back, conscious of Adrianna's proximity.

"Bashful English girl," he whispered, his green eyes twinkling as they mocked her.

"Overexuberant Texan cowboy," she replied.

Gabe threw back his head and laughed. "Come on. Adrianna is going to show us around the place."

It was only as Gabe spoke that Livvy glanced around and realized there were no other visitors. "Where are the other tourists?"

He tilted his head to one side. "It's closed. They're only hosting us today."

Livvy raised her eyebrows and gave a slight shake of her head. "How did you manage that?"

Gabe winked. "I have my ways."

Livvy chuckled. "Well, even though you are incorrigible, I really appreciate the gesture."

They spent the rest of the day learning how the aquarium helped rescue injured and orphaned dolphins. The facility put them through a rehabilitation program in the hope of returning them to the wild. Gabe listened intently and asked lots of questions. As they were getting ready to leave, he made a generous donation to the center. Although he could easily afford it, his philanthropy still struck a chord with Livvy, and she fell a little deeper under his spell.

"Thank you for today," Livvy said as they climbed back into the car.

His fingers lightly brushed hers, causing a shiver of delight to creep up her spine.

"You're welcome."

IF SHE THOUGHT the dolphin encounter would be the highlight of their weeklong vacation, Livvy couldn't have been more wrong. Gabe whisked her all over the country to all manner of events and experiences, from renting out an entire ice rink—where Livvy discovered she was a *terrible* ice-skater—to hot-air ballooning at dawn over New Mexico. He topped off the week with a visit to a rodeo in Texas, where they also paid his mother a visit.

As their vacation drew to a close and they headed back to Los Angeles, a sense of loss ran through her. Even though she would be traveling with Gabe on his business trip, it wouldn't be the same. He'd been devoted to her all week, yet now she would have to share him with the other side of his life—a very important one. She was being selfish by wanting him all to herself, but she couldn't seem to stop the errant thoughts from running through her mind.

They spent the night back at Gabe's place. Livvy kept calling it home in her head then had to correct herself because it wasn't her home. The problem was, she spent so much time at his house that she barely went back to her apartment. It was understandable how her mind drifted in that direction.

A weird feeling stirred in her chest. Even though Gabe

seemed committed to their relationship, he hadn't mentioned anything about the future. Livvy worried that she was significantly more invested than he was, and it made her nervous. Neither of them had come close to uttering the L word. Yet the fluttering she felt in her stomach every time he was near, the way he made her forget everything when they made love, and how safe and secure she felt around him told her it was already too late. She'd suspected her feelings ran deep before she and Gabe had gone away, but after their dream vacation, she knew for certain.

She'd learned to love again.

CHAPTER FOURTEEN

A FEW WEEKS LATER, Livvy and Gabe were in New York, preparing to attend a function to celebrate the acquisition of Gabe's latest business. He'd spent most of the day at his lawyer's offices, going over the final details before the deal was concluded.

"So who's going to be at this thing?" Livvy asked as she dabbed a tissue over her mouth to seal her lipstick.

Gabe stood beside her and straightened his bow tie. "The board of directors from both companies, plus the department heads and their partners, of course. I also instructed my people to invite the top talent from each regional office. It's good to show those folks how much they're appreciated and to set their minds at rest over the merger."

Livvy's gaze slid over him. Her man sure looked handsome in a tux. Gabe caught her checking him out, and his eyes darkened, even as a slight smirk curled his lips upward.

A faint flush crept over Livvy's neck. Even after all this time, Gabe could still make her blush like a teenager on her first date. "How many people?"

Gabe moved behind her and wrapped his arms around her

waist. He rested his chin on her shoulder. "A couple hundred maybe." His lips grazed her exposed neck, and she shuddered. "I like this dress. Blue suits you."

Livvy smoothed her hands over her hips as nervous tension bit at her insides. "That's a lot of people." She ignored his compliment because she was too damn anxious. This was the first time that she would be at his side during such a big function, and she desperately wanted to make a good impression.

"It makes no difference. I only have eyes for you."

"Sweet-talker," she said as she leaned back against him. She closed her eyes as his fingertips skimmed up her sides. Goose bumps broke out on her skin, but Gabe's touch made her stress levels recede. He grew hard, and as the flat of his palm pressed against her abdomen, he pushed her into his groin. A low groan eased from his throat.

"Do you think it would be bad form for the host to be late?" he murmured, his breath blowing warm air on the shell of her ear.

She circled her hips against his erection. "You're asking the wrong person, cowboy."

He groaned again, louder this time. "You up for this? It'll be quick."

Livvy nodded as desire made her stomach clench and wetness pool between her thighs. Gabe gripped the hem of her dress and gathered it around her waist.

"Spread your legs," he whispered, his voice low and husky.

Livvy did as he asked.

"Hands on the wall," he instructed.

Livvy repressed a moan. Over the last few weeks, their love-making had become more adventurous, and Livvy's confidence had grown so much that she instigated sex almost as much as he did.

As she leaned forward, Gabe's zipper came down. He tore open a condom and tossed the packaging on the floor. With one hand on the back of her neck, he moved her panties to the side and pushed himself in deep.

"Okay?" he gritted out as he stilled.

Livvy thrust backward. "Oh yeah."

He held on to her hips, and they moved in tandem, their breathing increasing with every thrust. Gabe's fingers played with her clit and took his cue from her. As he sensed her closing in on a climax, he squeezed hard. She exploded in an intense orgasm that made her legs tremble. If Gabe hadn't been holding on to her so tightly, she would have collapsed to the ground.

He groaned out his own climax, and as his breathing slowed, he gently pulled out of her.

"You make me feel about eighteen," he said with a chuckle as he discarded the condom and tucked himself away. "I can't resist you."

Livvy laughed as she smoothed her dress back into position. "Am I creased?"

He gave her the once-over. "Looks fine to me. Then again, you'd look gorgeous wearing a garbage bag."

She laughed again. "No need to sweet-talk me now. You've had your wicked way."

Gabe leaned in close, his lips brushing hers. "I call that putting down a deposit for later."

FLASHBULBS EXPLODED as their car drew up outside the Plaza Hotel in New York. The merger of Gabe's company with another equally huge one was a big story, but so far, he'd said very little to the press, which had increased their interest considerably. Still, he had no intention of spilling the details to hungry journalists yet. His new team deserved to hear from him first, then he would give the go-ahead for his publicist to release the prepared statement.

"Stay there," Gabe said to Livvy as he climbed out of the car. More flashbulbs went off as he made his way around to her side, and voices began shouting, all talking over one another. As he helped Livvy out of the car, she squinted against the bright lights.

"Don't answer any of their questions," he murmured in her ear. "Hold tight to me, okay? We'll soon be inside."

Livvy nodded and took Gabe's outstretched hand as they walked up the red-carpeted front steps and into the hotel.

"Wow," Livvy said as they stepped through the gold doors into the lobby. Gabe could understand her reaction. The interior of the Plaza was stunning—the highly polished tile, the opulent drapes hanging around the windows, and an impressive marble staircase to their right.

"Lovely, isn't it?"

She nodded as her eyes darted everywhere.

Gabe tucked her hand through his arm. "If you think this is nice, wait until you see the Grand Ballroom."

They set off through the hotel, and although Livvy was blissfully unaware, heads turned to watch them pass. Well, they turned to watch *her* pass. Livvy always shone, but tonight her star seemed brighter than normal. He didn't know if the cobalt-blue dress that clung so deliciously to her soft curves was what attracted interest from passers-by, or if it was that she'd put up her auburn hair, leaving her long, creamy white neck exposed. Or maybe it was simply her obliviousness to attention that drew the eye. But one thing was certain: people noticed Livvy. She oozed innocence mixed with wisdom. The combination had intoxicated him from the first moment he saw her, and his interest had grown every day since.

As they entered the ballroom, Livvy sucked in a breath. She tilted her head backward to gaze up at the ornate ceiling and the large crystal chandelier hanging from the center.

"This is amazing," she whispered, awe prevalent in her tone. "Look at the architecture."

"It is pretty special," he said as he spotted his marketing director, Edward, heading over.

The man wore a broad, triumphant smile. "Gabe." Edward stretched out his hand. "Today is a good day."

Gabe returned his smile. "It sure is. Edward, this is Livvy Hayes, my girlfriend. Livvy, this man here is someone I'd like you to talk to." As Livvy frowned, Gabe looked at Edward. "Livvy has a marketing degree. I'd like you to talk to her about opportunities within the firm." As Livvy drew in a sharp breath, Gabe squeezed her hand. "That is, if you're interested."

A smile inched across her face, and Gabe could swear she stood a little taller. "I would love the opportunity." Then she frowned. "But aren't there rules about taking on foreigners?"

"You let us worry about that," Gabe said. "We'll make it work."

She faced Edward, her eyes sparkling with excitement. "Then I'd be thrilled to join the firm. Of course, I don't expect any special treatment. I'm happy to start at the bottom and work my way up."

Edward chuckled. "I'm not sure I'll get away with having you open the mail, but don't you worry, Livvy. I have several ideas I think you may be interested in. Let's talk specifics later this week."

Livvy beamed, and Gabe's chest swelled with pleasure. Since she'd tentatively mentioned the idea of returning to work in some capacity, Gabe had hoped she would consider working for his firm. He'd taken a bit of a risk springing the idea on her, but it looked as though he'd gotten away with it.

After dinner and the speeches were out of the way, everyone began to relax and the mingling and partying began. A never-ending line of people waited to talk to them. Livvy seemed to have more than piqued the interest of not only his employees, but their partners too. As the night wore on, Livvy blossomed into someone far removed from the broken girl he'd met a few short months earlier.

With one ear tuned into Marianne, his HR director, he listened as Livvy discussed marketing strategies with Edward. It looked as though their idea to chat later in the week had been moved up, and from what he could hear, she had some stellar ideas. Edward's animated expression as he engaged with her told its own story.

A bite of jealousy gripped his insides, and Gabe had the sudden urge to take back the girl who'd enchanted half his board of directors. He touched Livvy's arm. "Would you excuse us please, folks? I must get this beautiful lady a drink."

Livvy frowned at her half-full glass of champagne, but she didn't argue as he took her by the elbow and led her to the far side of the ballroom, where a private bar had been set up to serve his guests.

"Are you trying to get me drunk?" she asked, holding up her glass and shaking the contents.

Gabe smirked. "Would you think I was a complete asshole if I told you that I was getting a little jealous back there?"

Her eyes softened. "No. I'd say it showed you care."

He gently lifted her chin and brushed his lips against hers. "I do, Livvy. Very much." He briefly closed his eyes and let out a soft sigh. "How did I get so lucky?"

Livvy replied quietly. "I think I'm the lucky one."

Gabe placed her glass of champagne on the bar. He held out his hand. "Dance with me?" He led Livvy onto the dance floor and pulled her close. "You know what I want?" he asked as he pressed his cheek against hers.

"What's that, cowboy?"

He smiled against her soft skin. "To get through the rest of the evening as quickly as possible so I can whisk you back to the apartment and peel you out of that dress." He felt a tremor flow through her body.

She tilted her head back and looked him in the eye. "And then what are you going to do?"

He touched his lips to the shell of her ear. "Fuck you until you can't walk straight."

She exhaled on a gasp then burst out laughing. "Flatterer."

He held her gaze. "I meant what I said earlier. You make me feel young again, Livvy."

She raised an eyebrow. "You're hardly old."

"I know, but sometimes when I think about the level of responsibility I have, which I've doubled after this merger, and the amount of people who rely on me to pay their mortgages, well, it can weigh a man down after a while. But with you, Livvy, the stress ebbs away."

As Livvy's gaze clouded over and she stared into the distance without responding, an uncomfortable feeling stirred in his chest. "Penny for your thoughts," he eventually said.

She refocused her attention on him, a glimmer of a smile on her lips. "If I hadn't gone to Sam's that day, we never would have met."

Gabe winced. "I'd rather not think about it."

"We must go back. It was my regular haunt for so long, Sam'll be wondering what's happened to me."

"I'll take you as soon as we get home."

Livvy grinned. "Can I sit in your chair?"

He snorted. "Of course not."

Before Livvy could respond, the song finished and Gabe silenced her retort with a kiss. As she wound her arms around his neck and slid her tongue between his lips, Gabe made a decision.

"Let's get out of here," he said. "I've done my bit."

As they made their way off the dance floor, Gabe heard someone calling his name. He ground his teeth and clenched his fists as he recognized the voice.

"Well, well, Gabe Mitchell. You have certainly changed. I can't remember you showing me any public displays of affection when we were together."

Gabe stiffened and automatically put his arm around Livvy. "Hello, Tabitha."

CHAPTER FIFTEEN

THE INTERNET HADN'T DONE Tabitha Hale justice. Beautiful wasn't a strong enough adjective to describe her. She had piercing blue eyes and dark, almost black, hair that fell in perfect waves over one shoulder, not to mention smooth olive skin, the kind that tanned evenly without a hint of redness. No sunblock required for Tabitha, unlike Livvy, whose pale complexion burned within five minutes of glimpsing the sun. And as if Tabitha hadn't been blessed with enough good fortune, she also had womanly curves and legs that went on forever.

"So who's this?" Tabitha looked Livvy up and down, her expression haughty and disparaging. She gave Livvy a stiff smile, which Livvy didn't return.

Gabe's hand tightened on her hip. "What are you doing here, Tabitha? Because I'm damn sure your name wasn't on the guest list."

Tabitha gave a husky laugh. "Don't be such a grouch, Gabe." She moved in and brushed her hand up and down his arm.

Gabe stepped to the side, pulling Livvy with him. "It doesn't matter, anyway. We were just leaving."

"Gabriel, don't be so rude." She flashed him an admonishing stare as she thrust her hand out in front of Livvy. "Well, if he won't introduce us properly, I will. I'm Tabitha. And you are?"

Gabe was holding on to Livvy's hip so tightly, she was sure she would have a bruise there in the morning.

"Livvy." She shook the outstretched hand of Gabe's ex while praying Tabitha didn't feel her slight tremble.

"My girlfriend," Gabe added. Livvy risked a quick glance up at him, hoping to catch his eye. *No such luck.* His face smoldered beneath barely hidden fury, making the hairs stand up on the back of Livvy's neck. This had been more than a long-term relationship coming to a natural end. Something had gone terribly wrong between these two.

"Girlfriend?" Tabitha's head tilted to one side then the other, reminding Livvy of an eager puppy. She repressed a giggle.

"Yes," Gabe bit out. "Now, if you'll excuse us."

"So you can finish what you started on the dance floor?" Tabitha asked. "You certainly have changed, Gabe. When we were together, you would barely hold my hand in public. Of course," she added with a girlish giggle, "you made up for that when we were alone. You couldn't keep your hands off me as I recall."

A surge of jealousy stole Livvy's breath. She had no right to be envious—everyone was entitled to a past—but something about Tabitha's manner set Livvy's teeth on edge.

"That was a long time ago." Gabe's jaw was clenched tight, a nerve beating in his cheek. "I'm with Livvy now."

Tabitha's answering smile reminded Livvy of a lion before it ripped out the throat of its prey. "Well, they say change can be refreshing. This one is certainly a change." She turned her attention to Livvy. "If you want the skinny on how to keep him interested in bed, give me a call."

"That's *enough*, Tabitha, or so help me God—" He stopped

when Livvy twisted out of his tight embrace. "Where are you going?"

"I-I need the restroom," Livvy said, desperate to escape the terrible atmosphere caused by the untimely appearance of Gabe's ex.

He frowned but also nodded. "Okay. I'll meet you in the lobby."

Livvy didn't reply as she made her escape. The ladies' room wasn't far from the ballroom, and fortunately, it was empty. She stepped into a stall, locked the door, and plunked herself down on the toilet seat. The hatred—which wasn't too strong of a word—dripping from Gabe had been hard to watch. What could an ex-girlfriend have done to make someone who used to love her despise her so? And if he could show such hatred towards Tabitha, then what was to stop him from turning on Livvy?

No, she wasn't going down that road. Gabe had given Livvy no reason to doubt his affection for her. She resolved to ask him about his ex-girlfriend later when they were alone. Apart from the one time he'd shut her down when she asked about Tabitha, she hadn't pressed. But now that Livvy had met her and seen Gabe's reaction, she wanted to know and understand what had happened.

After finishing up, she headed to the washbasin as the door to the ladies' room opened. She paid no attention to the new arrival, removing a towel and thoroughly drying her hands. As she dropped the towel into the laundry basket, she turned around. Standing by the door, arms folded across her chest, was Tabitha.

"Can I help you?" Livvy asked.

Tabitha gave Livvy a sympathetic look. "I'm sorry you had to see that. And I'm sorry if I came across as a little... bitchy."

Livvy shrugged. "It's fine." She tried to move around Tabitha, who put her arm out.

"Wait, please. I want to talk to you."

Livvy swallowed. "Why? What could we possibly have to say to each other?"

She sighed and looked Livvy directly in the eye, her lips pressed together in a slight grimace. "You need to know who you're dealing with."

A nervous laugh bubbled up in Livvy's throat. "I know who I'm dealing with, thank you. Now please step aside. Gabe will be waiting for me."

Tabitha pulled herself upright. "You have absolutely no idea who you're dealing with. Has he told you he loves you yet?"

Livvy held back a wince. He'd come close but hadn't quite taken the final leap. "That's none of your business."

"Look, I'm not trying to be mean. I don't want someone else to go through what I went through, that's all. You need to understand the type of relationship Gabe and I had. We loved each other fully and completely. We were *obsessed* with one another."

A burning sensation passed through Livvy's chest, one she recognized as pure envy. "I'm not sure why I need to understand that. Still, if he loved you so much, why aren't you together?"

Tabitha dabbed at the corner of her eye, although Livvy wouldn't lay a bet that she was crying a real tear.

"Because something happened to me that he didn't like, that he didn't agree with, that *inconvenienced* him."

Livvy's mind began to race. What in God's name was Tabitha going on about? Livvy had an urge to push past her, to leave and never look back, but something kept her rooted to the spot.

"Has he told you why we broke up?"

Livvy shook her head but remained silent. Something about Tabitha's demeanor already made Livvy feel outmaneuvered. She wasn't about to give the woman even more of an upper hand.

"I got pregnant. It wasn't planned, but I guess a lot of pregnancies are mistakes."

Livvy's breath hissed through her teeth. *Pregnant?* No, surely not. Gabe would have told her about something so huge, especially considering her history. With all the things she'd shared with him about losing Daniel and about her two miscarriages, he wouldn't keep such a huge part of his life from her. Would he?

"So you have a child together?" Livvy whispered, barely trusting her ability to form a coherent sentence.

Tabitha paused then took Livvy's limp hand inside her own and squeezed. "I'm so sorry to have to tell you this, honey, but the perfect man out there—the one you seem so taken with—decided a baby wouldn't be good for his career. He made it clear he couldn't, or rather wouldn't, be a father to our child. At the time, I simply wasn't strong enough to raise a child on my own. He gave me no choice. I had to abort our baby."

Livvy inhaled on a gasp, her eyes widening in shock. She began to shake. No… he wouldn't. The man Livvy knew wouldn't do such a thing. But then again, how well did she really know this man who'd brought her back from the brink and given her a reason to live again? She so desperately wanted to believe in him.

"You're lying," she said, her voice quiet and wary.

Tabitha vigorously shook her head. "I'm not lying. What could I possibly hope to achieve by lying? It's not as if I want him back. After what he put me through, I wouldn't touch him again if he paid me."

A horrible sick feeling churned in Livvy's gut. Something about Tabitha's vehemence while recounting the terrible event told Livvy it was true. Tabitha had been pregnant, and she'd had an abortion. *Oh God.* She was going to be sick.

With a deep, cleansing breath, Livvy pushed past her nemesis, but as she wrenched the door to the restroom open, Tabitha grabbed her arm.

"Be careful, okay? Gabe is not who you think he is. You're wrong for him. Leave now before you get hurt."

Livvy shook off Tabitha's hand and ran towards the lobby. She needed air before she threw up over the undoubtedly expensive carpet running along the hallways of the Plaza.

As she burst into the lobby, she sprinted towards the exit.

"Livvy, wait! What's wrong?" Gabe's voice reached her, but she couldn't stop.

With her heart thundering in her chest, she burst through the doors and onto the steps outside. The press was still clustered around, clearly waiting for the party to finish and the guests to leave. They looked startled at the whirlwind running down the steps of the Plaza but recovered quickly. Their cameras flashed in case she was someone worthy of a story. Except she wasn't worthy. She was no one.

Livvy didn't break stride as she turned left and sprinted down the street. With no idea where she was going, she continued to weave in between hordes of people enjoying the sights of Manhattan. When her lungs were fit to burst and her feet started cramping inside her shoes, she drew to a halt and took a deep breath.

The man she thought she knew—the man she loved—wasn't a nice person. Forcing a woman to make such a terrible decision because a baby would ruin his perfectly ordered life made him a monster.

She'd been sharing her bed with a monster.

As her brain continued to whirr with questions that had no answers, a limousine pulled up to the curb, and the rear window opened.

"Livvy, get in the car."

Gabe's calm voice had the complete opposite effect on Livvy. Pain seared through her chest as she looked into the earnest expression of the man she'd envisaged spending her whole future with.

"I'm not going anywhere with you," she snapped. Her tone was cold, even as anger simmered beneath the surface. This man that she'd entrusted with her heart didn't deserve it.

Turning her back, she set off walking. As she heard the limo idling alongside her, she darted down a one-way street, knowing the car couldn't follow.

"Livvy, for fuck's sake," Gabe shouted behind her.

A car door slammed, and she quickened her footsteps but couldn't outrun him. He took hold of her arm, but Livvy wrenched her shoulder upward, making him lose his grip.

"What the hell is going on?" Gabe frowned at her furious expression. "Please tell me what I did."

As he made another move to touch her, Livvy raised her hands, warding him off. "Go away. I don't want to talk to you right now."

"I'm not going anywhere, Liv." His voice was soft and gentle. "Not without you."

"Did you really think I wouldn't find out?"

Gabe took a step back and studied her face, his brows drawn low. "Find what out?"

Livvy shook her head. "Forget it. If you're going to try to play the innocent, then there's nothing more to say."

Gabe let out a sigh of exasperation. "I don't know what you're talking about, but let's go home and discuss it."

"No."

Before Livvy could move, Gabe gripped her elbow. "We're going home now."

Livvy tried to shake him off, but Gabe's grip was too strong. He opened the back door, only then releasing her. He waved his hand. "Get in."

She knew why he'd let her go, of course—to give her a choice. She could go with him or walk away. If she did the latter, then how would they get past this? Although right at that moment, she didn't know how she would ever be able to forgive him for such a callous move.

With a sigh, Livvy got in the car. Gabe climbed in beside her. A nerve beat in his cheek, his jaw was tight, and his nostrils flared, although whether that was from exertion or anger, she didn't know.

He instructed the driver to head for his Manhattan apartment then turned to her. "Okay, so catch me up, Livvy. You go to the restroom and agree to meet me in the lobby. Next thing I know, you're running outside like a pack of tigers is on your tail, and now, all of a sudden, I'm the bad guy. Throw me a goddamn bone, would you? I'm not a mind reader."

Livvy met his frustrated gaze and got ready to unleash, but the words wouldn't come. As the seconds scraped by without either of them speaking, Gabe expelled an irritated sigh.

"I'm a patient man, Livvy, but even I have my limits."

Livvy chewed her lip. Either Gabe was a great actor, or he really didn't have a clue. Could Tabitha have been lying about carrying Gabe's child? No. Livvy didn't think so. As anger and doubt warred for equal head space, Livvy's brain began to hurt.

"Tabitha followed me to the restroom," she said.

Gabe pressed his lips into a straight line. "What did she want?"

"To warn me off you."

His eyes widened, and his head jerked backward. "She did what?" he asked through clenched teeth.

"Apparently, you're not the man you pretend to be," Livvy said. "You're no good for me, according to your ex."

Gabe sighed. He swept a hand down the back of his head. "Look, I know I haven't told you much about my relationship with her—because it's in the past—but Tab and I didn't end on the best of terms. I thought she'd moved on. Clearly, I was wrong."

"I'll bet you didn't end on good terms." Bitterness filled Livvy's tone. "It's hard to *move on* when your boyfriend forces you to abort your child because he found it an *inconvenience*."

Livvy had always thought that the old cliché "you could cut the atmosphere with a knife" was a stupid phrase, but as Gabe's hands curled into fists and his face flushed bright red, she couldn't think of anything more appropriate to describe the climate inside the car. It was as though a cold blast of air had been forced through the vents, and she shivered in response.

"She said what?" Gabe asked, his voice low and menacing.

Livvy pressed herself against the door, putting as much distance as she could between her and Gabe. She'd never seen anyone so angry, but Gabe's fury didn't result in punching walls or screaming at the top of his voice. No, his rage was cold, calculating, and the scariest thing that Livvy had ever seen.

"Is it true?" she asked.

Hurt flashed across his face before he schooled his expression into that of a stranger rather than the man she shared her bed and her life with. Nervous tension bit at Livvy's insides. Had she made a mistake? One she couldn't take back?

"If you can ask me such a question, Livvy, then you don't know me at all." He twisted his head and gazed out the window.

An uncomfortable silence grew between them, and Livvy considered leaping out at the first red traffic light—anything to escape the hideous car journey.

Eventually, the car drew to a halt outside Gabe's apartment, and he climbed out. Ever the gentleman, he normally opened her car door for her, but not this time. Livvy peered through the window and watched as Gabe jogged up the steps before disappearing into the building. With a sigh, she considered her next move. Should she ask the driver to take her to JFK and get a flight back to LA, or should she be an adult, go inside, and have it out with Gabe?

She made her decision and got out of the car.

CHAPTER SIXTEEN

LIVVY STOOD outside Gabe's apartment, but as she lifted her hand to knock, she lost her nerve. His reaction was that of a hurt man, but did it make him an innocent man? She didn't doubt that Tabitha had been pregnant; otherwise Gabe would have instantly refuted the claim. But was Tabitha's version of events the whole truth?

Only one way to find out.

She rapped on the door and waited. She could hear Gabe moving about inside. He opened the door but barely gave her a glance before leaving her standing in the hallway as he walked away. Livvy closed the door behind her with a quiet click and bent down to remove her shoes. Gabe had unfastened his bow tie but left it hanging loose, his top button undone. Despite the heavy atmosphere, her heartbeat kicked up a notch. Christ, he was handsome.

Their eyes met briefly, but when his gaze became shuttered, she lowered hers. Her abdomen clenched as she waited for him to break the silence—except he didn't. As her chin came up and their eyes met once more, it became obvious he wasn't going to do the running. It occurred to Livvy that this was their first proper fight. All the other spats had been meaningless in the grand scheme of things, but this one felt serious. *Was* serious.

She blew out a soft breath and leaned against the wall. Gabe stood too, hands deep in his pockets. His eyes were smoldering, and not in a good way.

"Okay, so do you want to tell me your side of the story?" she asked, breaking the silence.

"Do you want to hear my side?" Gabe's tone dripped ice. "Or have you already decided to only listen to my ex?"

Livvy closed her eyes and bit her tongue. If they were going to get anywhere, she needed to be the calm one, because it was obvious by his voice—not to mention the stiffness with which he held himself—Gabe was far from calm. Beneath the surface, he was seething.

Livvy's expression changed into one of sympathy and openness. "Of course I want to hear your side." Her rage had cooled, but she still didn't know what to believe or *who* to believe. "She took me by surprise, that's all. And with my history, I guess I'm not always… measured when it comes to babies."

Gabe scraped a hand through his hair before shrugging out of his jacket. He tossed it on the couch. "I should have told you what happened with Tab, but it was an awful time, and not one I like to look back on, because when I do, I swear, Livvy, I could kill someone… her preferably."

"Was she pregnant with your child?"

Gabe nodded. "Tab was the first woman I ever fell in love with." Livvy repressed a wince, which he clearly didn't notice because he pressed on. "She was my everything, and I'd have done anything for her. I knew she was ambitious—she was an up-and-coming model—but I was fully supportive of her career. I never wanted a trophy girlfriend, one whose only job was to look good on my arm, so when things took off for her, no one was more thrilled than me."

He crossed over to the bar and poured bourbon into a

couple of glasses. He held one out to her, and she pushed off the wall and wandered over to take it from him.

"She never told me she was pregnant. I found the test, and when I asked her about it, she admitted it. She told me a child didn't fit in with her career aspirations." He took a sip of his drink. "I begged her to reconsider, but she was adamant. The next day, she took herself off to a clinic, without me knowing, and…" His eyes fell shut at the memory.

Livvy's heart squeezed at the pain that tightened his features. Her forehead fell onto his shoulder, and she was more than relieved when he didn't shake her off.

"I'm so sorry." Tears pricked her eyes, and she let them fall. "She told me it was you who didn't want the child."

A tremor ran through Gabe's body. He jerked his shoulder, making her lift her head. "And you believed her?" Disappointment and incredulity were prevalent in his tone.

"I didn't know what to think. She hit on my weak spot, and she was so convincing…"

"Oh yeah," Gabe said bitterly. "Tab can be *very* convincing."

"What happened after she… you know?"

"I told her I never wanted to see her again. She begged and pleaded with me to reconsider, told me all she wanted was a few years at the top of modeling, then she'd give it all up and we could have a whole football team. But it was too late. She'd broken my trust and my heart."

Hearing Gabe talk about another woman, one he'd loved so completely, wasn't easy, but then he probably felt the same when she mentioned Mark. They both had a past, but it was the future that mattered.

"I can't imagine how difficult that was for you."

"After our breakup, I kind of went off the rails. I wanted to hurt her as badly as she'd hurt me. I was determined that I'd never let anyone cause me so much pain again, so I kept my relationships, if you can even call them that, very shallow. I wouldn't let anyone close to me—until you."

Livvy's breath hitched as Gabe took her face in his hands. He kissed her, softly at first, then more insistently. But before she could sink into the kiss, he drew back. As their eyes met, his flashed with anger and disappointment.

"Don't doubt me again, Livvy," he said. "I can't bear it."

She began to answer, but before she could utter a word, his mouth crashed into hers. His big body pressed against her, pushing her backward until she hit the wall. He captured her hands in one of his and held them over her head. Desire rushed through her veins as his erection nudged her abdomen through the barrier of his trousers. This wasn't gentle Gabe. This was intense, burning, all-consuming Gabe, who took what he wanted without apology.

His tongue surged into her mouth as he dry-humped her against the wall. A moan eased from her throat, and her skin heated under his fervent touch. He let go of her hands, gripped the hem of her dress, and bunched it around her waist. His fingers dipped inside her underwear, and he pushed two through her slick folds.

"Jesus, Liv," he muttered as he nipped and sucked his way from her earlobe to her throat. She heard his zipper go down, and be

she could say the word "condom," he hooked her legs over his hips and pushed inside her.

Her mind went wild as to what this change could mean, but soon, her thoughts scattered as Gabe began to thrust, hard, his hips clashing with hers. Their breathing was intermingled with soft moans from her and shallow grunts from him. She held on, her hands threaded into his hair, her thighs gripping him tightly. This was nothing like any of their other sexual encounters. There was a heat, an intensity driven by anger, frustration, hurt, and desire… and she *loved* it.

Her body tightened, and as she crested and fell into a mind-blowing orgasm, Gabe groaned out his release, his breath hot against her neck. Their damp foreheads touched, and they remained connected as their breathing slowly returned to normal. Only then did he pull out of her and tuck himself away before smoothing her dress back into place. When he raised his head, the earlier anger and disappointment in his eyes had been replaced with love. His hands curved around her cheeks, and he touched his lips to hers.

"Marry me, Livvy."

CHAPTER SEVENTEEN

THE WORDS WERE out of Gabe's mouth before he realized what he'd said, and for a moment, he panicked. But then a sense of calm and a feeling of utter conviction settled over him. Livvy, on the other hand, wasn't in the same place. Her mouth opened and closed, her eyes widened in shock, and a flush spread from her neck up and over her cheeks.

"Marriage?" she whispered. "But we've only known each other a few months."

"So?" Gabe shrugged. "During our time together, I've shown you more of who I am than I've shown to people who I've known for years."

Livvy shook her head. "You haven't even told me you love me."

He brushed aside a stray lock of hair that had fallen across her face and tucked it behind her ear. "It's implied, Liv."

She jerked her head back. "Well, maybe I need more than implied. Maybe I need to actually hear the *words*," she said, incredulity leaching into her tone.

Gabe laughed as he picked up her hand and kissed her

knuckles. "Do you think I'd ask you to marry me if I didn't love you?"

"I don't know what to think." She began to wear out the carpet as she paced. "I never thought I'd get married again," she said more to herself than him.

Gabe reached out as she was on her third tour of the living room and circled his arms around her waist. He tilted his head towards her, touching her forehead with his. "You don't have to answer now. Take your time."

He didn't want her to take her time. He wanted a "yes" right then because he had a sinking feeling that the more time that he gave her, the less likely she was to agree. However, the tension in her shoulders and the stiffness in her spine told him she wasn't ready yet. If he pushed, he would get a definite no.

She twisted around, and he withheld a sigh of relief as her arms curved around his neck. She looked into his eyes. "Are you still in love with Tabitha?" The tightness around her mouth told him she dreaded the wrong answer.

"No." His response was immediate and emphatic. "She killed any love I had for her when she aborted our baby." He exhaled softly. "It was a long time ago, Liv. I didn't know she would be there tonight. I don't even know how she got in. I'm sorry she made you doubt me."

Livvy's face crumpled. She rested her head against his chest and tightened her grip on him. "It's me who should be apologizing. I never even gave you a chance to explain."

Gabe brushed his thumb across her plump lower lip. He was going to fucking kill Tab when he got a hold of her. "You don't need to justify your actions to me, Livvy. Tabitha can be very convincing, and I'm not surprised you reacted the way you did —especially given your history. But you have to believe me when I say things were over between us a long time ago. The only feelings I have for Tab now are contemptuous. *You* are all I want."

Gabe gently cupped her chin and tilted her head backward.

Her eyes held sorrow, regret, and a tinge of uncertainty. His abdomen clenched. He wanted to wash away those doubts and negative feelings. So he kissed her. When he drew back, she offered him a faint smile.

"You're very good at distraction techniques."

Gabe chuckled. "I like distracting you."

She touched her hand to his cheek. "Give me some time."

He nodded solemnly. "I can do that."

As she walked across the living room towards the bedroom, he called out to her.

"I love you, Liv."

Her slow, beautiful smile made a surge of affection rush through him. "I love you too."

As THEIR PLANE landed the following day, Gabe squeezed Livvy's hand. "I'm sorry, darlin', but I have to stop by the office. I'll have my driver drop you off at my place. I'll be home as soon as I can."

"Actually, can he drop me off at my place? I could do with picking up a few things, and I wouldn't mind doing a workout." She patted her stomach and groaned.

"As if you need it," Gabe scoffed.

"I will if I keep eating all this rich food."

Gabe shook his head and ignored her. Livvy had been so thin when they'd met. It was nice to see that she had put on a couple of pounds. It showed that she was happier, more settled, and that visits to the dark place she'd told him about were becoming fewer as time passed.

His driver pulled up outside his office building, and Gabe kissed Livvy's cheek before heading inside. The minute the car drove away, his smile fell, and as he rode up in the elevator, his fury at Tabitha grew. He'd held his anger in check while he was with Livvy, but now that he was alone, his throat was dry, blood pounded in his ears, and his vision kept clouding over.

As he stomped towards his office, his executive assistant held out a file of paperwork. She'd been with him a long time, and one look at his face told her that he wasn't in the mood for chitchat.

He swiped the file from her hand. "No interruptions, Alana."

"Certainly, Mr. Mitchell," she said, reverting to a rarely used formal address as he slammed the door behind him.

Gabe tossed the file on his desk and paced, trying to calm himself down before he picked up the phone to call Tabitha. He hadn't seen the damned woman in months, not since her last hapless attempt to convince him they should get back together, but that had been long before he met Livvy. He'd hoped Tab had disappeared for good, but this time, she'd gone too far. To insinuate what she had to Livvy—no, not insinuate, but downright lie—meant she'd wanted Livvy to believe her untruths. And that also meant she hoped it would split him and Livvy up. He briefly wondered if Tab had known about Livvy before they met at his company event in New York. He wouldn't put it past Tab to follow his every move. She was a woman who liked to be in control, to make the decisions. When he looked back, he was surprised they'd been together as long as they had because they were a mirror image of each other rather than complimentary like he and Livvy were.

He sat at his desk and steepled his fingers under his chin. Swiveling around in his chair, he stared out the window at the Los Angeles skyline, a place he'd grown to love. He still missed Texas, but as his business interests were split between the East and West Coasts, he'd had to choose one. Los Angeles had been the easy choice—great weather, beautiful beaches, and even more beautiful women. The sight of the downtown skyline usually soothed him, but not today.

He reached for his phone and dialed Tab's number. He had half a mind to get back on a plane to New York so he could rip her head off in person. But then Livvy would want to know why he was returning when they'd only just gotten home, and he didn't want her any more worried than she already had been.

"Gabe." Tabitha's smooth, practiced voice set his teeth on edge. "How lovely to hear from you. Have you gotten bored with your English rose already?"

Rage burned within him. "I know what you said to Livvy, Tab. And I'm warning you. Stay the fuck away from us."

Her laugh tinkled through the phone. When they were together, he'd found it alluring. Now it irritated the fuck out of him. "I only told her the truth."

Gabe almost choked. "You said I made you abort our baby. That's a fucking lie, Tab, and you know it."

"Oh, that." He could visualize her gesturing dismissively with her hand. "Well, yes, I might have stretched the truth there. I thought you meant the part where I told her she was all wrong for you, because that *is* true."

Gabe sucked in a breath. He was going to have to play hard-ball because anything less wouldn't cut it. With his free hand, he clenched his fist, his nails digging into the palm of his hand until he drew blood.

"You are a manipulative, vicious, selfish woman. I have no idea what I ever saw in you, but know this, Tabitha. If you come near me or Livvy, I will make sure that you never work as a model in this country again."

Tab gasped. "You wouldn't."

Gabe laughed derisively. "Try me, sweetheart. My reach is far and wide. By the time I've finished with you, you'll be lucky to get a job flipping burgers. I've given you fair warning. You'd do well to heed it."

He didn't wait for her response before cutting the call. That would be the end of it. He'd tolerated Tab's woeful attempts at reconciliation, even relished the boost to his ego, though he'd had no intention of reuniting with her. But since he'd gotten together with Livvy, everything was different. He knew Tab's career meant everything to her—the termination of their child was a testament to that. She wouldn't risk him carrying out his threat. She was smart enough to know that bluffing wasn't his style.

An hour later, Gabe walked through the door of his house. Silence greeted him, and he remembered that Livvy had asked to be dropped off at her apartment. He instantly headed for the garage, grabbed the keys to his BMW, and set off for Livvy's place. The earlier tension had left his shoulders now that he'd resolved the Tabitha problem.

He parked outside Livvy's apartment building and jogged the thirteen flights of stairs to her floor. He smiled as he recalled the very first day he'd knocked on her door and gotten no answer. He'd decided to hedge his bets and wait for her to come home. He remembered the punch to his gut as he'd seen her coming towards him with perspiration flattening her hair to her skull. He'd known he would have to treat her carefully so he didn't scare her off.

He wondered if she'd thought any more about his proposal. He'd thought of nothing else. Several times on their way home that morning, he'd opened his mouth to ask her but then promptly shut it again. He was impatient, wanting to know her answer. He hoped for the best but was prepared for the worst. If she refused, he had a whole convincing speech ready to go.

He rapped on her door, and when she opened it, he swept her into his arms. His mouth came down on hers, cutting off her girlish giggle.

As they broke apart, laughter erupted from her. "Blimey, that's a hell of a greeting."

"I missed you." He crossed the threshold into her apartment as she stepped back.

"You saw me"—she checked her watch—"three hours ago."

He closed the door behind him. "Felt like a lifetime."

"Everything okay at work?"

He considered telling her about his conversation with Tabitha but then decided against it. They wouldn't hear from her anymore so there was no real point in upsetting or bothering Livvy with the details.

"All good. So have you eaten yet?"

"No."

"Good," he said. "Let's eat out."

"On one condition."

"Name it."

"Take me back to Giovanni's," she said. "And this time, I promise not to run away."

AFTER GIOVANNI HAD ROLLED out the red carpet and fussed over Livvy so much that Gabe almost popped a blood vessel, he left them alone with a crisp, cool Pinot Grigio and enough pasta to feed a small town.

"To us," Livvy said, clinking her glass against Gabe's. "And to surviving our first fight."

Gabe laughed. "Darlin', if they all end like that one did, I'm going to instigate more of them."

Livvy's skin flushed hot, and her stomach twisted with need at the memory. She squirmed in her seat and clamped her thighs together, a move not missed by Gabe. His lips twitched, and he brushed his calf against hers. In response, Livvy shoved a forkful of pasta in her mouth before she was tempted to do something very inappropriate in public.

"So are you still okay about me working for your firm?" she asked in a bid to get her mind out of the gutter.

He nodded. "Of course. Edward has already contacted HR to get the process started. It'll take a while to get the paperwork through the various bureaucratic channels, but Edward will push hard, and I'll get involved if I need to."

Livvy grinned. "I'm really looking forward to using my brain again. I won't let you down. I promise."

Gabe expertly twisted spaghetti around his fork. "I know you won't." He chewed thoughtfully. "You really impressed Edward."

A dart of excitement shot through her. "I did?"

"Yep. And believe me, he's hard to impress."

As dinner progressed, Livvy's mind turned to Gabe's proposal the previous night. It might have come out of the blue, but their lives were already so intertwined that marrying Gabe was a natural next step. And as that thought crept into her mind, she knew. She'd asked for time, but that was only because her natural English reserve had risen to the forefront when he'd asked her. She didn't need time. She needed him.

Her teeth grazed her bottom lip. "I've been thinking."

Gabe stiffened, although he kept his voice light. "About what?"

"Your proposal."

He sucked in a breath. "And?"

She lowered her chin and looked up at him through her lashes. "It's a yes… if you'll still have me."

He paused for a heartbeat, then a broad smile spread across his face. He pushed back his chair and walked around to her side of the table. He took her hands in his and eased her to her feet. Once she was standing, Gabe wrapped his arms around her and twirled her in the air, causing several diners to turn their heads and watch them.

"This amazing woman has just agreed to marry me," Gabe said to the roomful of strangers—and Giovanni, who had just appeared from the kitchen. "I'm the luckiest man in the world."

Livvy blushed as the restaurant patrons began to applaud. Giovanni clapped the loudest and called for a bottle of champagne.

She giggled. "Put me down before you do your back in."

He placed her back on her feet and gently ran his knuckles down the side of her face.

"I promise to make you happy, Liv."

She swallowed as her vision blurred with tears. "You already have," she whispered.

CHAPTER EIGHTEEN

"Oh, Livvy," Ches said with tears in her eyes as Livvy smoothed her hands over her hips and gazed into the mirror. "You look stunning. No, strike that. You *are* stunning."

"I agree, darlin'," Heather said. "You're like an angel. My son is a lucky boy."

Livvy smiled as happiness coursed through her veins. The last four weeks had sped by in a whirlwind of venues, cars, cakes, and dresses. Once she'd agreed to marry Gabe, he hadn't wanted to wait. Heather had almost fainted when he'd told her that she had such a short time to organize the wedding, but she'd rallied beautifully, taking all the worry and concern away from Livvy and leaving only the fun stuff behind.

Livvy turned to the side. The dress certainly played to her best features. The off-the-shoulder chic lace camisole top allowed her to show off her neck. The fitted satin skirt gave her more curves than she was entitled to and finished in a puddle train that—with any luck—she wouldn't trip over. The bridal gown was simple yet elegant, exactly what she had hoped for. And even better were the full-length lace sleeves, which covered the scars on her wrists. She didn't want to be reminded of her past pain. Not today.

She turned to Heather. "Would you mind giving me five minutes with Ches?"

Heather immediately picked up her purse from a nearby chair. "Not at all, sweet pea. It's time I went, anyway. Need to make sure that son of mine is standing in the correct spot." She took Livvy in her arms and pressed a kiss to her cheek. "I can't wait to have a daughter again."

The conversation Livvy had had with Gabe all those weeks ago came rushing back. He'd refused any further attempts to discuss his brother and sister, and Heather didn't mention them, either. In fact, this comment was the first time she'd alluded to having another child. Gabe must have told his mother that Livvy, at least, knew the bare bones.

"And I can't wait to have a mum," Livvy whispered back, her words making Heather's eyes glisten. Gabe's mom dug a tissue from her purse and dabbed the corners of her eyes. With a last lingering glance at Livvy, she closed the door behind her.

"You okay, Liv?" Ches lightly brushed her fingertips down Livvy's arm. "You're covered in goose bumps. Are you cold?"

Livvy shook her head as she swallowed past an enormous lump in her throat. "Tell me honestly, Ches," she blurted. "Do you think I'm being disloyal to Mark by marrying Gabe?"

Ches's eyes widened in surprise at Livvy's query. "Absolutely not, Livvy. After everything you've been through, you deserve to be happy. Mark wouldn't want you to live out the rest of your life alone. You're so young, and you have your whole life ahead of you."

She put her arms around Livvy, being careful not to brush against her delicately crafted chignon. After hugging her so tightly that Livvy almost passed out, Ches stood back and gave Livvy a no-nonsense shake of the head.

"It was terrible what happened to Mark and Daniel, Liv, not to mention all the trauma you went through at the time—and since—but you've paid your dues. You mourned for them both so deeply. Now it's your turn to be happy." Ches paused. "Gabe *does* make you happy, right?"

Hot tears brought on by an intense feeling of love welled behind Livvy's eyes. She nodded. "Ecstatically happy."

"Then let yourself feel it, Liv. Every wonderful moment in his company. Every sensation he makes you feel. Every time he touches you." She winked. "*Especially* when he touches you."

Livvy gave her a mischievous grin. "Yeah, he's pretty good at that part."

"All right," Ches said with a faux pout. "No one likes a bragger."

Livvy laughed as a knock at the door interrupted Ches's teasing. She went to answer it, but Ches stopped her.

"I'll go. It'll be John. Are you ready?"

Livvy took one last look in the mirror, patted her hair, and nodded. "As I'll ever be."

As Ches opened the door, she made sure that she blocked John's view of Livvy.

"Get ready, Pops," Ches said. "Tissues at the ready." Standing back, she dramatically bowed and waved John into the hotel room.

As he set eyes on Livvy, his hand flew to his mouth and his eyes shone with pride. "Oh, Liv." He held his arms out to the side. "Let me look at you." As Livvy did a quick twirl, John walked closer. When she came to a halt, he took her hands in his. "I wish Beth could have been here to see this." His voice was rough and hoarse, but as Livvy opened her mouth to comfort him, he squeezed her hands and shook his head.

"Since the day you married my son, I've been so proud to call you my daughter, and that's what you'll remain. But today is all about you and Gabe, and I, for one, couldn't be happier." He leaned forward and whispered in her ear. "And so would Mark. You made him so happy, Livvy. But it's time to move forward, to leave the past behind, where it belongs. Gabe is your future." He stood back then and blinked away tears before they had a chance to fall. "You chose well."

Livvy couldn't hold her tears back. Praying the waterproof mascara lived up to its name, she let them roll down her cheeks. "I know, John. I know."

LIVVY HOVERED outside the hospitality suite where she was due to marry Gabe and took a deep, cleansing breath. The hairdresser made a few last-minute adjustments to her hair, and the beautician Heather had hired was touching up Livvy's makeup, which was much needed because she'd discovered that waterproof mascara was, in fact, a big, fat lie.

After they slipped inside and closed the doors behind them, John turned to Livvy. "Ready?"

She couldn't trust herself to speak in case more tears fell. Beyond those doors her happily ever after was waiting, yet her mind turned to her first wedding all those years ago. Unlike this one, her previous wedding had been much smaller, but no less happy. She glanced over her shoulder. Ches stuck her thumbs in the air and nodded encouragingly.

Livvy tilted her head back and looked up. "Goodbye, Mark," she said so quietly that she knew neither John nor Ches heard her. Turning to John, she gave him a wavering smile. "Okay. Lead the way. I'm ready."

John tucked her arm in his and patted the back of her hand. He gave a brief nod to the hotel staff that opened the doors. As Livvy and John stepped inside with Ches close behind, Livvy was met with a sea of people... so many people. Her stomach flipped. Jesus, there must have been at least two hundred guests, most of whom, she speculated, were Gabe's friends, colleagues, and business associates. Heather had kept all the organization away from Livvy. All she'd asked for was a list of names of people Livvy wanted to invite. It had been a *very* short list.

Her eyes swept up the aisle, falling on Gabe standing by the altar, his best man beside him. Gabe smiled softly, an intense expression on his face, appraising and appreciating her. Livvy took a deep breath and straightened her spine.

The wedding march began, and on shaky legs, Livvy moved forward with John. Vaguely conscious of the scores of people staring at her and whispering what she hoped were kind words, Livvy kept her gaze firmly on the man she was about to marry. Heather was sitting in the front row and caught Livvy's eye. As they briefly looked at each other, Heather wiped away a tear and reached out to squeeze Livvy's arm as she passed by.

When she reached the altar, John removed her arm from his and placed her hand into Gabe's outstretched one. As John stepped back, Livvy looked into the eyes of the man who was about to become her husband. As the reality of how fast things had gone came crashing down, she wavered on trembling legs, but as Gabe reached out an arm to steady her, all her nerves dissipated.

He bent down, and as his lips brushed the shell of her ear, a shiver of delight ran through her.

"You look so beautiful, Livvy. You eclipse every woman in this room. And soon, you'll be all mine." His voice was husky and raw. As he moved away, Livvy realized his emotions were as close to the surface as hers.

"And you'll be mine," she whispered.

Wearing smiles, they both turned to face the preacher as he began the ceremony.

"Dearest friends…"

"Almost ready to leave, Mrs. Mitchell?"

Gabe had his arms around Livvy as they stood in the middle of the packed dance floor, gently swaying together.

She trembled with delight at her new name. "You read my mind."

"Good. Because I can't wait much longer to make you my wife—in every way possible," he added seductively.

Livvy's insides did a double backflip. She studied his face, then curved her hands around his neck. Standing on tiptoes, even in the four-inch heels, she only just managed to touch her lips to his ear.

"Then lead the way, cowboy."

"You got it." He placed a warm hand against the small of her back and ushered her through the crowd. But as they headed towards the exit, Livvy spotted Heather and John chatting near the bar.

She tugged on his arm. "We should say goodbye to your mum and John," she said, nodding in their direction.

Gabe groaned. "If we must."

As they got closer, Heather looked up with a beaming smile and held out her arms. "You kids okay?" she asked, gripping tightly onto Gabe's upper arms.

Gabe leaned in and kissed her on the cheek. "We're going now. I'll call you in a few days."

"Okay, darlin'." She gave him a squeeze before letting him go. "It's been a long day. You must be tired." She winked suggestively at Livvy, who felt a hot flush race to her cheeks.

Gabe rolled his eyes. "Very funny, Mother."

He shook John's hand, and as the two men shared a few words, Heather whispered in Livvy's ear. "My son chose well, Livvy. You and he are made for each other. Be happy, sweet pea."

Her kind words brought tears to Livvy's eyes. As John pulled her close for a hug, she let them fall.

"Thank you for coming," she managed to get out between sobs.

"Now, now." John dug into his pocket and pulled out a crumpled tissue. He dabbed it against her cheeks. "I wouldn't have missed it." He turned to Gabe. "You take good care of my girl, now."

Gabe nodded. "Yes, sir." His arm curved around her waist. "Come on, darlin'. Time to go."

With a last glance back at Heather and John, Livvy reluctantly allowed Gabe to lead her towards the exit. As they stepped through the doors, a loud voice called out to them.

"Hold it right there, Hayes."

Livvy turned around and spotted Ches making her way through the throng of people.

"You've got one minute," Gabe said to Ches. "And it's Mitchell now." He wagged his finger at her, making her chuckle.

"Shit. That's going to take a bit of time to get used to. Okay, one minute. Now shoo," she said, directing him elsewhere. "I want to talk to my girl in private."

Gabe walked away, giving them room to chat. Ches enveloped Livvy in an enormous hug. "God, I'm going to miss you so much. Call me when you know where you land."

"I will. I'll miss you too. Make sure John gets home okay."

"Don't you worry about a thing. Enjoy the honeymoon. Be happy, Liv."

Livvy choked back tears as Gabe returned. He kissed Ches on the cheek. "Safe trip back to England. We'll be in touch."

He put his arm lovingly around Livvy's waist and ushered her out the door. She glanced over her shoulder and gave Ches a quick wave before her best friend disappeared from sight.

CHAPTER NINETEEN

"SO WHERE ARE WE GOING?" Livvy's voice had a slight petulance to it, but Gabe loved to surprise her so she hadn't grilled him too much.

He peered over the top of the newspaper he was reading and grinned. "On our honeymoon."

She laughed. "I know that, idiot." Trying another tactic, she teased, "What if I haven't brought the right clothes or shoes for what you have planned?"

His lips twitched upward. "Oh, Livvy, will you never learn?" He folded the newspaper and placed it on the table in front of him. "Firstly, as you well know, I had Bea pack everything you need, and unlike you, my housekeeper knows our full itinerary. Secondly"—he held up his finger as she began to interrupt—"in the unlikely event we have forgotten anything, there are these amazing places called 'stores,' where we can buy whatever we need."

"Fine," she said. "I'll play along."

"Good." Gabe crossed one ankle over his opposing knee and picked up the newspaper again. "Just as well. You don't get a choice."

Livvy stuck her tongue out, even though he couldn't see her. With a bored sigh, she removed a book from her carry-on bag, but after flicking through a few pages, she tossed it to one side. She stared out the window, but there was nothing to look at apart from blue sky above and white clouds below.

After eight hours in the air, Livvy's ears popped as the plane began to descend. Excited, she glanced out of the window, and as they broke through the clouds, she scanned the ground below for landmarks or anything that would give her a clue where they were headed. Nothing stood out. With a huff, Livvy slumped back in her seat. Her eyes slid over to Gabe, who was sitting with an amused grin on his handsome face.

"In a mood, Livvy?" he asked, his tone teasing and light.

She crossed her arms over her chest. "We're almost there. Surely *now* you can tell me?"

He leaned back in his chair and clipped his seat belt into place, nodding for her to do the same. "When we land," he said in a tone that told her she would be wasting her time if she pressed any further.

"Mr. Mitchell." The pilot's voice came over the intercom. "We've been cleared to land, sir. No clouds or mist today, thankfully, so we won't have to divert."

Gabe met Livvy's gaze, a secretive smile making his lips twitch. "Good news. Thanks."

Livvy narrowed her eyes. "We might have had to divert? To where?"

Gabe tapped the side of his nose. Livvy made a growling noise, which made him laugh.

She went back to looking out the window. As they got closer to the ground, she saw they were surrounded by mountains so high that the clouds cut off some of the tops. That meant they were at altitude. In the valley below, there were lots of low-rise buildings. So they weren't traveling to the middle of nowhere, then.

A thrill ran through her at what was to come. One thing

Gabe had been willing to share was that they would be away for eight days. He'd wanted it to be longer, but he'd taken too much time away from work as it was. He was CEO of a large multinational company, and despite having a very capable team, his business needed its leader at the helm. She also had a job to get back to. She'd insisted that starting at the bottom of the marketing department was the right approach. She figured it would be hard enough to convince her colleagues that she hadn't been given favorable treatment because she was the boss's wife. If she went straight into a senior position, it would make her situation untenable.

She was really looking forward to starting work again. Too much time had passed since her last job. Mentally, she hadn't been in the right place to take on such a commitment, but now she definitely was.

As the plane landed with a bump and a screech of tires, Livvy grinned across the table at Gabe.

"We're here," she said.

"We are." Gabe unclipped his seat belt after the plane came to a halt. He stood and held out his hand for Livvy to take.

"So?" she prompted as she curled her hand inside his. "Where's here?"

Gabe bent his head and brushed his lips against hers. "Peru."

With her stomach in knots of excitement, she squeezed his hand. "The Inca Trail," she whispered. "You remembered."

Very early in their relationship, Livvy had mentioned she'd always wanted to hike to Machu Picchu, but neither Mark nor any of her friends had been interested in that type of trip, so she'd put her desire on the back burner and forgotten all about it. When she'd brought the subject up with Gabe, he'd nodded and listened, but she'd gotten the sense that he hadn't shared her excitement about it.

"Of course I remembered." He tapped the side of his skull

with his finger. "When it comes to you, Livvy, I never forget a thing."

She threw her arms around him. "Thank you. Oh God, thank you so much."

Gabe bent his head. "Happy honeymoon, Mrs. Mitchell," he said against her lips.

THE TAXI PULLED up outside their hotel in Ollantaytambo, the place where they were staying for a couple of nights while they acclimatized to the altitude. After that, they were heading back to Cusco, where they would begin their hike to Machu Picchu.

Gabe glanced over at Livvy. He could tell she was exhausted even though she kept assuring him she was all right. The only thing keeping her going was the excitement and the adrenaline.

"You okay, darlin'?" he asked as they waited for the taxi driver to bring their bags.

She nodded. "My chest feels heavy, and my muscles are aching, sort of like after a hard gym session. But I'm fine, honestly."

"It's the altitude," he said. "After a couple of days relaxing, you'll feel much better."

He took her hand as they walked into the hotel. He couldn't help but steal glances at her, his wife. A shiver crept up his spine as he watched her looking around, taking everything in. How the fuck he'd gotten this lucky was something he questioned regularly. The horrific time with Tabitha and his man-whore rampage following her betrayal seemed like a different life that had happened to a different guy. With Livvy, he'd found his intellectual equal and his soft place to fall—his soul mate.

They checked in and went up to their room. Gabe opened the door and ushered Livvy inside. "It's not exactly the Plaza."

"I don't care," she said with a wide grin as she rubbed her

hands together. "This is going to be the best holiday ever. *You're* the best ever."

Gabe waggled his eyebrows. "Careful, darlin'. My ego is barely held in check most of the time. You rub it with those talented hands of yours, and you may just unleash it."

Livvy laughed. "Don't worry. If that happens, I'll think of something suitable to bring you back down to earth." She drifted over to the window. "Wow, look at that view," she said, encouraging Gabe to join her.

He crossed the room and stood behind her. His arms curved around her waist, and he rested his chin on her shoulder as they stared up at the mountains surrounding the hotel. They almost felt close enough to touch.

Livvy twisted her head for a quick kiss. "Isn't it gorgeous?"

"*It* is very nice. *You* are gorgeous."

Livvy turned in his arms and curved her hands around his neck. Her fingers twisted in his hair, a habit of hers that he loved. Her lips parted, and her skin flushed. Gabe recognized those tells as desire.

"How tired are you?" she murmured.

He touched his hand to her cheek, his middle finger playing with her earlobe. "Ask me, Liv."

Her breath hitched, and she swallowed. "Take me to bed."

His hands curved underneath the ass he couldn't get enough of, and he hitched her legs over his hips. She bent her head, allowing him to capture her mouth. With a groan, he took her over to the bed and gently laid her down. Their lovemaking the previous night had been hurried, desperate, and passionate. Tonight, he was going to take his time, to savor every inch of his perfect wife's body. He might have been tired and lethargic because of the thin air that high up, but if she could find the energy to make love, so could he.

He shucked his own clothes and tossed them into a heap on the floor, but he removed Livvy's clothing piece by piece, stopping every few seconds to put his hands, his mouth, or his tongue on her.

When he'd fully undressed her and she lay naked before him, he sat back on his heels and drank her in. It wasn't simply Livvy's body that turned him on. She really was the whole package. Quietly intelligent and with a great sense of humor, Livvy had suffered but had come out the other side. She was a strong woman, a survivor. Her experiences had given her a deep sense of what was important: family and friends, not money and material things.

All those elements made her his perfect partner because he knew that Livvy didn't care at all about his wealth. She wanted him for him, not for what he could give her financially.

Her warm body made him want to press closer, and as he did, as their damp flesh connected, he ached to be inside her. *Not yet, Mitchell.* Something about Livvy made him almost lose his mind. With other women, except Tab—at least before he knew what a manipulative bitch she was—he'd been able to remain detached from the emotion of the physical act. He might as well have been doing laundry for all the emotional connection he'd experienced. Yet with Livvy, every touch, taste, and smell of her made him go crazy for more.

His mouth found its way to her neck, and as he kissed her there, she moaned loudly and tilted her hips, rubbing herself against him in a way that wasn't helping him take things slow. As he fought for control, Livvy took matters into her own hands. Or rather, she took *him* into her own hands. As her damp palms curved around his shaft and she guided him inside her, Gabe almost exploded. He bit hard on his lip as Livvy began to move. Her hands gripped his ass, and she wrapped her legs around his waist.

"Faster, please," she murmured against his ear.

Oh shit.

He thrust into her, but before he'd had anywhere near his fill, her muscles clenched around his cock and nature took over.

An orgasm erupted from him, and as he rode it, Livvy pulled him closer even though he must have been far too heavy.

As his breathing slowed, he rolled off her. He nestled her head against his chest as his whole body relaxed.

"Gabe?" she murmured lazily, her eyes already closed.

"Yeah, darlin'?"

"Thank you for saving me."

His heart squeezed because he felt exactly the same way. They'd saved each other. He tightened his arms around her. "I love you, Livvy Mitchell."

CHAPTER TWENTY

LIVVY ROLLED over and opened her eyes. She was alone. She reached across the mattress. Gabe's side of the bed was warm, meaning that he hadn't been up for long.

"Gabe?" she called out.

He appeared in the doorway to the bathroom, his mouth full of toothbrush. He winked at her before disappearing again.

Livvy flung the covers off of her and swung her legs over the side of the bed. She climbed out and shrugged into a bathrobe that Gabe had helpfully left at the foot of the bed. She drifted over to the window to check out the weather. Excitement for the day ahead made her stomach clench. Today they were heading back to Cusco, where their hike to Machu Picchu would begin.

"Bathroom's free," Gabe said, appearing at her side. "At least it's not raining."

Livvy leaned on his shoulder. "I wouldn't care if it was." She reached up and pecked his cheek. "You're making all my dreams come true, cowboy."

Gabe snaked his arms around her waist. "This is only the beginning, Liv."

"Well, you've set the bar high. I hope you haven't peaked too soon."

Gabe threw back his head and laughed. "Oh, I have lots of things up my sleeve, and I have a lifetime to share them with you. Now scoot." He playfully slapped her backside. "We're meeting our guide in a half hour."

They had a quick breakfast in the hotel restaurant. Gabe brought their backpacks down from their room, and Livvy couldn't help but notice that hers was significantly lighter. She frowned at Gabe as he hoisted his much larger, and clearly much heavier, backpack onto his shoulders. As she opened her mouth to tell him off, he gave a firm shake of his head.

"Don't even go there, Liv. I'm not being benevolent. I'm making sure you have enough energy left at the end of the day. A newly married man has needs."

And with that, he headed outside. Chuckling under her breath, Livvy followed him. At the front of the hotel, they were met by their guide, Piero. After the introductions had been made, Piero pulled out a map and laid it on the hood of the jeep. With his finger, he traced the route they would follow that day. Twelve kilometers didn't sound very far, but when combined with a three-hour car ride to get to the start of the trail, and the fact that the terrain wasn't exactly like walking along a beachside promenade, it would still seriously test their fitness. Not only that, but their altitude would also be an issue. The lack of oxygen in the air would take it out of both of them even though they'd spent the last couple of days acclimatizing.

As they passed through picturesque villages, Livvy stared out the window, trying to take in as much as possible during this trip of a lifetime. Their guide pointed out landmarks along the way. The closer they got to the starting point, the more excited Livvy became.

Finally, they reached their destination, and after a quick check to make sure nothing had been left behind, they shrugged into their backpacks, added plenty of sunscreen to any exposed skin, and set off. Despite the fairly cool temperatures by California standards, the sun was very strong.

"This is the Vilcanota River," Piero said as they followed the trail to the right that climbed steeply. On either side of the river, rust-colored rock gave way to bushes and trees embedded into the rock face.

Livvy removed her camera from her pocket and hung it around her neck. She paused to take several pictures before slipping her hand inside Gabe's once more as they continued to follow the direction of the river.

After a hard hike, Piero drew to a halt. He lifted his hand and pointed in the distance. "That's the Inca hillfort," he said, indicating an arched ruin made out of stone bricks. "We can stop for a moment if you want to drink something."

Livvy peeled off her backpack and greedily drank some water. The altitude certainly took its toll, and they were only on day one. After quenching her thirst, she picked up her camera and took more photos, determined that she and Gabe would be able to look back on this trip in years to come and have the physical memories even as their own began to fade.

"You hanging in there, darlin'?" Gabe asked as he held out her backpack so she could slip her arms inside the straps.

She smiled up at him. "I'm fine."

They set off once more, and after another seven kilometers or so, they reached the village of Wayllabamba, which was set about three thousand meters above sea level.

"Normally, the people I guide stay here, but there are some prettier campsites a little further on if you're up to it," Piero said.

Gabe looked over at Livvy, who nodded and said, "Yep. Let's keep going."

It was the right decision, because when Piero stopped once more, the view was utterly breathtaking. Clouds settled over the mountains, and as the wind blew them across the valley, the peaks disappeared and reappeared in a constant harmony.

Gabe and Piero set up the tents, and after a quick meal, Livvy promptly fell asleep.

The next two days were some of the best of Livvy's life. The climb became more challenging, and she got blisters on her feet, but none of that mattered. When she rose on day four after spending the night on the floor of the crammed Trekkers Hostel, she didn't care that her back ached and her legs felt like lead. Nothing could take away the sense of excitement coursing through her. Soon, she would get to see one of the seven wonders of the modern world, something she'd dreamed of many times. And the man stuffing their belongings into their backpacks beside her was the one to bring her dream to life.

Outside, dawn was still an hour or so away, but they had to leave at this time so they could watch the sun rise over Machu Picchu. Gabe took Livvy's hand as they, along with many other groups, set off towards what would undoubtedly be a very emotional experience.

As they reached the final set of steps, which would lead them to a view of Machu Picchu, Livvy turned to Gabe. Her excitement was mirrored in his eyes.

They followed Piero up the steep stairway. By the time Livvy reached the top, her lungs were burning from the exertion, but nothing could have prepared her for the sight that greeted her. As the sun rose, it cast a golden light across the ruins far below them.

"Oh, Gabe." She clutched her hand to her chest. Hot tears pricked her eyes at the spectacular sight, which many coveted but, in reality, would never see. "Thank you for bringing me."

His lips touched her ear as he spoke. "This is just the start. I want to give you the world, Livvy. And I will."

CHAPTER TWENTY-ONE

"We're home, darlin'."

Livvy murmured something unintelligible and forced her eyes open. Despite sleeping through most of the plane ride back to the US, she'd still managed to drop off again in the car, which had stopped outside Gabe's home in LA. Correction—*their* home in LA. She'd let her apartment go before they got married.

Gabe climbed out and came around to her side. After setting foot on the driveway, she found herself swept up in his arms.

"I can walk, you know," she grumbled, her eyes still refusing to open all the way.

"Yes, I know. But it's traditional for the groom to carry his bride over the threshold."

Of course. They hadn't been back to the house since their wedding day. Livvy accepted her fate and buried her head in Gabe's neck as he strode through the front door. She expected him to set her down in the hallway, but instead, he took off upstairs.

He kicked open the door to their bedroom suite and

deposited her unceremoniously on the couch at the foot of their bed. Livvy yelped.

Gabe grinned. "At least that woke you up."

Livvy frowned at him. "That is no way to treat your new bride."

Gabe bent over and kissed her furrowed brow. "Don't frown. You'll get lines, and you're too young for Botox."

He left her alone for a few moments, returning with a bottle of champagne and two glasses. "I know you're exhausted after all the excitement and traveling, but as this is our last night before we return to work tomorrow, I thought we should celebrate."

Livvy pushed herself upright and held out her hand for a glass. "I hope I don't let you down on the work thing," she said, chewing on her lip.

Gabe paused with the champagne bottle in midair, his brows pulled low. "Why would you let me down?"

Livvy wiggled her glass at him, encouraging him to pour. As the champagne fizzed to the surface, she sipped quickly to avoid spillage. "It's been a while since I've worked. I know I have a marketing degree, but that counts for nothing given how much time has passed since I've used it."

Gabe set the bottle on the floor and joined her on the couch. He clinked his glass against hers. "I have a feeling you're a natural." With a twinkle in his eye, he added, "Although if you're terrible at your job, I won't hesitate to fire you."

Livvy narrowed her eyes at him but then couldn't help but giggle. "If I'm terrible, I'll resign. How's that?"

"Deal." Gabe slung his arm around her shoulder and pulled her to his side. "So what do you want to do to the house?"

Livvy looked up at him. "Nothing. I love this house."

"But you must want to do something, put your own stamp on it?"

She shook her head. "Honestly, Gabe, I hadn't even thought about it."

"Well, do. I want this to be a home for both of us. I can sell it if you'd rather we choose somewhere together."

Livvy gave him a horrified look. "Of course I don't want you to sell it."

"Okay, then *we* won't sell it," he said, his emphasis not lost on her. "But remember it's yours to do with as you wish."

THREE WEEKS after their return from their honeymoon, Livvy left Gabe's offices in downtown LA and jumped into her car. Things were going well at work. Actually, things were going really well at work. She couldn't wish for a better boss than Edward—the guy really knew his stuff—and Livvy was already learning heaps from him.

Things with Gabe were even better, if that were possible. He catered to her every whim. He was attentive, loving, kind, and seriously hot between the sheets. When she looked back, she could barely remember those terrible two years after Mark died, and the black days that used to be so prevalent were now just a distant nightmare that belonged to someone else.

The only blot on the landscape was her lack of energy. She was tired *all the time*. And she simply could not shake a lingering cold. The minute the sore throat and sniffles disappeared, another virus followed straight afterward. Gabe had suggested it might be best if she took a break when she'd mentioned it to him, but Livvy had immediately cast the idea aside. She'd only just started work. It was hardly going to endear her to her colleagues to start slacking off now.

She figured her lack of energy correlated to her lack of exercise. Apart from the bedroom workouts with Gabe, she hadn't been exercising regularly. And that was why she was on her way to meet Paul. A few sessions with her personal trainer would sort her out.

Ten minutes after leaving work, Livvy parked outside the

gym. As she climbed out of her car, Paul was already heading towards her.

"Livvy Hayes, well, look at you." He gave her a quick hug.

"It's Mitchell now, although I'm still getting used to my new name."

Paul cast his eye over her. "You look well. A bit out of shape, but nothing a hard session in the gym won't fix." He cocked his head at the building behind him. "Let's see what you've got."

It turned out that Livvy didn't have much. By the time the end of the hour arrived, she was totally spent. Paul had drilled her like never before, and she had absolutely no energy left. As she collapsed on the floor, Paul brought her an energy drink.

He sank down beside her and shook his head. "Well, Mitchell, I don't know what you've been doing in the last couple of months since I've seen you, but you're out of shape. We're going to need to work hard to get you back into it."

Livvy frowned. "I don't understand it. How could I have lost so much condition in such a short space of time?"

Paul patted her arm and encouraged her to finish the rest of her drink. "Try not to worry. I'll pull together a program and get some regular sessions scheduled. We'll soon have you back on track."

Livvy nodded, thankful he was in her corner. As she got to her feet, she wobbled slightly. "Whoa, head rush."

Paul clutched her arm. "Take it easy, Liv." He appraised her, his head tilting to one side. "Hey, Livvy, don't take this the wrong way, but could you be pregnant?"

Livvy violently shook her head. "No. Absolutely not."

He shrugged. "Okay, it was only a thought. It might explain why you're so out of shape and why you're tired all the time, but you know your body best."

"Yes, I do, and that's not even remotely possible," she insisted.

Paul dropped his questioning and walked her back to her car. As Livvy put the car into reverse and pulled out of the parking lot, she waved at Paul, but her bright goodbye was tainted with concern. All the way home, his words rang in her ear.

"Could you be pregnant?"

Surely not. She and Gabe had been extremely careful. She'd always taken the contraceptive pill, having suffered crippling periods since her teenage years. The only time she'd stopped was when she'd been trying for a baby with Mark. Certainly, during the whole time with Gabe, she'd religiously taken the little tablet each morning before breakfast. No, there had to be another reason. She was probably tired from the whirlwind her life had become ever since Gabe had entered it. Despite giving herself a good talking to, on the spur of the moment, she pulled into Walgreens. *Only one way to find out for sure.*

Ten minutes later, she parked the car in the garage, took the pregnancy test into the house, and shot straight upstairs to their bedroom. She unwrapped the package and scanned the instructions. Pee on the stick, and if two blue lines appeared, well, she would need to sit Gabe down and have a serious talk.

Livvy plunked herself on the toilet, but the tension tightening her insides stopped her bladder from doing what nature intended. No matter how much she concentrated, she couldn't pee. Deciding to leave the stick on the vanity unit, Livvy wandered back into the bedroom to lie down and wait for her bladder to play ball. She stripped off her workout gear, threw the sweaty clothes in the laundry basket, and although she really should have taken a shower, she slipped under the covers and promptly fell asleep.

"LIVVY."

Gabe's gentle shaking of her arm dragged Livvy from slumber. She forced open her eyes to find him sitting on the bed, his face full of concern.

She pushed herself upright and rubbed her eyes. Gabe was holding something that Livvy couldn't quite make out because it was all fuzzy. After a second eye rubbing, her vision cleared… and her heart dropped to somewhere around her feet.

"Livvy, what's this?"

Shit.

"It's a pregnancy test," she mumbled, utterly mortified. This was the last way she wanted him to find out she might be pregnant.

"I know what it is. I mean what is it doing in our bathroom, clearly unused?"

Livvy tried to work out whether he sounded angry or amused, but the tone of his voice gave no clue as to his state of mind.

"Something Paul said made me wonder."

Gabe frowned. "Who the hell is Paul?"

Livvy patted his arm in reassurance. "My personal trainer. I went to see him today, and he worked me to death. Then I was telling him how tired I am all the time, and he suggested I might be pregnant. I don't think for one minute he's right," she added quickly. "But I need to be sure."

"So why haven't you used it?"

Livvy gave an embarrassed grin. "I couldn't go."

He wore an amused smirk. "You couldn't pee? Oh dear. I can see how that would be a problem." He was openly laughing now, which made her relax. He didn't appear remotely concerned with the result.

"So wanna see if you're going to be a mommy?" he asked, waving the stick in the air.

Livvy grimaced. "I don't know. I'm scared."

"What are you scared of, darlin'?" he gently coaxed. "Worried it'll be like last time?"

She shook her head. "Yes and no. I don't know what I'm more scared of—whether it's positive or negative."

Gabe grinned. "Well, Liv, I'm guessing it's going to be one

or the other. I think this is one of those fifty-fifty situations." He held out his hand. "Come on. There's only one way to find out."

Livvy gave him one of *those* looks. "You're not bothered?"

"Bothered how? Look, I know we haven't talked about having kids, but let's look at it this way. If it's positive, I'll be thrilled. Having kids with you, well, it's all my dreams come true. And if it's negative…" He grinned again. "We can have lots of fun trying, can't we?"

Gabe looked at her in a way that made Livvy's insides melt. Christ, she was fortunate to have him as her husband.

She took his hand and blew out a breath. "Okay, let's do this."

Livvy closed the bathroom door, leaving Gabe on the other side. She sat on the toilet, held the stick in place, and waited for nature to take its course. After finishing up, she opened the door to find Gabe lounging against the wall. He turned to her, his face expectant.

"We have to wait a minute," she said.

"Oh, of course."

They waited together, both anxious. After the allotted time had passed, Livvy held the stick towards the light. She and Gabe stared at the two vertical blue lines. Livvy felt a rush of emotion, and tears welled up in her eyes.

Gabe looked between her and the stick then back again. "What does it mean?"

"It means I'm pregnant." She couldn't say the words *we're going to be parents* because with her history, that outcome was far from certain.

Gabe let out a whoop of joy and swung her around the room. Livvy wanted to match his broad grin with one of her own, but she couldn't bring herself to. Stretching her mind ahead, all she could see was week after week of worry that her body would reject this baby like it had rejected all of the others.

Even when she'd gotten past the dreaded first trimester, she'd still failed to protect Daniel.

After a few seconds, Gabe sensed her lack of excitement. He placed her back on the floor, his arms around her waist. "I know you're scared," he said, picking up on the nub of her concerns. "And you have every right to be. But you will have the best care money can buy. I guarantee it." He chewed his lip. "I know how much you're enjoying working, but if this news makes you want to reconsider, then don't worry about it."

"Let's see what the doctor says first," she said. "No point jumping to conclusions. I promise I'll take whatever advice I'm given."

A COUPLE OF DAYS LATER, Livvy and Gabe arrived at the office of Dr. Wilson, an ob-gyn that Gabe's family doctor had recommended. The fact that he'd managed to secure an appointment so quickly made Livvy's head spin. She wouldn't have been able to secure an appointment with a doctor in the UK nearly as fast.

As they sat in the reception area, Gabe was the epitome of relaxed, and Livvy was the complete opposite. When she started chewing her nails down to the quick, Gabe's hand curled around her wrist to stop her. He gave her a warm smile and squeezed her hand as the door to the doctor's office opened. A woman in her early forties with kind eyes and the thickest dark-brown hair Livvy had ever seen stepped through.

"Mr. and Mrs. Mitchell?" She held out her hand and shook first Livvy's then Gabe's. On unsteady legs, Livvy made her way into the doctor's office. As she sat on one of two visitor's chairs, her heart began thundering in her chest. Recognizing the signs of anxiety, she took several deep breaths to slow down her speeding pulse.

Dr. Wilson sat in a large leather chair behind her desk. "So how are you feeling, Mrs. Mitchell?"

Livvy glanced at Gabe then at the doctor. "Did you receive my medical records?" she asked, unsure of what Gabe had already passed along.

"Yes, I received them." Dr. Wilson leaned forward. "This must be a worrying time for you."

Livvy nodded. "I'm terrified." Her voice sounded small and lost.

Gabe reached for her. He knitted their fingers together, and she drew strength from his warmth.

Dr. Wilson gave her a sympathetic nod. "I doubt there is anything I or anyone else will be able to do to allay your fears, Mrs. Mitchell, but be assured you will receive the very best care. We'll monitor you closely at every stage of your pregnancy."

"I'm quite tired, but I guess that's normal?"

"Completely normal. I'll prescribe some prenatal vitamins as a precaution. Any nausea?"

"No, none at all."

"Good." Dr. Wilson got to her feet. "Okay, shall we see how far along you are?"

"You can do a scan right now?" Livvy asked, more than a little taken aback.

"Yes. We'll try the ultrasound first, but if you are newly pregnant, we may need to do an internal scan. Let's see how we go."

Dr. Wilson passed her some water, and once Livvy had drunk as much as she could, she climbed up onto the bed. She clung to Gabe's hand, and it was clear to see how fascinated he was with the whole process. He watched the doctor closely as she squeezed cold gel onto Livvy's abdomen and moved the wand over her belly while she focused on a monitor to the side.

After a few moments, she pressed some buttons, and the image froze. "There. See it?" She pointed to what looked like a kidney bean. "You're about eight weeks pregnant."

Livvy blinked rapidly. She shared a look with Gabe. It must have happened in New York on the night they had their fight about Tabitha—the night of angry, passionate sex. He winked, letting her know he'd worked out the timing too.

"Does it look okay?" she asked the doctor.

"Everything looks fine, Mrs. Mitchell." Dr. Wilson's eyes slid to Gabe then back to Livvy. "Want to hear the heartbeat?"

A thrill ran through her. "Oh God, yes. If we can." Livvy couldn't take her eyes off the tiny form on the monitor.

The doctor moved the wand again and clicked a couple of buttons, and then the sound of their baby's heartbeat came through the monitor. It was clear and strong and totally overwhelming.

Unable to utter a word, Livvy began to cry, and as Gabe's arm came around her, he looked as though he couldn't trust himself to speak, either.

"Would you like a picture?"

Livvy gave an enthusiastic nod to Dr. Wilson, who wiped the gel from Livvy's stomach as they waited for the printer to spit out a picture that she would cherish.

Gabe eased her upright then helped her down from the bed. He pulled her into his side and gently kissed her temple. "Well done, Mrs. Mitchell," he whispered, his eyes bright and full of love.

Dr. Wilson handed over a black-and-white picture. Livvy could clearly see the tiny blip, which, God willing, would turn into a healthy baby. Her hand automatically went to her flat stomach, and she sent up a silent prayer that it wouldn't stay flat for long. *Please let me take this one to term.* She'd suffered enough. Surely this time, she deserved to walk away with the top prize— a son or a daughter.

They sat in front of the doctor's desk once more. "I'll have a prescription for some vitamins sent to your local pharmacy," she said. "Now, with your history, I want to see you every week, at least until you're through the first trimester. You can make the appointments with my secretary. And if you have any concerns at all, day or night, call me."

"I will."

"Are there any further questions at this point?"

"I don't think so," Livvy said.

"I have one." Gabe's eyes cut to hers, and he winked before turning back to Dr. Wilson. "Should we refrain from having sex, given Livvy's prior history?"

Livvy's mouth fell open. Oh, she was going to kill him. Fortunately, Dr. Wilson must have heard similar questions a hundred times over because her lips didn't even twitch.

"Not at all, Mr. Mitchell. You're both young and perfectly healthy. There's no reason why you can't enjoy a full sex life right up until the birth."

"Excellent." Gabe grinned. Livvy did not. First chance she got, he was getting a firm dig in the ribs.

"I'll see you next week, then, Mrs. Mitchell."

Livvy made an appointment for the following week, and as soon as they were outside, she turned to Gabe with a glare. "Sex? Really? *That's* what you wanted to know?"

Gabe's answering grin couldn't have been wider. "Come on, darlin'. Let's go home."

CHAPTER TWENTY-TWO

THE NEXT FEW months passed by in a contented haze. Livvy successfully negotiated the first trimester, resulting in all-round relief. The only downside was her continuing fatigue. Despite taking every pill the doctor had thrown at her and sleeping at least eight hours per night, Livvy's exhaustion was bone deep. And so the previous Friday, Gabe had put his foot down and insisted she begin her maternity leave even though she was only five and a half months into her pregnancy.

On Monday morning, she was sitting in the rocking chair in the nursery that Gabe had already decorated, waiting to go to her regular doctor's appointment. When Gabe walked in and found her, he couldn't hide the concern etched into the line of his jaw. Livvy knew what he was seeing—dark circles beneath her eyes, an almost gray pallor to her skin, and she was thinner than she should be, especially given how far along she was.

"Ready, Liv?" he asked gently.

Livvy nodded and held out her hands for him to pull her up from the rocking chair. As she collided with his broad, firm chest, she rested there for a moment, enjoying the sound of his heart beating rhythmically beneath her ear.

He cupped her face and bent to kiss her before his arm came around her waist. "I got you."

Twenty minutes later, they arrived at Dr. Wilson's office. They were ushered straight in.

"How are things, Livvy?" Dr. Wilson asked after the pleasantries were out of the way.

"Everything's fine except I'm still so tired. I've taken every pill, and I'm sleeping lots, but I still don't have any energy."

Dr. Wilson tapped her pen against her pad. "Let's get you up on the examination table so we can have a look."

Livvy gave herself over to the physical exam as Dr. Wilson felt up and down her arms then over her breasts and stomach. She had Livvy sit upright so she could listen to her chest and lungs.

Once Livvy was lying flat once more, the doctor's eyes narrowed. "Livvy, can you put your right arm over your head for me?"

Livvy obeyed as the doctor examined her right breast again. Dr. Wilson frowned slightly. Livvy wasn't sure whether it was in concentration or concern, but regardless, her pulse spiked, and her heart began to thunder against her ribcage. She didn't like the look on the doctor's face. Neither, apparently, did Gabe.

"Is something wrong?" he asked, his tone brusque and hoarse.

"Give me a moment please, Gabe," Dr. Wilson said in a dismissive tone, which caused Gabe's scowl to deepen. "Put your arm down, please, and do exactly the same with your left."

As Livvy's left breast was prodded and kneaded, her sense of dread and foreboding grew. Dr. Wilson gently placed Livvy's arm by her side, softly sighed, and pulled up a chair next to the bed.

"Livvy, have you noticed any changes to your breasts recently? I mean apart from those related to your pregnancy?"

Livvy swallowed. "No."

"So you haven't noticed a small lump underneath your right armpit?"

Lump. Livvy's heart began to gallop, and her mouth emptied of saliva. She swallowed past a throat that had closed over.

"No," she replied quietly.

"What does that mean?" Gabe demanded.

"It's hard to tell. It may be nothing at all, but I'm going to make a couple of phone calls and get some tests organized."

"Will I have to go to the hospital?" Livvy asked.

"No. We can do them as an outpatient in the clinic next door."

Livvy swallowed. Surely a lump only meant one thing. She forced herself to form the words and ask the question. "Do you think it could be cancer?" Her voice sounded cold, detached.

Gabe increased the pressure on her hand, squeezing her tight enough to cut off her blood supply.

"It's highly unlikely." Dr. Wilson patted her shoulder. "Let's not jump to any conclusions until we know more. You're young and healthy. It's much more likely to be a benign cyst, some fatty tissue that's completely harmless."

"What tests will I need?" Livvy's voice sounded strained.

"A mammogram to see what the lump looks like, and then if needed, we'll do a fine-needle aspiration biopsy. That's just a fancy term for inserting a very thin needle into your breast and removing a small amount of tissue. It stings a bit, but it's over quickly. We'll also take some blood."

"How long will we have to wait for the tests to be done?" Gabe asked.

"I should be able to get you in today. Take a seat in the waiting room, and I'll see what I can do."

A couple of hours later, Livvy and Gabe headed back to their car after her tests had been completed. As they climbed in, Gabe started the engine but didn't set off. Silence stretched between them, and after a few minutes, she couldn't stand it any longer.

"Say something," she whispered.

Taking her completely by surprise, he twisted in his seat and captured her mouth. His lips were insistent, almost as though he thought it might be the last time he would be able to kiss her. When he broke off their kiss, his eyes smoldered.

"I don't want you worrying about this until we know whether there's something to worry about."

"But—"

Gabe's hand shot up. "Let's wait for the results, Liv. Like the doctor said, it's probably nothing."

Livvy nodded even as her insides twisted. A lump in the breast was every woman's worst nightmare. It was impossible to stop her mind from taking her to dark places full of fear and terror.

She turned to stare out the window, the landscape blurring as they passed.

It's just a cyst. It's just a cyst.

But what if it wasn't? What if, once again, her happiness was about to be snatched away? A gigantic wave of terror made a sob catch in her throat.

"Liv." Gabe blindly reached out his hand and captured hers. "I'm here."

"I know," she said as she continued to look out the window. Her heart began to thunder in her chest as she feared the worst. She couldn't even manage to hope for the best. Her history had taught her she wasn't a lucky person. If something bad could happen, it would happen to her.

She curled her free hand into a fist, her fingernails digging into her palm. She wanted to shut her brain off, to pretend none of this was happening, but the screams echoing inside her head made that impossible.

"We're home," Gabe said, jerking her from her innermost thoughts. Still unable to speak, she nodded glumly and followed him inside.

"What can I do, Liv?" Gabe asked as she brushed by him and headed for the stairs.

She glanced over her shoulder. "Give me some space."

Ignoring the flash of pain that crossed his face, she turned her back and trudged upstairs.

———

A COUPLE OF DAYS LATER, the initial shock had worn off, and Livvy was feeling much more positive. She was, however, beginning to go stir crazy. Gabe refused to go into the office, although he took various calls at home, despite her insisting she would be fine on her own. Livvy was sure some women would have loved being pampered and not being allowed to lift a finger, but his overzealous attention was driving her crazy.

As she heard him jogging down the stairs, Livvy pulled her hand away from her breast. Since the doctor had pointed out the lump under her armpit, she couldn't stop fiddling with it, sort of like when she would bite the inside of her cheek then keep running her tongue over the bump. The problem was, every time Gabe saw her with her fingers in her armpit, he gave her the evil eye. He thought she was making her worry more intense by constantly playing with it. Livvy wasn't so sure.

"Why didn't you wake me?" Gabe asked as he entered the living room to find Livvy curled up on the couch with a book in her lap—and her fingers nowhere near the telltale lump.

"Why would I do that?" She moved her legs so he could sit down beside her. "I can get myself downstairs and make my own coffee, you know." She tried—and failed—to keep the irritation out of her voice.

Gabe raised an eyebrow. "Am I crowding you?"

Livvy sighed. "A little maybe."

He picked up her feet and rested them across his lap. "I'll give you some space today. I have some calls to make, anyway."

Before Livvy could respond, she felt a fluttering sensation in her abdomen. After a couple of seconds, she realized what it was, and she smiled at Gabe. "The baby's kicking. Here." She grabbed his hand and put it over her bump.

After a couple of seconds, the baby kicked again. "Amazing," Gabe said in awe. "Gonna be a quarterback for sure."

"Not if it's a girl."

"Sure she can. My daughter can be anything she wants."

They began a playful argument about what their baby may or may not be when Livvy's cell rang. As she picked it up, all the blood drained from her face and her stomach tied itself in knots.

"It's the doctor's office," she said.

Gabe removed the phone from her hand. "Here, let me."

After a few yeses and a couple of nods, Gabe announced, "We're on our way."

With nausea churning in her abdomen, Livvy met his gaze. "My test results are back?"

"Yes."

Livvy swallowed. "Did she give any indication of whether they were bad or good?"

Gabe shook his head and rose from the couch. He leaned forward, captured her hand in his, and helped her to her feet. "Do you want something to eat before we go?"

Livvy shook her head. The idea of food made her already-churning stomach rebel. "But you should get something."

"I'll be fine."

They drove to the hospital in silence, each of them lost in their own thoughts. Scared out of her wits, Livvy spent the time running pointless scenarios. Her mind wouldn't stop racing.

Gabe stopped the car outside the front entrance and instructed her to wait while he parked. Livvy leaned against the wall, her legs barely holding her up. Their future hung on what the doctor said. A week ago, their happiness seemed assured. Now it could be in jeopardy.

Gabe only took a couple of minutes to park. As they entered Dr. Wilson's office, Livvy's knees buckled. Gabe's arm shot around her waist, and he helped her into a seat before whispering in a low voice to the receptionist, who tapped on a computer then indicated for him to take a seat alongside Livvy.

They weren't kept waiting for long, and when the door to Dr. Wilson's office opened, Livvy's stomach headed south. She could barely keep her breathing under control, and Gabe's worried expression didn't help matters. He was always so strong, so assured, yet the pinched lips and furrowed brow gave the game away—he was as scared as she was.

The doctor made sure they were settled before she opened a file in front of her. She glanced down then peered at them both over her glasses. "Thank you for coming in at such short notice."

Believe me, if I had a choice, I wouldn't be here.

"No problem," Livvy murmured. "Do you have my results?"

"I do. We carried out a variety of tests to see why you were suffering from such fatigue, and as you know, you also had an aspiration of fluid from the lump in your breast." She paused and glanced from her notes to them again. Livvy held her breath, but before the doctor spoke, she knew.

"I'm afraid it's bad news, Livvy. I'm so sorry. You have breast cancer."

CHAPTER TWENTY-THREE

THE BOTTOM completely fell out of Livvy's world. Her breath rasped, and her mind shut down. *I have cancer.* She was only thirty, for Christ's sake. She'd suffered immeasurably, yet whoever was up there—if anyone *was* up there—clearly didn't think that she'd suffered enough.

She felt Gabe touch her shoulder, but she couldn't respond to him or to the doctor, whose voice sounded as if it were coming from very far away.

Numbness swept through her, and as her fingers tingled, she began to shake her hands as if she were trying to remove mittens on a cold winter's day. Then her whole body began to tremble.

Gabe knelt in front of her and took her hands in his. Her hands were freezing, whereas his were warm, vital, and alive. She was dead. Or she would be soon.

"Livvy, look at me. Please, honey, look at me."

He never called her honey. Why had he changed his term of endearment for her? Was she already fading from his mind? Honey seemed so impersonal. She tried to focus, but Gabe's face was blurry, as if she needed glasses to see it properly close up. He squeezed her hands, which lay limp in her lap. It was as though he thought he could pass his life force to her. Except he couldn't. He was wasting his time.

"Livvy, we're going to get through this—together. You and me. You're strong, Liv. The strongest person I've ever met. We can beat this. Please, baby, come back to me."

And there was another endearment, another new term he'd never used before. Why was he changing? Why was he talking to her differently? Was this how it would be from now on? Him slowly becoming a stranger while her body gradually turned to dust?

Livvy tried to speak. She could hear the worry in Gabe's voice, and she wanted to take it away. Her vision cleared, but as she saw the pain etched in his face, she wished it hadn't. She couldn't deal with his agony as well as her own.

In slow motion, she watched him turn to Dr. Wilson in panic.

"This is a normal reaction, Gabe. Let's give her a moment, shall we? Please take a seat."

Livvy took a shuddering breath as Gabe moved off the floor to sit beside her once more. Her hands were still covered by his much larger ones. The three of them sat in silence while Livvy tried to rewire her brain, to face her new reality. She couldn't lose it, not now. She needed to face this head on if she were to have a chance of beating it. And to beat it, she needed information.

She forced her eyes to look at the doctor, relieved when she didn't see pity, only determination on Dr. Wilson's face.

"Okay, give it to me straight. What are my options?"

A flash of surprise crossed the doctor's face at Livvy's about-face from "freak-out" to "strong, confident woman."

"You'll need to be referred to an oncologist. I hope you don't mind, but I took the liberty of contacting one of the best, Dr.

Anderson. She's waiting outside. She'll be able to explain your options much better than I can. Are you okay if I bring her in?"

Livvy nodded.

Dr. Wilson rose from her chair and disappeared. Livvy wrung her hands and stared at the floor.

"Liv?"

She shook her head. She couldn't look at him. "Don't. Let's just see what the doctor says."

Dr. Wilson returned with Dr. Anderson in tow. The oncologist had the look of a determined and experienced woman. Livvy took an instant liking to her and immediately felt safe in her hands.

Dr. Anderson took a seat to the side of Dr. Wilson's desk.

"Mrs. Mitchell, I believe Dr. Wilson has already given you your test results. I'm sorry the news isn't better, but if I can give you any reassurance, it's that you're young, strong, and otherwise healthy. I'd like to get started on your treatment as soon as possible, preferably tomorrow."

"So soon?" Gabe couldn't hide his shock.

"Yes. The sooner the treatment begins, the greater the chance of making a full recovery. Every day we wait gives the cancer an extra day to spread."

"But the chances of recovery are good?" Hope filled his voice.

"We'll need to do more tests," Dr. Anderson said noncommittally.

Livvy straightened her spine. "Okay, so let's get started. Will I need to bring an overnight bag with me tomorrow?" Her tone was all business. She wanted this *invader* out of her body.

The doctor shook her head. "I'm afraid there's a complication."

Livvy's pulse jolted. As if having breast cancer wasn't enough of a complication. "Which is?"

"Your pregnancy. I'm afraid that changes things considerably."

Livvy frowned. "I don't understand. Changes things how?"

Dr. Wilson shifted uncomfortably in her chair and fiddled with a clip that was holding her hair off her face.

"Because you are pregnant, a lot of treatments are not available to me," Dr. Anderson said. "I can surgically remove the tumor or perform a lumpectomy if that's the better option when I see what I'm dealing with, but looking at the size of the tumor, you'll definitely need chemotherapy. I'm afraid your baby wouldn't survive the treatment. Therefore, in cases such as yours, we normally recommend…" A sympathetic tilt of the head sent shock waves through Livvy as she guessed the next sentence before it was out of the doctor's mouth. "Termination of the pregnancy as the best course of action."

Livvy leaped to her feet, and the chair made a horrible scraping sound as she shoved it backward. It rocked on its legs before settling back in place.

"No!" she screamed, her hands gripping and pulling at her hair. She couldn't breathe. A pain seared through her stomach then moved upward, like a tight fist closing around her heart. Any minute, she was sure it would explode because it couldn't continue to beat so hard, so fast, and so painfully without something terrible happening. Except something terrible was happening. She would *not* allow them to take her baby.

Gabe launched out of his chair, his arms coming around her, but she didn't want him. She didn't want to be there. She shoved him in the chest, hard. "Get off me," she hissed.

He stared at her, his face creased with worry. "Liv, please sit down. We need to talk this through."

Livvy sucked in a quick breath and stiffened her spine as she read his words in the way he spoke and held his body. Hurt rolled through her. He was actually considering what the doctor had said as a viable option. This man, who she trusted, who she loved, who she'd married was on the doctor's side. She was alone in this. Well, she'd been alone before, and she'd survived.

Whatever happened, she would not kill her own child, even if it meant killing herself.

She poked her finger at the doctor then at Gabe. "All of you, listen to me. I am *not* terminating my pregnancy. That is *not* an option."

Dr. Anderson half rose from her chair. "I understand this is a huge shock, and there is a lot for you and your husband to discuss and take in. Why don't we meet again tomorrow?"

"There's no need," Livvy said coldly. "Find another way." And with that as her parting shot, she strode from the office. She slammed the door behind her, nearly taking it off its hinges. As she spilled onto the steps in front of the hospital, Gabe caught up with her.

He took a firm hold on her arm. "Livvy, stop. Please, come back inside. We need to talk to the doctor. This is important. This is about your *life*."

Livvy wrenched her shoulder away from him. She hated him. In this moment, she despised him for siding with the doctor, for even *considering* ending their baby's life before it had begun. She watched him recoil as she glared at him with pure venom.

"You talk to her if you're so fucking keen. I'm done talking." She jabbed her finger in his chest. "You listen to me. There is no way that I am terminating this pregnancy. This is my baby, my body, and *I* will decide. Not you, not her, not anyone. Do I make myself perfectly clear?"

She whirled around and blindly set off running—to where, she didn't know, but she couldn't stay there. As she heard Gabe's footsteps behind her, she twisted around and held her hand out, palm facing him. "Don't follow me!"

Her voice cut through the air, causing several people milling about the hospital entrance to take an interest in the commotion.

"I don't want you anywhere near me right now."

She turned around before the stunned hurt on his face made

her reconsider what a bitch she was being. But she couldn't think about him. She could only think about her and her precious child. Whatever happened, this baby was going to live. *This one* would have a chance at life even if the decision ended hers.

As luck would have it, a cab pulled up, and as a couple climbed out, Livvy threw herself inside and locked the door. "Drive, please," she begged the cabbie, who gave her a sharp nod and hit the gas. She glanced over her shoulder. Gabe had his hands in the air, a look of complete devastation on his face. As he disappeared from view, Livvy began to cry.

"Are you okay?" the cabbie asked. His kindness increased her tears, especially when he passed her a box of tissues over his shoulder.

After she'd pulled herself together, she apologized to him— which he simply shrugged off—and gave him her address. God, she wished she'd kept hold of her apartment. She had no choice but to go back to their place, and she knew Gabe would be on his way.

As soon as the driver stopped outside her house, she thrust some money at him and ran inside, heading straight upstairs to the bathroom. She desperately needed some personal space to absorb everything that had happened. She locked the bathroom door, knowing Gabe would be about five minutes behind her, tops. And when he arrived, she had no clue what he would do.

She shivered and touched her palm to her forehead. Every part of her was cold, and as a tremor ran down her spine, Livvy flicked on the shower. Maybe the hot water would warm her from the outside, even though her insides were frozen.

When steam rose over the glass partition, Livvy removed her clothes and slipped inside, but the enormity of the double blow —she had cancer, and both her doctor and her husband thought aborting her baby was the only choice—meant she couldn't hold her own weight any longer. She slid down the wall until her bottom hit the base of the shower, and closing her eyes, she began to sob, her tears washed away by the flowing water.

Why her? Wasn't it someone else's turn to suffer? Perhaps she'd been a terrible person in a previous life and now karma had decided it was payback time. And boy was she paying.

As her tears continued to stream down her cheeks, a loud banging started on the bathroom door. Only one person could be outside.

"Livvy, are you in there? Please, open the door."

Livvy clamped her hands over her ears, and her sobs grew louder.

"Livvy! For fuck's sake, open this goddamn door."

She didn't react. The next thing she heard was Gabe clearly shoving his shoulder into the bathroom door. There was a loud crack before the door burst open.

Gabe took one look at her sitting on the floor of the shower in floods of tears, and his face crumpled. "Oh, darlin'," he whispered.

He slid the shower door open, stepped inside, fully dressed, and sat down on the floor. His arm came around her shoulders, and he pressed his left hand to her forehead, easing her head to rest against him.

They sat there in complete silence, her naked, him fully clothed, until her wracking sobs were replaced with a gentle, quieter crying. Gabe cautiously knelt in front of her. He curved his arms around her back and under her knees then gently lifted her, cradling her close to his body. He carried her out of the shower and into the bedroom, grabbing a warm bath towel from the rack as he passed.

With great care, he placed her on the bed and dried every bead of water from her skin even as his own soaking clothes clung to his body. Livvy sat there, legs dangling, as Gabe wrapped her in a fluffy warm robe. He left her then but was back in seconds holding the hairdryer. He proceeded to dry her hair, slowly and carefully.

Livvy couldn't respond, couldn't form the words to tell him how much his quiet ministrations meant to her on the inside.

When Gabe was satisfied she was warm and dry, he quickly changed and sat beside her, expelling a deep sigh. "Liv, please talk to me. Tell me what you're thinking. You're scaring the shit out of me."

She forced her head up, and when she caught sight of his expression, full of concern for her, she began to cry again. "I don't want to die." Her voice was quiet, soft, and scarcely audible.

His face got tight. "Darlin', you're not going to die. I'm here for you. I will *always* be here for you."

She caught hold of herself, because if she didn't, she might lose who she was for good. "I can't terminate the baby, Gabe. I feel him inside me. He's *real*. He moves. He kicks. He sleeps. For God's sake, we've seen him on the scan, and he sucks his thumb. I won't have to hang on long. With modern medicine, they'll be able to get him out early—but not this early. I can hang on. I can do it. I know I can. I'm strong, right? You've said it yourself, how strong I am. Please… I've lost three babies. I can't lose another. Even if by giving life to this baby, I risk my own, it will be worth it."

As her words came out in a manic jumble, his face crumpled.

"I get it, Liv. I understand where you're coming from, but please, look at this from my point of view. I can't lose you. We can have more babies. We can have as many rounds of IVF as you need. But we can't do that if you're not here. You know how much I love our baby already. The thought of losing him or her is abhorrent to me. But the thought of losing you is so much worse."

Tears pricked her eyes as Gabe poured out his feelings. Her lip trembled, and she bit down on it. "I can't," she whispered.

His shoulders dropped, and he let out a long sigh. He took

her hands in his and squeezed. "At least have the surgery. Please. For me."

She leaned forward and softly kissed him. "Let's talk to the doctor about options. But the abortion is off the table."

He pulled her into his arms. "Thank you, darlin'."

CHAPTER TWENTY-FOUR

GABE STROKED Livvy's hair until she fell into a fitful sleep. Her eyebrows were crushed together, and her lips were pressed tightly together in a grimace. He stiffly got to his feet and walked downstairs, his steps calm and measured, but inside of him, a storm was brewing. The swirling in his stomach and the pain in his chest wouldn't go away, and if he didn't get the anger out, it would eat him up from the inside.

Gabe's hand formed a fist, and he hit the wall. Pain shot up his arm, but he didn't care. He sucked on his scraped knuckles as he carried on walking down into the basement. He pushed open the door to his gym, stripped off his clothes, pulled on a pair of gym shorts, and stuffed his feet into his tennis shoes.

He started on the punching bag, pounding into it until his knuckles weren't only scraped but bloodied. He welcomed the physical pain, a far-more preferable feeling than the emotional turmoil tearing him up.

Half an hour later, with sweat dripping from his face and dampening his chest, Gabe sank to the floor, heartbroken. He hugged his knees to his chest and cried.

After his private breakdown, he showered, changed, and

jogged back upstairs. He dabbed some salve on the torn skin on his hands and flexed his fingers. Unsurprisingly, they were stiff and sore. No doubt Livvy would ask what had happened and worry about him when she needed every ounce of concern for herself. But if he hadn't gotten that out, he would have exploded, and him losing his shit was no use to anyone. He had to be strong and let Liv be the one to fall apart.

He wanted to keep her all to himself, but he knew he couldn't do this alone.

He grabbed his cell and made three difficult calls.

"How are you feeling today, gorgeous girl?"

Ches was fussing... again. As she plumped the pillows behind Livvy's head, Gabe's lips twitched when Livvy scowled.

"I'm fine. Will you leave those bloody pillows alone?" She twisted and punched them flat, making Gabe's half grin turn into a full-on smile.

"You're braver than me, Ches," he said. "You know Liv."

Her scowl turned on him, but even when she gave him her best icy glare, he couldn't love her more. *Two more weeks.* That was all they needed before the doctors assessed whether their baby would be viable without the need for medical intervention. They would perform a C-section, and as soon as Livvy was strong enough following the birth of their child, they would start her cancer treatment. She'd had a lumpectomy the week after her diagnosis, but through the regular scans, the doctor had assessed she would still need the mastectomy as soon as possible.

Gabe could tell she was suffering. The dark shadows under her eyes—almost like bruises—were combined with a gray pallor that made his heart clench. The one thing keeping her spirits up was the knowledge that she would soon hold their child in her arms. Livvy had always been a mother—without a child. In his quiet moments when she would fall asleep in his arms, her breathing soft and steady, Gabe would send up silent prayers to anyone who might be listening. He would promise the earth if they let both Livvy and his child live. He could only hope his prayers were answered.

"I am perfectly capable of plumping my own pillows. I am not an invalid." Livvy gave his mother a beseeching look. "Tell them, Heather."

Heather's hands shot up in the air. "Oh no, darlin'. I'm not getting in the middle of this."

Livvy turned her eyes to his. "Can you take me downstairs?"

Both his mother and Ches opened their mouths to protest, but he shot them down with a single look. "If that's what you want, darlin'."

She nodded. "It is. And can you make me some of your special scrambled eggs?"

Gabe couldn't hide his delight. Livvy's appetite had waned of late, making her even more ill as the baby took what nutrients it needed, leaving her weak and exhausted. He moved over to the bed, tossed back the covers, and lifted her into his arms. Ches scrambled to open the door.

Once downstairs, Gabe settled her on the couch and headed into the kitchen. He could hear Livvy and Ches arguing, and a smile crept across his face. Since Ches had arrived a few weeks earlier, she'd been an immense support to both him and Livvy. Fortunately for them both, Ches's firm had immediately granted her a leave of absence as soon as she'd explained Livvy's situation. John wasn't well enough to travel, but he regularly Skyped Livvy, and she always brightened for a short while afterward.

Gabe glanced over his shoulder as his mother slipped onto a stool at the breakfast bar. "You doing okay, darlin'?"

"I'm not the one you need to worry about," Gabe said as he cracked eggs into a bowl.

"I disagree."

He turned, bowl in hand, and began to whisk the eggs. "I'm fine, Mom."

Heather sighed. "No, you're not. You're running on empty, determined Livvy won't see your pain, but you don't have to hide things from me."

Gabe's face crumpled, and he dropped the bowl containing the egg mixture on the countertop. "What if it's too late, Mom?" His voice was barely above a whisper in case Livvy heard. "What if they get the baby out but then find the cancer has spread and there's nothing they can do?" He covered his face with his hands. "I can't lose her."

Heather was off the stool in an instant, and her arms went around him. "You listen to me. That girl is strong. She must be, given all she's lived through. And she loves you so very much. She will fight with everything she has."

He nodded and pulled back, searching his mom's face for answers he knew she didn't have. "I hope it's enough."

CHAPTER TWENTY-FIVE

A COUPLE OF WEEKS LATER, Livvy woke with anxiety and excitement—a strange mix of emotions—rolling through her stomach. She was going to meet her baby later that day. The hospital was performing her C-section at two that afternoon. That was the excitement part. The anxiety part was in relation to what would come next.

The mastectomy. The chemotherapy. The fear of the unknown.

Livvy craned her neck. Gabe remained asleep beside her. The worry lines he wore during the day were relaxed in sleep. Her decision to put their baby first had been so difficult for him to accept, but once he'd seen that she wasn't going to change her mind, he'd reluctantly acceded to her wishes. But he'd also withdrawn from her physically. Sure, he still touched her, still dropped the occasional kiss on her lips, still carried her when she was too weak to walk far, but it all felt clinical and detached. The passion that had been their mainstay was absent.

As though he sensed her scrutiny, his eyelids flickered before his gaze fell on hers. In the depths of his captivating green eyes,

Livvy saw fear even though he tried to hide it behind a bright smile.

"Mornin', beautiful." His hand cradled her cheek, and Livvy leaned into the rare caress.

"Morning."

"How are you feeling?"

Livvy shrugged. "Excited. Nervous. Can't wait to meet him or her and then get on with the rest of it."

He nodded. She didn't have to explain any more.

"We'd better get up. We need to be there soon."

Gabe gave Livvy a hand out of bed and helped her into the shower. Even though she was still four weeks away from a normal pregnancy term, her belly was enormous, which made bending down impossible. But even as she relished the feel of his hands on her body, it reminded her more of a caregiver than a lover and a husband.

She closed her eyes as Gabe squeezed shampoo into the palm of his hand and began massaging the soapy suds into her scalp. After he'd washed her, he made sure she stood directly under the hot spray while he shampooed his own hair and bathed. He flicked off the shower and wrapped Livvy in a huge fluffy towel then slung one around his waist. Despite the cancer and the pregnancy making her weak and exhausted, she couldn't help but slide her gaze over him. Her eyes flickered over his abdomen before settling on the thin line of hair that trailed from his navel and disappeared beneath the towel.

When her head came up, her eyes met his. The resounding green of his irises seemed even richer, and for a moment, the gaze that settled on hers reminded her of how things used to be. He cradled her face and kissed her. It wasn't a gentle kiss as had been his recent habit—almost as though he was scared she would break—but a hot, hard kiss, the kind he used to treat her to before she became sick. Her hands clutched his upper arms, and the muscles beneath his soft skin bunched as he ran his fingers up and down her back.

Livvy moaned into his mouth as his tongue tangled with hers. It had been so long since he'd touched her with such raw passion. Like a woman starved of oxygen, she clung to him, returning the strength of his kiss with an intensity of her own.

Gabe pulled back, his chest heaving. "No, Liv." He held her at arm's length, which made all the warmth he'd generated leave her body in a whoosh, replacing it with an icy chill that slowly crept down her spine.

Her eyes sank to the floor, and she grazed her teeth over her bottom lip. "I miss you," she whispered, unable to look at him for fear of what she would find. "I miss us."

He tilted up her chin. "I'm still here. I'll *always* be here."

"Then why do I feel so alone?"

Gabe blanched, the color leaching from his skin, and his mouth slackened. "I'm here, darlin'. You're not alone. As long as I have breath in my body, you'll never be alone." He tilted his head to one side when she remained tight-lipped. "I want to touch you. I want to make love to you so very much, Liv, but you've been so tired…"

His voice petered out, and his hands fell to his sides.

"I'm not tired now," Livvy whispered. But Gabe had already walked away.

GABE PICKED up her prepacked hospital bag, and they slowly made their way downstairs. They found Ches in the kitchen, a half-empty bowl of cereal in her hands.

"You guys want anything to eat before we go?" she asked.

They both shook their heads. Livvy's eyes went to Gabe, who looked pale beneath his tanned skin. He gave her a tight smile and took her hand with his free one. "Ready, darlin'?"

Livvy swallowed down the panic that had bubbled up into her throat. *Focus on the baby, not the cancer.*

"Yes, I'm ready."

Ches scraped the remains of the cereal into the trash and slung her bag over her shoulder.

"And so am I. Can't wait to meet my goddaughter." Her bright tone and the direction of conversation was clearly meant to distract Livvy. "I am going to be the godmother, right?"

Livvy gave a brief smile. "'Course you are."

Ches made a dramatic sweep across her forehead with the back of her hand. "Phew. That could have been awkward."

Livvy's mood lightened, and she squeezed her friend's arm. "Thank you for being here. For everything."

Ches's answering smile was full of love. "Nowhere else I'd rather be, Liv."

"Okay, then let's get this show on the road," Livvy said.

Gabe led her outside, only letting go of her hand to put her bag in the trunk. It gave her ten seconds alone with Ches, who leaned in and whispered, "You are going to be okay, Olivia Mitchell. Do you hear me?"

Choked up, Livvy could only nod as hot tears stung her eyes. "I wish John were here."

Ches grimaced. "Not as much as he does, but with his blood pressure being so high, he couldn't get clearance to fly. We can Skype him later, though, once the baby's here."

Livvy brightened. "I'd love that."

Ches pulled Livvy in for a quick hug before Gabe opened the passenger door, helped her inside, and clicked her seat belt into place. Ches got in the back as Gabe wandered around the front of the car and climbed in beside her. Livvy glanced over at him. She wished that time would stand still and that she could be in *this* moment a little while longer, with her baby still safely inside her womb and her pre-surgery body still intact. But all too soon, Gabe turned the car onto the hospital grounds and parked outside the labor ward.

Livvy spotted Heather waiting for them on the front steps. She'd had a routine appointment at the hospital and had agreed to meet them there. Livvy waved and tried to put on a brave smile.

Heather walked across to them and opened Livvy's door. "Okay, sweet pea? Ready to meet your little bundle of joy? Because I know I am."

Heather's easygoing manner calmed Livvy's stuttering pulse. "I'm more than ready." Livvy rubbed her distended abdomen. "It's been a long time since I've seen my feet."

Gabe chuckled and put an arm around Livvy's waist. "How you doin', Grandma?" He leaned down to kiss his mother on the cheek. "Everything okay?"

Heather flashed him a broad grin and dismissed his concern for her health. "I never thought I'd be happy with such a title, but I'm thrilled."

The four of them walked into the hospital, and as they approached the reception desk, Livvy drew on their combined strength as fear of what came after the baby rolled through her once more.

"One step at a time," Gabe whispered in her ear.

Livvy gave him a grateful smile. He regularly guessed what she was thinking without her having to say the words. Perhaps it was the way that her face tightened every time her thoughts turned dark, or maybe he simply understood her better than most.

After the paperwork had been signed, Livvy was quickly checked in. A nurse showed her to a private suite, which looked more like a posh hotel than a hospital room. It was painted in a pale pink with matching bedcovers and drapes, and the only thing that gave away its true purpose were the rails on either side of the bed.

Livvy wandered over to the window. Her room looked out onto the hospital gardens, which were small but definitely provided a nicer view than the parking lot.

Gabe laid her stuff out on the bed, but before Livvy could

get to it, Ches and Heather pounced, and in seconds, her things were all safely tucked away in drawers.

Livvy tossed her purse on the nightstand and sank onto the bed. This was it—the moment she'd been hankering for and dreading in equal measure. She couldn't wait to hold her baby in her arms, but beneath the joy was the nauseating fear of the upcoming mastectomy and chemotherapy.

She hadn't voiced her concerns to Gabe, but on the rare occasions she was alone, she would worry that he wouldn't find her attractive once her body was covered in scars. And what about all the side effects? Hair loss, mouth ulcers, the fact that she would lose what few curves she had. They seemed like such ridiculous thoughts to have, given the alien eating her from the inside out, but she couldn't help it.

As Livvy tried to erase such dark thoughts, Dr. Wilson arrived.

"Hi, Livvy, Gabe." She shook hands with both of them, and Gabe introduced her to Ches and Heather. "How are you feeling?"

"Excited and a little bit sick," Livvy answered honestly. Gabe squeezed her arm.

"That's normal," the doctor said. "Do you have anything you need to ask me?"

Livvy shook her head.

"Okay, well, relax, settle in, and I'll see you in the operating room with Dr. Morgan. He's one of the best surgeons at the hospital, so you're in good hands." Dr. Wilson smiled before turning on her heel and leaving the room.

Livvy fiddled nervously with her wedding ring until Gabe sat down beside her and took her hands in his.

"You'll soon be a mommy."

His words swept away all the terrible thoughts going through Livvy's head. She only needed to focus on one thing today, and that was meeting her son or daughter. All the other stuff could wait.

She leaned her head on his shoulder. "And how are you doing? Ready to be a daddy?"

Gabe grinned. "Not sure, if I'm honest, darlin', but if I can manage a boardroom full of egos, I'm confident I won't be outdone by one tiny person."

Heather laughed. "That's what you think."

The mood in the room lightened at Heather's teasing. Livvy took hold of the joyous moment and held on tight. She couldn't let her cancer detract from the fact that she was finally going to be a mother. This was *her* time to fulfill her destiny. She was going to be a really good mum, and Gabe would be a wonderful father. He had patience in abundance, but he would also set boundaries, and he had so much love to give. She should know. She'd blossomed under the strength of his love—despite her illness—and their child would do the same.

As a nurse entered the room, pushing a wheelchair, Livvy's pulse jolted. "Ready to go to the operating room, Mrs. Mitchell?"

Livvy nodded as she blindly reached for Gabe's hand. She sat in the wheelchair even though she was perfectly capable of walking… okay, waddling. But it seemed that wasn't permitted. Ches squeezed her shoulder and whispered, "See you on the other side, Mummy Mitchell."

Heather brushed the back of her hand down Livvy's cheek. "See you soon. Take care of her," she said to Gabe, causing him to roll his eyes and give her a playful nudge.

"Yes, Mother."

The operating room wasn't very far away, and as the nurse pushed Livvy through the double doors, she directed Gabe to a side room to change into scrubs.

Inside, the operating room was full of people. Livvy couldn't quite believe that she would need so many medical staff for one operation. As her gaze fell on the familiar sight of Dr. Wilson, her heart rate slowed.

"Do you remember Dr. Morgan, Livvy?" Dr. Wilson asked.

She nodded and smiled at the gray-haired surgeon that she'd previously met.

"Ready, Livvy?" Dr. Morgan asked as Livvy was helped onto the bed.

"As I'll ever be."

After Livvy's epidural was administered, she was laid on her back and a cloth screen was put up to prevent her from seeing the action below her waistline. When Gabe appeared at her head, Livvy burst out laughing. He looked so out of place in baggy blue scrubs, with his hair tucked into a silly hat, especially considering his penchant for smart, well-fitting clothes.

His lips twitched. "I look hot, don't I?"

"Oh yeah. I hope they let you take that outfit home."

He laughed as he took a seat beside her head and wrapped his fingers around her left hand.

"Can you feel that, Livvy?" Dr. Morgan asked.

"Feel what?"

"Good. Okay, we can begin. Just relax and get ready to meet your son or daughter very shortly."

Apart from a tugging sensation, Livvy felt very little during the procedure. It didn't stop her pulse from racing or a faint sheen of sweat from dampening her forehead. Gabe's hand tightened around hers the longer the operation went on. His head snapped up as a sucking noise started, sort of like the sound one would hear from a dentist's tool.

As he rose from his chair, Livvy dragged him down. "No chance," she said.

He gave her a soft smile and dabbed a damp cloth to her forehead. She had no idea where he'd conjured it up, but thank goodness he had because she was burning up.

"Fair enough, Momma," he said. "You in any pain?"

Livvy shook her head as the tugging sensation increased. And then she heard it.

The wail of a baby.

"Oh God." Her voice choked as Dr. Wilson held up a tiny,

honest-to-goodness person with a mop of dark hair and a hell of a set of lungs.

"Congratulations, Livvy, Gabe. You have a perfectly healthy little girl. We'll get her cleaned up, and then you can hold her."

Livvy burst into tears.

Gabe leaned over her and buried his head in her neck. His arms curved around her as he hugged her tightly. When he pulled back, his eyes were glistening. "She's perfect. Just like you."

Livvy clung to him as words failed her. She'd done it. Finally. After so much heartache, she'd finally brought a life into the world. At times, she'd believed that she was cursed, but no longer. Gabe had rescued her, and now he'd given her what she'd always craved—a baby.

"Thank you," she managed to croak.

Gabe kissed the top of her head. "No, thank you. I love you, Liv. So very much."

A few minutes later, Dr. Wilson appeared around the screen with their daughter wrapped in a green sheet, her head covered. "Here she is. Ten fingers and ten toes. Six pounds, one ounce. I'll leave you three to get acquainted while we stitch you up. You can nurse her if you feel up to it." And without a moment of further delay, Dr. Wilson placed the tiny baby on Livvy's chest.

Her arms automatically closed around her daughter, and she placed a soft kiss on her forehead. As an intense peace settled over her, she stiffened her resolve to fight the cancer with everything she had.

"How do you feel?" she asked as her gaze settled on Gabe's mesmerized expression.

"Ecstatic." He bent to plant his own kiss on his daughter's soft cheek as Livvy steeled herself to say what she knew had to be said. He wasn't going to like it.

"If anything happens to me—"

"No, Livvy." Gabe's tone brooked no argument. He even held his palm up for added emphasis.

"Listen." She wrapped her hand around his wrist. "Listen to me."

He shook his head. "We're not doing this. Not now. Not ever. You've just given birth to our daughter."

"Gabe, please."

A tear spilled down his cheek, and he shook his head again, this time violently. "I can't, Liv." His voice cracked. "Please don't ask me to. Not now."

An intense pain speared through her chest, stealing her breath. To feel her own fear was one thing, but to see his, so raw and honest, was quite another. The conversation would have to be had, because if things didn't go well, plans would need to be made. But for now at least, she would push aside the upcoming horror and simply let the happiness soak into her bones.

"Okay," she said softly. Gabe rewarded her with a soft brush of his lips against hers.

After the doctor stitched her wound, an orderly took her up to her room, and a nurse brought the baby along in an incubator. Even though she'd given birth four weeks early, her daughter needed no medical intervention. The steroids the doctor had administered to speed up the forming of her baby's lungs had worked as they should.

As she and Gabe arrived back at her room, Heather and Ches greeted them, their faces wide with smiles.

"Well?" Heather asked as Livvy was pushed inside on a gurney.

"A girl." The pride in Gabe's voice couldn't be missed.

Heather clasped her hand to her chest, and Ches let out a whoop, but as they both crowded over the incubator, Livvy could swear Gabe growled. She gave him a sympathetic glance and squeezed his hand.

"Oh, Liv. She's gorgeous," Ches said. And then as she looked between Livvy and Gabe, she chuckled. "Although, look at the gene pool she comes from. The kid had to be a stunner."

Gabe chuckled. "That's all Livvy," he said as he threw an

arm around his mother's shoulders and kissed her temple as tears streamed down her face.

"And how are you, sweet pea?" Heather choked out through her tears as her gaze fell on Livvy.

"I'm fine." Livvy beckoned her mother-in-law over and patted the bed. "Want to hold her, Grandma?"

Heather nodded vigorously. Gabe lifted their baby girl in his arms and—Livvy could tell—reluctantly handed her over. She repressed a giggle. Clearly, her husband was going to have a problem letting anyone touch their daughter.

"So what are you going to call her?" Ches asked. "I can see her tag says Baby Mitchell, but you can't leave her like that for long."

Livvy glanced at Gabe, and he nodded at her, happy for her to introduce their daughter.

"Meet Sophia Annabel Heather Mitchell. I know it's a mouthful, but we wanted to get my mum's name in there too."

Gabe's mum sucked in a sharp breath, and more tears fell. "Your sister would be so happy."

"It was Livvy's idea."

Heather clasped Livvy's hand and squeezed. "Thank you with all my heart."

Livvy smiled and allowed her head to fall back against the pillow. Exhausted, she closed her eyes while listening to Gabe, Heather, and Ches talk excitedly. Not for the first time, relief that Gabe and Ches got on so well swept over her. If anything happened to her, Gabe would need Ches and she would need him.

"We should let Livvy get some rest." Gabe's voice reached her through her sleep-deprived haze.

"No," Livvy mumbled. "I like hearing your voices. Please stay, all of you."

"Okay, darlin'."

Gabe's voice was the last she heard before sleep claimed her.

LIVVY WOKE the following morning and, for the briefest of moments, couldn't remember where she was. Then her memory came rushing back. She went to sit up, but a sharp pain across her stomach reminded her of the operation. The pain meds must have worn off.

With a struggle, she managed to ease into a half-sitting position. Her eyes scanned the room. Gabe was sleeping in what looked like a very uncomfortable chair, his head resting on the palm of his hand. Ches and Heather were nowhere to be seen. He must have sent them home after she crashed.

Her eyes fell on her daughter, fast asleep in the crib, her chest going up and down at quite a rate. Her plump cheeks were flushed, and her eyes were squeezed shut. A rush of love raced through her, so intense that Livvy found it difficult to catch her breath. Then horror clutched at her chest. She hadn't fed her baby since the previous day.

"Gabe," Livvy said urgently. "Wake up."

He woke with a start, his eyes wide with concern. "Liv, what is it? Is everything okay?"

"I haven't fed the baby since yesterday," she said, panic leaching into her tone. "I'm a terrible mother. She must be starving. Why isn't she crying?"

A smile crept across his face, and he eased out of the chair. "Calm down, Livvy. I wanted you to rest so I hired a nurse to help. Sophia has had all of her regular feeds."

She clamped her lips into a thin line. She accepted that her baby wouldn't be able to be breast fed all the time, especially with Livvy's upcoming treatment, but *she* wanted to administer the feeds, whatever form they took. "I don't want a nurse feeding my baby. I'm her mother."

Gabe sat on the edge of her bed and took her hands in his. "Liv, we'll need the help when you..." His voice faded, and a flash of pain crossed his face before he put his mask back in place.

As her baby stirred, she nodded at the crib. "Can you bring her to me? I can't get out of bed," she said, ignoring his comment.

Gabe nodded and crept over to the crib. Sophia grumbled as he lifted her into his arms. He cradled her close to his chest, his eyes full of love and wonderment. Livvy's heart constricted as she watched them together. Thank God for Gabe. At least Sophia wouldn't be short on love when Livvy couldn't give her as much attention in the coming weeks and months.

As he placed Sophia in Livvy's arms, a rush of love almost overwhelmed her. Tears welled in her eyes as Sophia woke up, her mouth opening into a wide yawn. Whatever happened to Livvy, no one would ever convince her that she'd made the wrong decision by choosing this precious life over her own.

No one.

CHAPTER TWENTY-SIX

"GABE, TALK TO ME."

Livvy set firm eyes on her husband, who refused to meet her gaze. The day of her mastectomy operation had finally arrived. As it had crept ever closer, Gabe had become more and more withdrawn, refusing to discuss his thoughts and feelings. She could feel him pulling away from her, which she could understand—to a point. In his shoes, she might have created some distance so that if the worst happened, it might make things easier. But what worried her more was that he was also pulling away from Sophia. He was still doing everything a doting father should—feeding her, changing her, playing with her—but he acted almost like he'd been with Livvy before the birth. Everything felt too *clinical.* The closeness was missing.

"What about?" he asked in a too-bright tone. "Here, give her to me while you check that you've got everything you need." He held his arms out for the baby, and with a resigned sigh, Livvy handed Sophia to him.

She watched from the corner of her eye as he cradled their four-week-old daughter in his arms. He hummed softly under his breath and held out his pinky, which Sophia dutifully sucked into her mouth. To the outside world, they must have looked like the perfect family, but in reality, that was not the case. Livvy might as well have been fighting two battles: one with the cancer quietly stealing through her body, and the other with a husband who was gradually slipping away.

Livvy closed her bag and clipped the locks in place. She picked it up, shaking her head at Gabe's offer of help, and quietly left their bedroom.

She dropped her bag at the bottom of the stairs, wandered into the kitchen, and slid onto a stool at the breakfast bar. She couldn't stop herself from expelling a heavy sigh.

"You okay, darlin'?" Heather asked as she heated up a bottle of expressed milk for Sophia—the last breast milk Livvy would ever be able to provide for her daughter. Sorrow swept through her, and she clutched a hand to her chest while giving Heather a warm smile. Her mother-in-law didn't need to witness Livvy's sadness right at that moment.

"Keen to get it over with now."

Heather nodded sagely. She placed the bottle of milk on the counter and sat down beside Livvy. "She's in safe hands with me," Heather said, squeezing Livvy's hand.

"It's not Sophia that I'm worried about."

Heather frowned, but before she could say anything more, Gabe came into the kitchen. "Hey, Mom." He smiled at his mother in a way that he didn't smile at Livvy these days.

"Darlin'." His mom held out her arms and hugged him tightly. "Where's my grandbaby?"

Gabe jerked his head towards the stairs. "Asleep in our room."

"That's good. Now, you two, remember you don't have to worry about a thing." She turned to Livvy, pulled her into a warm hug, and whispered in her ear. "Get through the next couple of days, and then we'll talk." Then louder, for Gabe's benefit, she said, "Sophia will be just fine here with me."

Livvy nodded as her face became tight and her vision clouded. "I know she will." Her voice was thick with emotion.

Gabe picked up Livvy's bag and took hold of her hand. He squeezed, although the affectionate touch didn't soothe her ravaged heart.

"Call me later," Heather said.

Gabe nodded and silently guided Livvy outside and towards her fate. There was no going back.

"I'm going to give Ches a call," Livvy said once she was settled into bed in her private hospital room. "I promised I'd call her before the operation. She's still feeling bad about having to go back to work, and I want to reassure her."

"I'm sure she'll appreciate that," Gabe said, wondering where his reassurance was.

Livvy gave him a warm smile. "Why don't you go and grab me a glass of water?" The message that she wanted to be alone was clear, especially as she wasn't allowed to eat or drink anything before her surgery.

Gabe tried to ignore the crushing pain in his chest, but it was becoming harder and harder. He felt as though he were losing Livvy, and the closeness they'd shared in the couple of days following Sophia's birth had disappeared. He knew he was the one creating the distance, but somehow, his terror of losing her had manifested in him retreating into himself—and withdrawing from Sophia and Livvy in the process.

He wandered down the hall and found himself in the hospital cafeteria without remembering the journey there. He grabbed an extra-shot coffee and sat down by the window. California was having a rare downpour, and as the rain lashed against the panes of glass, Gabe couldn't help but wonder if the bad weather was an equally bad omen.

"Hello, Gabe. Mind if I join you?"

His head snapped up to find Dr. Wilson pulling out the chair opposite.

"Dr. Wilson. Of course not. What are you doing here?"

With a weary sigh, she flopped into the chair and dropped her paper coffee cup on the table. "Visiting my father-in-law. He's had triple-bypass surgery."

"Oh, I'm sorry. I hope he's going to be okay."

She shrugged. "Me too. So how are you holding up?"

Gabe rubbed a hand across his face. "I've had better days."

She nodded in understanding. "I heard that today was Livvy's operation. How's she doing?"

He shrugged. "Better than me."

Dr. Wilson frowned. "What do you mean?"

He sighed. "I'm so scared." He wondered why it was easy to say those words to a doctor but not to his wife.

Dr. Wilson sat back in her chair and wiped a napkin over her lips. "Those are normal feelings, Gabe."

He took a sip of his coffee and winced. *Too bitter.* He shouldn't have had the extra shot. He put the cup on the table and pushed it away. "Doesn't make it any easier to cope with."

The doctor patted his hand. "Hang in there. If you need to talk, I can recommend someone."

"I'm my father's son," he said. "We Mitchells have never found it easy to share our feelings with strangers."

"Well, if you find your inner Californian, give me a call."

His answering laugh sounded strange to his ears. He certainly hadn't had much to laugh about recently. He left Dr. Wilson to finish her coffee and went back to Livvy's room. She'd finished her phone call and was lying back, her head propped up against the pillows.

As she spotted him, she gave him a bright smile. "Where's my water?"

Gabe forced a smile. "You could have told me to go, that you wanted to talk to Ches in private."

"Busted." She laughed, and despite his inner turmoil, Gabe joined in, his spirits momentarily lifted.

"How is she?"

"Worried about me and, as I suspected, feeling guilty because she can't be here. Honestly, between her and John, they're like a pair of mother hens. I told her I was fine. I've got you—right?"

He sat down on the side of her bed and swept a lock of hair away from her forehead. "You do."

She captured his fingers and pressed his palm against her cheek. Gabe reveled in the rare moment of intimacy even though it was his fault they didn't have more loving moments. He leaned forward until his lips were close to hers. She raised herself up and kissed him, lovingly rather than passionately, but considering she was about to go in for major surgery, it was hardly surprising. Even so, his stomach clenched, and his breathing quickened.

As they broke apart, the door opened, and an orderly pushed in a gurney. Dr. Anderson followed a moment later.

"Ready, Livvy?" the doctor asked.

Livvy set her jaw and nodded. "Let's do this."

CHAPTER TWENTY-SEVEN

"Livvy? Can you hear me? Open your eyes now. Come on."

"Go away," Livvy mumbled. "Need sleep."

"You can sleep as soon as you've opened your eyes for me. Come on, sweetie. You're in recovery, and it's all over. Now open your eyes, hon."

All over? What's all over? The baby? No, she'd had the baby. Precious Sophia. Where was she?

"Baby, where's baby?" On some level, she knew she wasn't making any sense but couldn't seem to form coherent sentences. What was wrong with her? Briefly, her eyes flickered open to find a nurse peering at her.

"Your baby's fine, Livvy. You've had your operation. All went well."

"Want to sleep," she muttered.

"That's fine. You'll wake up in bed soon, sweetie."

Livvy's last thought was that she wished the nurse wouldn't call her sweetie. It sounded too much like "sweet pea," and only Heather was allowed to give her that endearment.

"Liv?"

Her eyes flickered again, but this time, her surroundings were different. The walls were a pale pink instead of stark white. She groaned and closed her eyes again. Everything hurt, from the top of her head to the tips of her toes.

"Are you in pain?"

She tried to focus on the voice that was concerned, loving. Familiar.

Despite the weights, which must have been glued to her eyelashes, Livvy forced her lids open. She licked her lips, and as a straw pressed against them, she sucked greedily. The water soothed her sore throat.

Her head fell back against the soft pillows, and despite her best efforts, she couldn't keep her eyes open any longer.

"Is she okay?" The voice was sharper now, demanding and dominant. *Gabe.* Her fuzzy brain began to clear in parts. She tried to speak, to tell him she was fine, but her tongue felt thick in her mouth.

"Yes, Mr. Mitchell. She just needs time to wake up from the anesthetic."

"Can I speak with Dr. Anderson?"

"Of course. She'll be here shortly."

Livvy swallowed and tried again. "Gabe." Her voice sounded weird, scratchy, and quite deep, very unlike her. But it had the desired effect because Gabe's face swam into her sightline.

"You okay, darlin'? What do you need?"

At the familiar endearment, Livvy managed a small smile. "More water."

A rustle sounded off to her right before he was back. He gently lifted her head and eased the straw between her lips. After she'd had her fill, he laid her back down.

"Are you in any pain?"

She nodded. "Are you sure I was taken to the OR and not run over by a truck?"

Gabe laughed, his relief showing in the lightness of his chuckle. "I'm sure, darlin'." He turned to the nurse. "Can we get her some pain relief?"

"She has a morphine drip," the nurse explained as she picked up a button and placed it in Livvy's hand. "Press this whenever you're in too much pain, hon, and your morphine will be increased."

"What if I overdose?" Livvy asked. Considering the way she was feeling, she would be pressing the button so often, she'd probably get repetitive strain injury.

The nurse chuckled. "You can't. Go ahead and press it as much as you need. If you're still in pain, let me know."

A few minutes later, Dr. Anderson arrived, and Livvy steeled herself for bad news. She couldn't hope for the best. With her track record, hope was a dangerous thing.

Dr. Anderson pulled up a chair. "How are you feeling, Livvy?"

"Sore."

She nodded. "I'm not surprised, but you don't need to be in pain so be sure to tell a member of the team if you are."

"How did it go, Doctor?" Gabe got straight to the point, for which Livvy could have kissed him. If left to her own devices, she would have taken ages, gradually working up to the only question that mattered.

"Very well." She smiled and patted Livvy's hand. "When we got inside, the tumor wasn't as bad as we'd feared. We're hopeful that the cancer hasn't spread outside the breast, despite the delay in starting treatment, but the lab tests will tell us more."

Livvy sucked in a breath, while Gabe muttered, "Thank God."

"Your reconstruction also went extremely well. Once the swelling goes down and your scars heal, I'm confident you'll be pleased with the result."

Livvy sagged against the pillows as tears welled up. She

reached out a trembling hand towards Gabe, whose warm fingers closed around hers.

"Does this mean she won't need chemotherapy?" Gabe asked.

Dr. Anderson grimaced. "I'm afraid we'll need to go ahead with that as planned. The tumor was still a fairly large size."

"I understand," Livvy said in a shaky voice. "But the prognosis is good?"

"Let's get the test results first. As soon as you've recovered from the surgery, we'll begin the next step in your treatment."

LIVVY DIDN'T FUSS when Gabe helped her out of the car. These days, she took whatever bit of affection he chose to dole out. But her dark mood instantly lifted when Heather came to the front door with Sophia. She'd only been gone three days, yet it felt like a lifetime since she'd seen her baby girl.

"Come on in, darlin'." Heather ushered them inside. "I've made you some tea."

Livvy smiled as she kissed the top of Sophia's head. Every step was painful, but she repressed a wince in case Gabe and Heather ganged up on her and sent her to bed. Even if she couldn't hold or rock Sophia until her scars began to heal, she could look at her, touch her, and smell her.

"I'll take your bag up," Gabe said with a smile that fell far short of his eyes. Livvy watched him as he took off up the stairs. Tears made her vision blurry, and she rapidly blinked to stop them from falling.

"Feel up to that chat?" Heather asked, reminding Livvy of their conversation a few days ago.

Livvy nodded. "Right now, I'll take all the advice I can get."

Heather led the way into the living room and put Sophia down in her bassinet, where she gurgled happily. She was such a good baby. They were lucky on so many levels. Livvy eased herself into a chair, flinching as a sharp stabbing pain shot across her chest.

"Do you need some painkillers?" Heather asked.

Livvy grimaced. "I took some before I left the hospital." She dismissed the pain. "I'm fine now. It's only when I move."

Heather's brow wrinkled. "Well, as soon as it's time for more, you let me know."

Livvy gave her a wan smile. "I will."

"So," Heather said as she blew on her tea. "Talk to me."

Livvy sighed. She glanced quickly over her shoulder to make sure Gabe wasn't there even though she would have heard him come downstairs. "I don't know what to do, Heather. I can't reach him. He won't talk to me. He won't tell me what he's thinking or feeling. And I know you'll probably deny this, but he's distant with Sophia too. I want the old Gabe back. I miss him so much." Her voice caught on a sob.

Heather leaned forward and squeezed Livvy's hand. "He's his father's son." She rolled her eyes, which in spite of everything, made Livvy chuckle. "Travis was exactly the same. Stubborn bastard. It must be in the Mitchell blood to think showing feelings means weakness when it's quite the opposite."

"So what do I do?"

"You reassure him, Livvy. He's terrified of losing you. You're being so strong, and yet he feels weak because he can't protect you—he can't take the pain away. You need to step up for him, fight for him. I know this might sound harsh, given you're the one fighting this awful disease, but"—she shrugged—"you married a Mitchell, darlin'."

Livvy paused to reflect on everything Heather had said. Her mother-in-law was right. Livvy had spent so long fighting, that to her, it was the norm, something she did without thinking. But through all of her pain and suffering and heartache, she hadn't stopped to consider Gabe's feelings. She'd made it all about her and had simply pulled on her big-girl pants and got on with it.

"Can you go and get him?" she asked Heather. "I'd go up, but it'll take me an hour to walk upstairs."

Heather grinned and patted her shoulder as she passed. "Good girl."

She returned five minutes later with Gabe in tow. Without saying a word, she picked up Sophia's bassinet and left the room.

"Mom said you needed me."

"Sit down, Gabe."

He did as she asked, concern and worry swirling in his green irises. Livvy's heart almost burst with love for this amazing, strong, dedicated man, who put everyone ahead of himself.

"I want you to do something for me."

Uncertainty about where she was going flashed across his face as he nodded. "Anything."

"Talk to me. Tell me what's in your head. Don't treat me like a china doll. You've never been like that, and it's one of the things I love most about you."

Gabe shook his head. "You have enough to deal with."

She reached out, even though it was painful, and took his hand. "Nothing is more important than you and me. I'm here for you, but you need to play your part. Don't hide things from me, Gabe. It weakens our relationship at a time when we need to be strong."

His eyes widened, and he swallowed hard before blowing out a heavy breath. "This isn't easy."

"Nothing worthwhile ever is."

A glimmer of a smile curved his lips upward. "Have I ever told you that you're one of the smartest people I know?"

She grinned. "Oh, I don't need you to tell me that."

He laughed then. Livvy memorized the sound and stored it away so she could call on it later.

"So?" she prompted when he didn't continue.

He dragged a trembling hand through his hair. "I'm so scared, Liv. All the time. I feel like such a failure."

He paused, but Livvy didn't interrupt. She needed to let him talk, and then she would have her say.

"I'm the man. I should be the one protecting you, and yet you're the one stepping up, being strong, being determined. I'm trying, Liv. Honestly, I am. But I just don't know what to do."

When he didn't say anything more but chose to stare at his hands instead, Livvy reckoned that was as much as she was going to get from him.

"Hold me," she said. "That's what you do, Gabe. You hold me."

He lifted his chin, pain creasing his handsome face. "Oh, Liv," he breathed as he scrambled from his chair and knelt in front of her. His arms came around her waist, and he rested his head on her knees.

She ran her fingers through his hair. "The best thing you can do is give me and our daughter love and affection. I need it, Gabe. This distance you've put between us has to stop. I am here for you, always, but I need you on the other side, an equal partner, a lover, not a caregiver."

His head bobbed in her lap. "No more," he said. "We fight this together."

A FEW WEEKS LATER, Livvy arrived in the hospital for her first bout of chemotherapy. Six was the magic number that Dr. Anderson thought she would need to kill off any lingering cancer cells. Even though the hospital had been fantastic, she'd spent the last few weeks researching what she could expect and had found some amazing blogs online. Those folks didn't pull any punches, so Livvy knew that she was in for a rough ride. She'd already made a couple of friends, people who were willing to answer questions she might not want to ask the doctors or want Gabe to know were on her mind. He was worried enough without her adding to the pressure. Since their chat after her surgery, the distance he'd created had dissipated and they'd grown closer than ever.

And however much suffering the chemo would bring, it was all worth it for Sophia. Her daughter was thriving, and every day brought a new change or discovery. Already Livvy missed her, but Heather was an absolute godsend, taking care of everything. Still, it didn't stop the odd spike of jealousy when Heather did something Livvy should have been doing, but the C-section and following mastectomy had taken their toll. No doubt the chemotherapy would make matters worse before they got better.

Livvy and Gabe sat in silence as the IV slowly fed the bright-red drugs into Livvy's system. It only took an hour. Livvy wasn't sure what she'd expected, but as they left the hospital, she felt the same as she had when they'd arrived.

That night, however, was amongst the worst of her life. The sickness, despite taking anti-nausea drugs, kept coming until there was nothing left in her stomach. Yet she continued to retch. Gabe suffered alongside her, holding her hair as she leaned over the toilet bowl for the umpteenth time, spitting bile into the pan as tears ran down her face. Then he would mop her brow and carry her back to bed until the next bout hit her.

Livvy collapsed into bed following her latest trip to the bathroom. Dawn had broken, and early sunlight brightened their room, lifting her spirits, although the complete exhaustion meant that she could barely find the energy to turn her head towards the window.

Gabe climbed in beside her. The dark shadows beneath his eyes told their own story. She wasn't the only one suffering. The sickness may have been happening to her, but the effects were felt equally by Gabe. He gently put his arms around her and nuzzled her hair, trying to bring her what little comfort he could.

"If you're still like this in an hour, I'm calling the doctor, Livvy. You must be getting dehydrated, and I'm really worried."

"They warned us this would happen." God, her voice

sounded so weak, even to her own ears. "I have to ride it out. If I can keep down the anti-sickness tablets, it will get better."

"But that's just it, darlin'. You're not keeping them down. If you carry on like this, I'm calling the doctor," he reiterated.

Livvy didn't argue, mainly because she had absolutely no strength to fight him. But over the next hour, she wasn't sick, and so Gabe agreed to hold off calling for medical assistance. He brought her some more anti-sickness pills, which she managed to keep down.

As the week progressed, Livvy's strength returned, and by Friday, she felt well enough to sit in the garden with Sophia. It was a beautiful, warm spring day, and as she rocked her baby, Gabe pointed out the different birds in the garden. Even though all Sophia did was gurgle, Livvy started to believe a happy future was within her grasp.

Unfortunately, Monday morning arrived too soon, and as Livvy and Gabe traveled back to the hospital for her second chemotherapy session, a heavy atmosphere hung over the car. The second time was much worse. Livvy couldn't keep anything down, even water. After twelve hours of hell and Gabe's frantic worry, Livvy relented and let him call the doctor, who gave her a shot that stopped the vomiting. But the nauseous feeling remained.

This time, Livvy didn't feel human until Saturday. Once again, she spent her weekend in the garden with Sophia. Her daughter had changed so much even in the last week. Sorrow at everything she was missing made her chest tight and uncomfortable. Heather was an absolute rock, but Livvy couldn't help her envious feelings. Gabe's mum was experiencing all the little changes that Livvy wasn't. She took to cursing the damn cancer that was robbing her of the important moments she would never get back. Heather and Gabe had started to make lots of videos, and Heather took to writing a daily journal of all the little changes in Sophia, but it wasn't the same.

The next four weeks were not only the longest of her life,

but also a living hell. The doctor had told her the effects of the chemotherapy would be cumulative, but knowing and experiencing were two very different things. Dr. Anderson assured her that once the final treatment had been administered, she would recover quickly from the sickness, although the bone-weary exhaustion would last much longer.

After the sixth bout of chemotherapy was over, Livvy spent the following two weeks getting her strength back. She'd lost so much weight. Every rib was visible, and her body ached constantly. Sometimes when she undressed for bed, she would catch Gabe in an unguarded moment, and the worry and concern on his face would make her heart ache painfully. But the moment he caught her looking, he would school his expression and smile warmly.

On the morning of her checkup at the hospital to see if the chemotherapy had worked, Livvy trudged downstairs. The smells coming from the kitchen making her stomach grumble. After weeks of even the idea of food making her nauseous, her appetite had started to come back. Luckily for her, she had a husband who was a fabulous cook.

As she spotted him moving about the kitchen, cooking breakfast, she hung around by the door and drank him in. They hadn't had the best start to their marriage—apart from Sophia—and she vowed to make it up to him now that she was feeling better.

"Morning, cowboy."

Gabe spun around, a broad smile lighting up his handsome features. "Morning, darlin'. You hungry?"

"Starving." She slid onto a stool at the breakfast bar and sipped a glass of juice. "Where's Sophia?"

Gabe rolled his eyes. "Where do you think?"

Livvy chuckled. "Heather?"

"Yep. They're in the garden. Breakfast will be a few minutes if you want to try to wrestle our daughter away from her grandmother for a quick cuddle."

Livvy stepped off the stool. "I'll give it a try."

As she wandered out into the garden, Heather's voice drifted across the lawn. She was humming to Sophia. She spotted Livvy and came straight across.

"Here's Mommy," she said, holding Sophia out for Livvy to take.

As she cradled her daughter in her arms, a sense of peace stole over her. She buried her head in Sophia's soft curls and breathed in her beautiful baby smell.

"How are you feeling today, sweet pea?" Heather asked, sweeping her hand briefly down Livvy's arm as a way of comfort.

Livvy forced a tight smile. "A little worried, but hopeful." *I can't do it again. I just can't.*

Heather nodded sagely. "Have you eaten?"

Livvy tilted her head backward. "Gabe's sorting breakfast now."

"He's a good boy."

Livvy chuckled. It always amused her when Heather treated Gabe like a child, although now that she had one of her own, she could understand.

Heather linked her arm through Livvy's. "Let's go and see what my clever son has rustled up."

LIVVY ARRIVED thirty minutes early for her appointment, as though that would somehow make the time go quicker. She and Gabe took a short walk around the hospital gardens to pass the time. After a few minutes, she spotted a bench, and the two of them took a seat.

Livvy reached for Gabe's hand. "I need to tell you something."

Gabe brought her fingers to his lips and kissed the tips. "What, darlin'?"

"If it's bad news—"

Gabe dropped her hand as his flew in the air, palm facing her. "No, Liv."

"Listen to me. I'm saying this whether you want to hear it or not. I thought we were past hiding." As Gabe's lips pressed into a thin line—his disapproval of the discussion evident—Livvy carried on. "If it's bad news, I want you to know that I don't regret a thing. I would choose Sophia over my own life every single time. She's my gift to you for showing me I could be happy again." She picked up his hand from where it lay limp in his lap and pressed it against her cheek. "Thank you for the best time of my life."

Gabe shook his head. "We have plenty more to look forward to. *All of us.* You, me, and our daughter."

Livvy didn't argue. She'd said her piece. There was no reason to labor the point.

As their appointment time drew near, they headed for Dr. Anderson's office and took a seat in the waiting room.

Five minutes later, the receptionist called out to them. "Mr. and Mrs. Mitchell, you can go in now."

Livvy's stomach sank, and she wiped clammy palms on her jacket before cautiously opening Dr. Anderson's door.

The doctor rose from her chair and shook both their hands. "Livvy, Gabe, please sit down. How are you feeling, Livvy?"

"Good. I'm still tired, but overall, I feel much better."

The doctor gave no sign as to whether Livvy's response was what she had expected. She opened a file and glanced at the papers within before she lifted her head and clasped her hands in front of her.

"I have your test results back, here. I'm afraid the chemo-therapy hasn't been as successful as we would have liked. The tests show a regrowth of some cancer cells."

Gabe sucked in a sharp breath, but Livvy couldn't even manage that. A horrible numb feeling swept through her, and she tapped her fingertips together as she would if she'd gotten an attack of pins and needles. Then the room began to swim. She felt herself waver before Gabe's arm shot out to steady her.

"Let me get you some water." Dr. Anderson walked over to the corner of her office and returned with a paper cup. She pushed it across the desk, and with a shaking hand, Livvy lifted the cup and drank the entire contents.

"What does that mean?" she managed to croak.

"It means our first shot across the bows wasn't as successful as we would have liked, but this is only round one. We'll get you on a second course of chemotherapy. We may decide to try a different type of drug, but I'll discuss the best course of action with my colleagues today, and we'll go from there."

Livvy nodded, while inside, her stomach twisted painfully. With quiet determination, she reached for Gabe's hand and squeezed. He hadn't said a word, but all the color had drained from his face. He squeezed back, his expression impassive.

"Okay, Dr. Anderson. When do we start?" Livvy said.

"Right away, if possible. I'd like to admit you this time so that we can keep an eye on how you react to the stronger dose and adjust our treatment accordingly."

"So I won't be able to go home?" Livvy asked in a quiet voice.

The doctor shook her head. "There's one more thing too. I don't recommend you see Sophia, at least not until we've completed the next round."

Livvy's eyes widened. "What? Why not?"

"Because your body is already weak, and the second course of chemotherapy will lower your immune system even more. As Sophia's immune system is still developing, she could inadvertently bring in bacteria and viruses. We can't risk you catching something that may derail our treatment plan."

"No!" Livvy jumped to her feet. "That's not possible. I can't forgo seeing my baby for six weeks. Please, there must be another way."

Gabe's grasp on her hand, which he hadn't let go of when she jumped to her feet, tightened.

"You'll be able to see her through the window of your hospital room, but unfortunately, I don't recommend you holding her or even having her in the room with you. Please, Livvy, you have to trust me on this."

Livvy sagged back into her chair as her legs gave out. Six weeks was a lifetime during which Sophia would change so much. Tears welled in her eyes, and she let them fall. Gabe's arms came around her. "It's okay, Liv. I'm here."

Dr. Anderson remained silent while Livvy cried in the arms of her husband. She didn't have it in her to be the strong one anymore. She was terrified of what was coming. Because this time, she knew what to expect. And it would be worse.

Oh God. I can't do it all again. I can't.

She was doomed never to be happy. Every time she believed her horror had come to an end, something else happened to disprove that.

The time had come to accept her fate.

CHAPTER TWENTY-EIGHT

GABE STOOD by helplessly as Livvy's second round of treatment began. With an awful sense of foreboding, he watched as the hideous bright-red poison slowly dripped into her veins. Anger bubbled up inside him. *Why her?* When the doctor had given them both the bad news, he'd watched the light go out in her eyes, and it had scared the hell out of him. He needed her to fight this thing with everything she had, but with the amount of trauma that her body had already been through, he couldn't blame her for thinking she couldn't go on.

He'd called Ches, who said she would jump on the next plane over. She should arrive in the next few hours. He'd heard the fear in her voice when he gave her the news, but it had been the call to John that had broken Gabe's heart. Still too ill to travel, John had sobbed into the phone, and it had taken all Gabe had to hold it together. As soon as he'd hung up, he'd been unable to hold back his own tears.

They'd given Liv a permanent IV this time so they didn't have to keep stabbing her with needles to get the drugs in. It didn't take long for the sickness to start, but this time, the nausea was accompanied by sweats and chills. Gabe spent his time either covering her with extra blankets or turning the air conditioner up. By the time Ches arrived, Livvy was out of it. Gabe wasn't sure whether she'd fallen asleep or her body had simply shut down, but Ches's gasp of horror as she stood over the bed was like a knife to his chest.

"Jesus, Gabe, look at her. And this is how many of round two?"

"One," he answered flatly.

"Fuck. How can her body take any more?"

Gabe clenched his jaw. "Not helping, Ches."

"Shit, I'm sorry." She gave him a hug and pulled up a chair. "It's the shock, you know."

You don't have to tell me.

"How's Sophia?"

He smiled. "Wonderful. She changes every day." His smile fell then. "I think that's what Liv has taken the hardest. Not being able to hold Sophia or touch her for six weeks."

Ches nodded. "I can imagine. And you, how are you holding up?"

Gabe rubbed a weary hand over his face. "I'm not. When she's awake, I manage to hold it together, to put on a brave face for her, but when she's asleep like now…" He swallowed past an enormous lump in his throat. "I'm terrified, Ches."

"Now you listen to me." She shook his arm. "Livvy might look slight, but she has the most immense inner strength I've ever seen. How many women do you know who could cope with everything she has and not only still be here fighting but have their sanity intact? She *will* come through this. You have to believe that."

"I want to, but I'm so damned scared." His voice broke. "We haven't had enough time."

Ches's arms came around him, and the two of them sat in silence and hugged.

BY WEEK FOUR, Livvy had lost so much weight, her bones were visible through her nightgown. Her immune system was at an all-time low, and as if her ravaged body hadn't been through enough, she'd caught pneumonia. She also began hallucinating and muttering all sorts of crazy stuff. Even the occasional visit from Sophia in which his mom would hold her up for Livvy to see didn't seem to brighten her spirits.

When the cold made her body wrack with shivers, Gabe climbed in beside her and wrapped his arms around her painfully thin frame as he tried desperately to give her some of his warmth. When her body would burn up, he would turn the air conditioner to high and press cold towels against her face and neck.

After the fifth session, Livvy regained some of her strength. The pneumonia had receded, and she begged to see Sophia. When his mom held her up to the window and Livvy saw that she'd sprung her first tooth, she began to sob.

"When did that happen?" she asked. But before he could answer, her crying grew. "I want to hold her. She needs me."

Gabe moved to sit on the edge of the bed. "Liv, God, please don't cry. I can't stand it." Despite trying to be strong for her, Gabe couldn't hold in his sorrow. As he wrapped Livvy in his arms, desperate to give her what little comfort he could, their daughter continued to smile her toothy grin at them both.

"I'm missing everything," Livvy said between hiccups as she tried to get a hold of her emotions. "And so are you. It isn't supposed to be like this. We should be having the time of our lives, bringing up our daughter together. It isn't *fair*."

Gabe couldn't find the words to console her, because whatever he said would be cold comfort to a woman who'd suffered more than anyone ever should. She shoved him in the chest and turned on her side. He knew her rejection of him wasn't personal, but it hurt like hell all the same. He looked over at his mother and shrugged. Heather's face crumpled. She mouthed, "We'll come back later," before disappearing with Sophia.

Livvy was right. She wasn't the only one missing out. They both were, and despite all the videos and journals, nothing would ever make up for the missed weeks and months with their firstborn.

When Ches returned from the cafeteria with a couple of coffees, she took one look at Livvy's curved frame and flashed a confused look at Gabe.

He shook his head and whispered, "Tell you later."

Over the next week, Livvy sank into a deep depression. She lay in bed, listless, barely uttering a word, and she wouldn't look at any photographs of Sophia. Even when the doctors set up her last bout of chemotherapy, not a flicker of emotion crossed her face. If her eyes weren't open, Gabe would swear she was comatose.

His heart grew so many cracks, he wasn't sure what was holding it together. He sensed his grip on his wife loosening, and no matter how hard he tried to hang on, it was as though his fingers were being pried away until eventually he would have no choice but to let go.

"She's no better, is she?"

Their nurse, Michelle, who Gabe had gotten to know really well, shook her head sadly. "I'm afraid not. The cancer has stopped growing, which is good, but until she regains some strength, we can't risk giving her another course of chemo."

"What can I do?" Gabe's voice was barely above a whisper.

"Exactly what you're doing. Keep talking to her. Tell her what's going on at home. Talk about how Sophia's doing. Give her something to fight for."

Gabe nodded. "I can do that. But is there anything else I should be doing? I'll do whatever is necessary."

Michelle patted his shoulder. "Pray."

THE PNEUMONIA RETURNED WITH A VENGEANCE, and Livvy slipped into a coma. No matter what her doctors did, it was as though her body had simply given up. Gabe spent his days by his wife's bedside and his evenings with his daughter so she wouldn't forget who he was. Then he would return to the hospital to sleep beside Livvy. At least he didn't have to worry about work. His deputy CEO had stepped up to the plate superbly. He only bothered Gabe when he had absolutely no other choice, which meant Gabe could focus all his attention on his family.

"How is she today?" Ches asked as she arrived holding a much-needed coffee.

He took it from her and gave her a grateful smile. "No change. Is John on his way?"

After Gabe had told John how bad Livvy had gotten, he'd begged his doctors to allow him to fly. They'd relented when Gabe offered his private jet and hired a doctor to accompany John back to the States. Whatever it took, Gabe would do. Livvy needed all those she loved around her.

"Yes. He'll be here this afternoon. I'll pick him up from the airport and bring him straight here." She tilted her head to the side. "Do you want to go home and take a shower or something, Gabe? You look awful."

He shook his head vigorously. "No, I'm not leaving her. What if she wakes, and I'm not here?"

"At least get something to eat."

He gave her another headshake. "I'm not hungry."

He shuffled his chair forward and gripped Livvy's hand. *Please wake up, Liv. I need you.*

"JOHN." Gabe rose from his chair and shook John's hand. "I'm so glad you could make it. How was the flight? Are you okay?"

"I'm doing all right. Still popping the pills." He gave a wan smile. "Thank you for sending your plane. I hated not being able to be here for Livvy."

John pulled up a chair, took Liv's hand, and pressed it to his cheek. "Oh, Livvy. What's going on? Come on now. Stop all this nonsense. You have a beautiful little girl at home who needs you. Come on back to us. Please, Livvy. I can't lose you too. "

John's voice cracked, and another splinter appeared in Gabe's heart. Livvy would leave so many heartbroken people behind if the worst happened.

Ches must have noticed that Gabe was close to losing it because she put her arms around his shoulders and whispered, "You don't have to hide it from us. We're your family."

A sob caught in his throat. "I don't know what to do. I can't live without her."

John nodded. "I know what you mean, son. I thought the same when Beth died, but life goes on. You have an amazing daughter who loves and needs you. Whatever happens, you have to go on, find a way through. But let's not think such terrible thoughts. She's a tough one, our Liv. Always has been. She's in there, fighting her way back to you, and if there is any way she can make it, she will."

It was the longest speech Gabe had ever heard John make, and he found comfort in the man's words. He swiped a hand across his eyes and vowed to drag Livvy back to health if it was the last thing he did.

"YOU LOOK A LOT BETTER, GABE."

Ches had finally convinced him to take a quick shower and had brought him a change of clothes. He'd also eaten a quick snack in the cafeteria, but he hadn't wanted to be away from Liv for too long.

"I feel it. Any change?"

"You've only been gone ten minutes. No change, but she's not any worse, either. Remember that."

He slumped into the familiar chair by Livvy's bed and took her cold, skinny hand in his. He rubbed his thumb over her knuckles. "Where's John?"

Ches grinned. "Heather brought Sophia by, and John couldn't resist. They've taken her for a walk in the gardens."

At the mention of his daughter, Gabe smiled. He missed her terribly. He hoped it wouldn't affect her too much having both her parents missing at such an important stage in her life. But what else could he do? He had to be around for Livvy. At that moment, she needed him more.

Gave felt a slight pressure on his hand. He thought he'd imagined it, but then it came again. Hope spiked within him. "Livvy? Was that you? Did you squeeze my hand? Try again, Liv, please."

Ches's head twisted around. "Are you sure?"

"I think so. I definitely felt a change in pressure. Come on, Liv. Do it again."

He felt another squeeze, barely there but real. Then her eyes flickered open.

"Christ, she's awake. Ches, go get the nurse and get John and my mom. Livvy, can you hear me, darlin'?"

She gave a brief twitch of her head and whispered one word. "Yes."

"Oh, Livvy. You've had us so worried."

The nurse rushed into the room, Ches following on her heels. She checked Livvy's vitals and called for the doctor.

"Gabe," Livvy croaked. "I can't see you."

He leaned over her, making sure his face was directly in front of hers. "I'm right here, darlin'."

"I don't feel well."

"I'm not surprised. You've been out of it for weeks. Take it easy, okay? The doctor is on her way."

Livvy blinked several times, then her breathing became labored. Her mouth fell open, and beads of sweat broke out over her face. Her chest rose and fell in an unnatural rhythm.

"What's going on?" Gabe's voice was panicked, frantic. "What's happening?"

"Step aside, Gabe. Quickly." The nurse shoved him out of the way and pressed a buzzer over Livvy's bed. An alarm sounded, and a team of people streamed in. A bag was put over Livvy's nose and mouth, and a doctor leaned over her and began chest compressions.

Gabe's legs trembled, and he clung to the back of a chair as he stood helplessly by, watching his wife lose her valiant fight. He shoved a fist in his mouth to hold back an imminent scream.

Then he heard Ches shout, "Do something!"

EPILOGUE

GABE STOOD over the grave and touched his hand to the tomb-
stone. He murmured a prayer then knelt to tug the dead flowers
from the vase before replacing them with a new bunch. A
couple of weeds had sprung up since he'd visited the previous
week, and he tugged them out and glanced around for a trash
can. He spotted one at the end of the next row and wandered
over to drop the weeds inside.

With a final glance at the grave, he trudged back to his car.
He started the engine and, with a deep sigh, drove out of the
cemetery. His grief settled over him, still raw, still painful. He
merged onto the highway and set off for home.

Twenty minutes later, he pulled into the driveway. The car
tires crunched on the gravel as he drove towards the house. His
gardener had planted spring flowers in the borders while he'd
been out, and he stopped to take a look. The spray of color
lifted his spirits.

He locked the car and strode to the front door. He pushed it
open and stepped into the wide hallway. Before he'd had the
chance to close the door behind him, Sophia came barreling
down the stairs, her dark auburn hair flowing behind her.

"Daddy! Where have you been?" Her voice was indignant and more than a little petulant.

He broke into a huge smile and picked her up, swinging her in the air. Pulling her close, he covered her face in kisses. Her peals of laughter were surely audible for miles.

"Hi, peanut. How're you doing?" He placed her squarely on the floor.

Sophia put her hands on her hips. "Stop calling me that. I've told you, Daddy, I'm not a little girl anymore."

He repressed a smile. She looked so much like her mother, her mouth forming into the perfect pout and one hip kicked out to the left.

"I am fully aware of that, Sophia Mitchell. You're a whole five years old. But you will always be my little peanut!" He picked her up again and tickled her until her delighted screams filled the house. God, how he loved her. She was the center of his universe, and every day his love for her grew.

She struggled in his arms. "Put me down, Daddy."

He did as she asked then theatrically sniffed the air.

"What can I smell? Is Bea cooking something wonderful again?"

"No, Daddy. She's on vacation, remember?"

Of course he remembered, but he loved to tease Sophia. He slapped himself on the forehead. "Oh, yes. Silly me. So, what's cooking, peanut?"

She glared at him, her hands on her hips once more. Then she flounced down the hallway, heading towards the kitchen. Gabe grinned and followed her. He paused for a second in the doorway, surveying the scene before him.

His beautiful wife was standing at the stove. Her hair was tied back, and her brows were drawn together as she tasted the food. Cooking wasn't her forte, but he loved the fact that she tried.

She hadn't heard him come in, so he put a finger to his lips, encouraging Sophia to be quiet. She mimicked him, lifting her own finger to her lips. He tiptoed across the kitchen, slipped his arms around his gorgeous woman's waist, and kissed her neck.

She startled and swiped at him. "Jesus, Gabe. I could have burned myself, you crazy man."

He chuckled and turned her around in his arms. His hands curved around her face, and he bent his head and kissed her.

She briefly kissed him back before pulling away. "Gabe," she said. "Sophia…" She nodded towards the breakfast bar, where their daughter had clambered up onto one of the stools.

Gabe rolled his eyes. "She doesn't mind seeing her mommy and daddy canoodling. Do you, Sophia?"

Sophia shook her head. "Nope."

"See," he said. "Now come here, Liv." He grabbed her again, and his mouth closed over hers. Six years on, and his desire for her grew with each passing day. As he drew back, he slapped her on the ass, making her yelp. "Now get on with dinner, woman. Your husband and daughter are wasting away here."

Sophia giggled as Livvy shot Gabe a withering look. "Carry on like that, and you won't be getting any food."

"Wouldn't be a bad thing." He winked at Sophia. "We both know Mommy can't cook."

Sophia's giggles grew. "Daddy, you're very brave. Mommy's cooking isn't so bad."

"Smells better than it tastes, usually," he said, bringing more giggles from Sophia.

Livvy rolled her eyes and turned back to the stove, but Gabe caught her soft smile. He could hardly believe his luck. Since the doctors had brought her back from the brink of death, he'd treated every day as a miracle. But as the years passed, the horror of that time began to fade.

"Can you set the table please, Sophia?" Livvy pointed at the cutlery drawer. Sophia immediately jumped down from the stool, eager to help.

Once her attention was diverted, Livvy turned to him. "How was it?"

"Hard," he replied. "I miss Mom so much, Liv. I can't believe it's been six months already. And the more Sophia grows, the more I realize how much she's missing out on not having her grandmother here."

Liv nodded. "I miss her too. Every day. I'm sorry I couldn't come today, but I think Sophia is too young to go to a cemetery. If Bea hadn't been on vacation…"

"It's fine, Liv. I agree with you. One day, we'll take her to see Mom, but not yet."

As they ate dinner, Sophia's constant chatter made his heart sing. They'd begun to clear the table when the baby monitor came to life. Their son made his feelings known by yelling at the top of his lungs.

Livvy set the plates on the side. "Back in a sec. Your son is obviously unhappy he's missing out on the family gathering."

"Hmm, funny that he's always my son when he's crying and yours when he's smiling."

"You know it," Livvy said with a grin before she disappeared.

Livvy jogged upstairs, eager to get to her little man. After the chemotherapy, the doctors weren't sure that she would ever be able to conceive again, but her luck had turned, and they'd been blessed with a beautiful baby boy. When she reached the nursery, Oliver was standing up in his crib, his face flushed from sleep, his fingers holding tightly to the bars.

As he spotted her, he held his arms out. "Mama."

A thrill ran through her. Ever since he'd uttered his first word over a week ago—which of course was "Dada"—she'd been dying for him to say her name.

She lifted him in the air and covered his face in kisses. "Hello, my big boy. Ready to join the family?"

He gave her the biggest grin, showing off his latest additions —two front teeth. Her heart constricted as memories flooded her mind of how she'd missed Sophia cutting her first tooth. But that was all in the past, and Livvy refused to let it be a part of her present or her future.

She propped Oliver on her hip and set off downstairs. The moment her little man feasted his eyes on Gabe, he struggled to be out of her arms.

"Dada." His voice demanded attention. Gabe rose from his chair and lifted Oliver out of Livvy's arms. He threw him in the air before catching him and repeated the whole process once more. Livvy swallowed down panic each time Gabe played this game, even though she knew he would never drop their son. Oliver's giggles were her reward, something she would never tire of hearing.

Livvy finished putting the plates away as Gabe placed Oliver in his high chair. She heated some baby food and handed it over to Gabe as Oliver started to bang his fists.

"Someone's hungry," Gabe said. "Ready, Olly?" He lifted the spoon high in the air, building Oliver's anticipation before popping the food in his mouth. A little dribbled down his chin, and Gabe expertly scooped it up. After their son had been fed, Gabe burped and changed him while Livvy watched. She cherished these moments, never taking them for granted.

"Why don't you take the kids to the upstairs living room, and I'll clear up in here?" Livvy began collecting the plates. "I'll be up in five."

Gabe nodded. He held Olly on one hip, hoisted Sophia up on the other, and scampered upstairs with both kids giggling in delight.

Livvy loaded the dishwasher, wiped down the counters, and headed upstairs to her family. As she neared the top floor, she could hear Sophia making her feelings known.

"No, Daddy. I've told you. I want to watch *Angelina Ballerina*."

Livvy grinned at the attitude. Sophia's personality had firmly asserted itself. Her daughter had bags of confidence, wasn't afraid to voice her opinion, and was extremely difficult to sway from a course once she'd made up her mind. She couldn't hear Gabe's murmured reply but didn't doubt that he'd given in. Gabe doted on Sophia. Their closeness was something Livvy had actively encouraged in case her cancer returned.

As she reached the living room, she paused by the doorway and watched the happy family scene. Sophia was lying on her stomach in front of the TV, and of course, her favorite program was playing. Gabe had Oliver cradled in his arms, the two of them relaxing on the sofa.

He glanced over his shoulder and held out his free arm, beckoning her over. "Come here, gorgeous."

Livvy settled down on the sofa and tucked herself into his side. His arm came around her, and Livvy sighed in contentment. They remained in the same position for a while until Oliver began to stir.

Gabe glanced at his watch. "Come on, Sophia. Time for bed."

"Oh, Daddy, ten more minutes. Please," she begged.

"No, Sophia," Livvy interjected before Gabe could give in to his daughter's demands. "Do as Daddy says. Bed."

Sophia hit Livvy with a glare. She stifled a giggle and schooled her face into a firm expression. With a pout, Sophia climbed to her feet and stomped out of the room.

Livvy grinned. "She's her mother's daughter, all right," she whispered in Gabe's ear, grazing his lobe with her teeth as she did so.

Gabe hissed and clutched her waist. "Hurry up," he said. The look in his eyes made Livvy's stomach clench with need.

She lifted Oliver from Gabe's arms and headed off towards the kids' bedrooms. After changing Oliver, she settled him down in his crib. She tucked the covers around him and brushed a lock of hair from his face. He was the most beautiful baby. He had his father's handsome features. For sure, he would break hearts when he was older.

"Night, baby boy." She gave him a kiss and cradled his head. As his breathing deepened, she backed out of the room and quietly closed the door.

By the time she reached Sophia's room, her daughter had already changed into her pajamas, her brief temper tantrum over.

Livvy read her a story before tucking her in. "Goodnight, my gorgeous girl. Daddy and I love you very much." She leaned over to kiss Sophia's soft cheek.

Her daughter gave her a sweet, angelic smile. "Night, Mommy. I love you so much."

Livvy's heart tightened in her chest, as it always did when Sophia uttered those precious words.

"Leave the light on, Mommy." Sophia's voice held a tinge of panic. She was at the age where darkness was something to be feared.

"Okay, baby. I'll leave the hallway light on and your door open. All right?"

Sophia nodded in agreement, and as Livvy turned her bedroom light off, Sophia snuggled beneath the covers, her auburn hair splayed out over the pillow.

As Livvy headed back to the living room, she counted her blessings for her happy, healthy children and her amazing husband. She found Gabe lounging on the couch. The TV was turned off, and soft music was playing. He held his arms out to her, and she willingly went to him.

"They okay?"

"Yeah. Sophia's strop didn't last long."

"Like her mother," he said with a grin.

Livvy rested her chin on his shoulder. "Gabe?"

"Yeah, darlin'?"

"Take me to bed."

LIVVY LAY SPRAWLED across Gabe's chest, listening to his steady heartbeat.

"Will it always be like this?" she mused, not expecting a real answer.

He briefly lifted his head and gazed at her with those amazing green eyes that had captivated her all those years ago.

"Well, darlin'," he said in his southern drawl, "it's been like this for six years. I can't imagine it changing anytime soon."

She grinned and kissed his chest. Now seemed like a good time to tell him her news. She sat up in bed, legs crossed in front of her. The scars from her mastectomy had long since turned to silvery lines, barely visible at a quick glance. She had no embarrassment sitting naked in front of Gabe, and he'd never shown her anything but love and support.

"I went to the hospital today," she said.

His eyes widened, and fear crossed his face. He sat up too. "Why?"

"A checkup."

"Why didn't you tell me?"

"You had more than enough on your plate today."

He shook his head. "I could have gone to Mom's grave tomorrow or the next day. You're what's important, Liv. You and the kids."

She ignored his reprimand. "Anyway, do you want to know what they said?"

"Of course I do." He tried to hide the tinge of anxiety in his voice.

Livvy took a breath. "I'm officially in remission. The cancer has gone."

Gabe inhaled sharply, and his arms came around her. He pulled her onto his lap. The tightness of his hold relayed his relief. "Oh, Liv." He kissed her hair. "Oh God, I'm so relieved." He frowned then. "But you shouldn't have been alone."

"I wasn't alone. I took the kids with me."

Gabe rolled his eyes. "That's hardly the same. Don't do that to me again, okay?"

"That's not all."

Another twinge of fear tightened his mouth, but as he saw the happiness on her face, he relaxed. "Okay, hit me with it."

She reached into the drawer of her nightstand to grab the white stick, then she dropped it into his outstretched palm.

As he glanced down, he spotted the telltale blue lines. His head snapped up. "Are you sure?" he whispered.

She nodded, a broad grin spreading across her face. "I'm going to need an extra pair of hands."

Thank you so much for reading My Gift To You. This was such a hard book for me to put out in the public domain, and I went two and fro on it for quite a while, but in the end, I decided Livvy's story, as difficult as it was, deserved to be told.

As part of the publication of this novel, I'd like to give a shout out to Breast Cancer Awareness. I'm sure most of us know someone who has been touched by this dreadful disease, the consequences of which are far reaching. Ladies, please check your boobs!

And now a plea for reviews!
Would you please, please consider leaving a short review on Amazon? You don't have to say much. A sentence giving your thoughts is more than enough. I know some folks are worried about leaving reviews, but you really don't need to be—and you'd be helping others discover books they may enjoy.

Next from me is a brand new series—The Brook Brothers, which centers around four…yep you guess it… brothers.

First up is The Blame Game which release in July 2018. Look out for a preorder soon.

Follow me on Amazon to be alerted when I have a new release out. Alternatively, you can also follow me on Bookbub and those kind folks will also let you know there's a new book for you to discover.

ACKNOWLEDGMENTS

Writing a novel is a little like raising a child - it takes a whole town! Therefore, at this point, I'd like to say thank you to a whole bunch of people who are a key part of my team.

To my editor, Neila Forssberg. This was our first time working together, but I'm sure it won't be our last. Thank you for your wisdom, and for making my words sing.

Delphine Noble-Fox and Incy Black - thank you so so much for reading an early version and providing your razor-sharp and inceitful feedback.

To Allison Irwin for your honesty, for giving up your valuable time to help me with those "Britishisms", and for the giggles you provided along the way!

To Pam Gonzales (Love2ReadRomance) for proofreading and catching those little niggles and making my work as clean as it can possibly be.

To my street team… I love you guys. You're the absolute best.

To my ARC team… the fact you voluntarily give up your time to read and review my books humbles me. Really, you're the bomb!! Each and every single one of you.

But the most important thank you is for YOU - the readers. Without you taking a chance on me and reading my books, well, this would be a whole lot less fun. Thank you, thank you, thank you, from the bottom of my heart.

ABOUT THE AUTHOR

Tracie Delaney writes contemporary romance novels that centre around strong characters and real life problem with, of course, a perfect Happy Ever After ending (even if she does sometimes make her characters wait a little while!)

My Gift to You is her fifth full length novel.

When she isn't writing or sitting around with her head stuck in a book, she can often be found watching The Walking Dead, Game of Thrones or any tennis match involving Roger Federer. Her greatest fear is running out of coffee.

Tracie lives in the North West of England with her amazingly supportive husband and her two crazy Westies, Cooper and Murphy who bring smiles and laughter every day.

Printed in Great Britain
by Amazon

29281070R00151